All You Can Eat . . . Before You Die

The official referee blew his whistle and the competition began.

Cheering erupted from the hall and children stood in their folding chairs to get a better view of adults eating in a way they'd be sent from the table for imitating. Roland held his own for the first three towering stacks of pancakes despite his heart troubles and his wife's admonishments to consider his health. The teenagers came on strong at the beginning but faded fast once the fourth and fifth stacks were placed in front of them. Only Alanza and Grandpa remained by the sixth stack of steaming cakes.

Grampa shifted in his seat in just the way he did every year at Thanksgiving to make room for pie. Alanza seemed to favor saturating the pancakes with so much syrup they dissolved into a pile of mush and needed no chewing. Only slowing to swat his beard out of his plate, Grandpa maintained a steady pace through his seventh stack. Alanza, however, began to slow down. Her shoulders slumped and her eyes became glazed. Squinting at her carefully, I noticed a bit of foam forming at the corners of her mouth. Before I could ask if she was all right she swayed gently, let out a deep moan, and pitched face-first into her plate . . .

Drizzled
WITH DEATH

Jessie Crockett

BERKLEY PRIME CRIME, NEW YORK

THE BERKLEY PUBLISHING GROUP
Published by the Penguin Group
Penguin Group (USA)
375 Hudson Street, New York, New York 10014, USA

USA | Canada | UK | Ireland | Australia | New Zealand | India | South Africa | China

Penguin Books Ltd., Registered Offices: 80 Strand, London WC2R 0RL, England
For more information about the Penguin Group, visit penguin.com.

DRIZZLED WITH DEATH

A Berkley Prime Crime Book / published by arrangement with the author

Berkley Prime Crime Books are published by The Berkley Publishing Group.
BERKLEY® PRIME CRIME and the PRIME CRIME logo are trademarks of
Penguin Group (USA).

For information, address: The Berkley Publishing Group,
a division of Penguin Group (USA),
375 Hudson Street, New York, New York 10014.

ISBN: 978-0-425-26000-5

PUBLISHING HISTORY
Berkley Prime Crime mass-market edition / October 2013

PRINTED IN THE UNITED STATES OF AMERICA

10 9 8 7 6 5 4 3 2 1

Interior text design by Kelly Lipovich.

This is a work of fiction. Names, characters, places, and incidents either are the product
of the author's imagination or are used fictitiously, and any resemblance to actual persons,
living or dead, business establishments, events, or locales is entirely coincidental.
The publisher does not have any control over and does not assume any responsibility for
author or third-party websites or their content.

PUBLISHER'S NOTE: The recipes contained in this book are to be followed exactly
as written. The publisher is not responsible for your specific health or allergy needs that
may require medical supervision. The publisher is not responsible for any adverse reactions
to the recipes contained in this book.

ALWAYS LEARNING   **PEARSON**

Acknowledgments

Writers write, but usually not without a great deal of support. I'd like to take a moment to thank the people who helped make this book a reality. So a big thank-you goes out to my agent, John Talbot; to my editor, Michelle Vega; and all the people at Berkley Prime Crime who work behind the scenes making sure the reader experience is the best it can be. Thank you also to Mary Anne Lasher-Dodge for creating the beautiful cover art for this book.

I'd also like to thank conservation officer Josiah Towne, for answering my many questions and for allowing me to ride along on a call. Thanks also to Maureen Steer and Jim White, who generously consented to answer my law enforcement questions. Thanks also to Lucy Zahray for sharing her expert knowledge of poisons.

Thanks goes out to my friends Betsy Baker, Amy Darling, and Jennie Palmatier for serving as willing taste testers for maple martini recipes, both magical and mundane.

My mother, Sandy Crockett, is always on the thank-you list both as a first and ideal reader and as a willing and dependable babysitter. My sister, Larissa Crockett, provided often needed encouragement as well as insider knowledge about syrup making. My sister, Barb Shaffer, seemed to know just when to call and ask how things were going.

I thank my children, Will, Jo, Theo, and Ari for their patience, kindness, and enthusiasm, and for taste testing more maple food products than they may have liked.

And finally, thanks to my beloved husband, Elias, without whom I would not be living my dreams.

One

I knew as soon as I lied to my mother, the night would turn out badly. Guilt sat in the pit of my stomach like a truck stop burger as I watched the lights of my grandparents' minivan fade down the driveway. I am not by nature a liar, but if I didn't get a couple hours to myself, I was going to end up headlining the local news. So I did what any devoted daughter would do and faked a migraine.

The holiday season brings on overachieving mania in my family every year. Preparations begin on All Saints' Day and reach toxic levels of holiday cheer by Thanksgiving. My mother festoons every room in our sprawling farmhouse with porcelain villages, twinkling lights, and creepy animatronic elves. Grandma turns the kitchen inside out crafting mince pies from actual meat, building gingerbread house replicas of famous castles, and challenging Switzerland to a chocolate production duel. My sister composes a holiday newsletter that puts many glossy magazines to shame. The year I was born, my grandfather added a dozen reindeer to our herd of cows and my father built a sleigh for them to pull through the center of town.

None of the preparations are all that overwhelming on their own, but set them to spin under the same roof and you've got holiday overload. The worst thing is the way everyone insists how much more I will enjoy the holidays when I have a special someone to share them with or, better still, a few kids of my own. I feel like I'm barely old enough to add a husband and kids to the bottom of my Christmas list, but everyone looks at me as if my stocking were full of coal when I sit down to the holiday table year after year unattached.

Thanks to my bald-faced fibbing, I was not helping the rest of the family set up for a fund-raising breakfast scheduled for the next morning at the grange hall. My grandparents met at the event over fifty years earlier when my grandfather came in second to his future father-in-law at the pancake-eating competition. Ever since then, our family has donated our syrup to the festivities. The firefighters' auxiliary, the Sap Bucket Brigade, counts on us to deliver the syrup and set it out on all the tables the night before the fund-raiser. I told myself they didn't really need my help. Besides there was some cleaning up to do in the sugarhouse after everyone had tromped through it fetching squat jugs of syrup for the breakfast.

The sugarhouse is my favorite part of the farm, especially at this time of year, when it is the only place free from tinsel and plastic garlands. With Thanksgiving less than a week away and holiday fervor gripping the household, I was hiding out there as often as I could. I slipped into a down vest, grabbed a bottle of Shiraz, and scooted on out the door. The sugarhouse sits back from the farmhouse far enough to be convenient to the trees but close enough to get to when the snow's antler deep on a nine-point buck. I crossed the quiet yard, the three-quarter moon shining its light down through the bare branches of the trees, and felt the lumpy frozen earth beneath my feet. The security light above the sugarhouse door winked on as I approached. Once inside, the familiar sights of the evaporator and the unadorned rows of syrup bottles drove any holiday stress right out of my mind. I sat the wine on the workbench, pulled the cork, and grabbed a glass from a cupboard. After pouring myself a healthy swig, I flipped on the radio, then grabbed a broom from the closet. Half an hour later all the dirt was gone and everything was tucked back into its place.

I sat on a stool and leaned back against the workbench to enjoy the tranquility. Taking a sip of wine, I scanned the room, a feeling of pride welling up. Over the past five years I had convinced my family to turn our hobby into a business. We'd modernized equipment, begun using hoses instead of buckets to collect sap, and started selling over the Internet. Just this past summer we'd added on a small shop to sell our own maple products and maple-themed gift items. The next thing on my list of improvements was organic certification. With a little luck we would have it in time for the upcoming sugaring season.

It hasn't been easy to get my family on board with the

new ideas. After four generations making sugar, they feel like our system doesn't need any tweaking. The farm has been in the family for over a hundred years so convincing everyone to try something new has been an epic battle. My age, birth position, and gender haven't helped. Being the baby of the family may have its advantages but it hinders you when it comes to garnering respect. My sister, Celadon, and my brother, Loden, just open their mouths and our elders start stringing those pearls of wisdom into necklaces. Me, I have to repeat everything at least a dozen times and then provide written documentation to back up my claims.

As I sat my wineglass back on the bench, I heard footsteps on the porch. The closest neighbor lived over a mile away, and I should have heard any cars coming up the drive. I slid off the stool and slipped toward the window. I was three feet from it when I saw the face. A tawny, furry, feline face filled the window. I took a step back, then another. The large amber eyes peering at me belonged to no tabby cat out for a night of carousing. My heart hammered in my chest. All my life I'd heard rumors of big cat sightings, but like most people, I had never taken them seriously.

The large eyes blinked and the big cat yawned. Four white teeth glowed in the moonlight. I blinked, too, sure I was not seeing what I was seeing. Bears are common here and moose have a pleasant habit of dropping by now and again. Deer cross the roads as often as people in some sections of town. But big cats, no way. Bobcats are a possibility even if they are a rarity, but this animal was far, far larger. I pulled my cell phone from the pocket of my

4

jeans and dialed the number for the police station. I used to date a guy that worked there so the number stuck in my head like an advertising jingle and I wasn't sure this qualified as a 911 call.

"Sugar Grove Police Department." I recognized Myra Phelps's raspy smoker's voice filling my ear. "How can I help you?"

"It's Dani Greene. Is Byron on duty tonight?" Byron is the part-time animal control officer hired by the department to deal with stray dogs, rabid skunks, and even deer that meet their maker in the middle of the highway.

"Sorry, Dani, he's away at his in-laws' for Thanksgiving. Is it important?"

"Has anyone ever reported a mountain lion?"

"Good Lord, yes, the darn fools."

"One's staring in my window right now." The cat blinked again then turned away. I crept closer, holding my breath as I watched it move down the porch, its long tail twitching behind it. "No wait, now it's sitting next to the stairs."

"I know you've got a real sense of humor, Dani, but this could be considered wasting police time."

"I know what I'm seeing. Isn't there anyone else you can send out?"

"I've been told to direct any animal calls to the Fish and Game Department."

"Well, would you do it? I'm here by myself and this thing looks big enough to swallow me."

"My beagle's big enough to swallow you." Myra let out a snort that turned to a hacking cough.

"It is not." My size is a bit of a joke in town. I like to tell people I am five feet tall, but the sad fact is that I'm barely four eleven. I weigh 103 pounds after making four trips through an all-you-can-eat buffet. Before you envy me, ask yourself how glamorous you'd feel buying all your clothes in the children's department.

"Are you sure it isn't a bobcat?"

"The tail's too stumpy. And the head's all wrong."

"Have you tried blinking? That always helps when people are seeing things in cartoons."

"It's stretching out on the porch like it intends to stay for the night. My bladder's full and there's no bathroom here in the sugarhouse. Could you just call Fish and Game?"

"All right, but don't be surprised when the guy laughs in your tiny freckled face." Myra herself wheezed out a laugh as she disconnected. I slipped my cell phone back into my pocket and stood staring out the window at the cat, wondering how long it would take to rouse an official from Fish and Game and for him or her to arrive. I watched it scratch its ear with a well-aimed hind foot, lap its paw with a long pink tongue, and turn over on its back to scratch those hard-to-reach bits on the porch floor. Within half an hour headlights winked up the driveway. The cat must have seen them, too, because it sprang to its feet in a sleek single movement and streaked around the back of the building. I raced to the back windows and caught a glimpse of its tail as it slipped off through the trees. Relief and disappointment filled me as I heard a vehicle door slam shut. I cautiously pulled open the sugarhouse door and peeked my head out.

"Hello, over here," I called to the man standing next to a state-issued truck. He strode toward me, lanky legs covering ground almost as quickly as the cat's. Dressed for the outdoors in cargo pants and a canvas jacket, he looked like he'd stepped off the cover of an L.L.Bean catalog.

"I'm Graham Paterson, from Fish and Game. Are you the one who reported a mountain lion?"

"I am. But it's gone. I think your truck scared it off." I looked up at him, suddenly aware I had no proof of my claim.

"Uh-huh." He looked down at me, his bottle blue eyes crinkling with skepticism.

"It was just here." I walked across the creaking floorboards to where it had been and pointed at the spot. "It sat right here for half an hour."

"Were you inside or outside when you spotted it?"

"Inside. Come on, I'll show you." I led the way into the sugarhouse and gestured toward the window.

"Are you sure it wasn't a bobcat?" he asked. "People make that mistake all the time."

"It wasn't a bobcat. It had a long swishy tail."

"Swishy, huh?" He smiled. "Bobcats have tails that swish, too, when they set their minds to it."

"It was long and swishy. About the same length as its body. No bobcat has a tail that long."

"Did you take a picture of it?"

"I didn't think of that. I guess I was just too startled."

I was starting to wish I hadn't called. His smile didn't feel friendly and pleasant; it felt pitying or condescending.

"That's what everyone says when they spot mountain lions. Or Big Foot. I've even heard it said about a monster someone saw in Lake Winnipesaukee."

"I'm sure of what I saw." I fought the urge to stamp my foot on the pumpkin pine floorboards. Graham shifted from peering out the window to scanning the room. His gaze landed on the wineglass.

"How much had you been drinking when you noticed the lion?"

"Only a few sips." I felt my cheeks ignite and something that felt like heartburn but was probably righteous anger welling up in my chest. "I thought when you'd had too much, you were supposed to see pink elephants, not big cats." I was not going to let my anger show. For one thing, it was beneath me, but more important, I look ridiculous when I get angry. My face gets splotchy and I break out in hives. My normally squeaky voice climbs up into dog whistle range and I sometimes punch the air with a fist scaled for a Barbie doll.

"In my experience with the department, I've noticed tippling causes all sorts of animal hallucinations."

"Then I won't offer you any." I tried not to flounce around in a huff but I know it was exactly what I did. I could see it as clearly as if I were having an out-of-body experience.

"I'm on duty anyway, so even if you had been so gracious as to offer, I could not have accepted." He sounded like a cop. After my disastrous and very public breakup with a local police officer, I didn't consider that a compliment.

"Since we agree this isn't a social call, shouldn't you do some investigating? Poke around looking for tracks or something?"

"Did you see which way it went, whatever it was?"

"The mountain lion went that way." I pointed behind the sugarhouse.

"I'll let you know what I find. Or don't." He descended the steps and was out of sight before I could get back inside. I hurried through the sugar shack and into the attached shop to get a better view of him. He walked slowly into the sugar bush, stopping every so often to inspect something closely. Before long he disappeared through the trees.

I turned away from the window and moved around the cold shop, touching a syrup bottle on one shelf, a maple leaf shaped stack of plates on another. Maple leaf shaped wrought iron sconces hung on the wooden walls. Spread on the floor in front of the cash register lay a maple leaf motif hooked rug. All through the previous summer I had sourced merchandise with a maple theme for the shop. Now the store was stocked with products ranging from maple wood cribbage boards to maple liquor. We had opened just in time for fall foliage season, and the leaf peepers visited in droves. Encouraged by the success of our opening season, I planned to spend the winter developing a line of specialty food items to sell bearing the Greener Pastures name. I was thinking about a maple-flavored

Jessie Crockett

cheese spread when I heard footsteps in the sugarhouse. I
hurried back out front and found Graham leaning over the
evaporator.

"I didn't find any tracks or scat."

"Did you really look? I don't think you went out there
with an open mind."

"I treat each and every call seriously, no matter how
far-fetched the claim." He crossed his long arms over his
chest, his stance wide and appearing rooted to the spot. It
occurred to me he might still be here when the rest of the
family returned if I didn't hurry him along. Then I'd be
forced to explain how my migraine led me to entertain a
visitor in the sugarhouse rather than to lie down in a dark
room. Knowing them, they'd gleefully assume there was
something romantic going on and I'd have to endure more
disappointed tongue clucking when I explained what really
happened.

"Well, don't let me waste any more of your time." I
crossed to the door and yanked it open.

"I need to jot down a few notes to write up a report."
He pulled a small notebook from a pocket in his uniform
jacket. "Do you have a pen?"

"Aren't you supposed to be like a professional Boy
Scout? I would have thought you'd always be prepared."
I shut the door, crossed to the workbench, and handed
him a pen.

"Let's say I never got all the badges. Since you seem
to be in a hurry, I'll just get a couple of particulars and
fill out the rest later. Let's start with your name."

"Dani Greene."

"Is Dani short for Danielle?"

"No, it is not." I wasn't about to tell him what it was short for either. The last man I'd shared that with got a splinter in his cheek from rolling around on a hardwood floor laughing.

"We'll leave it at Dani then. Age?"

"Twenty-seven."

"Really?" I didn't think he was trying to flatter me. Most people think I'm nineteen, maybe twenty. Sometimes I even get asked for my license when I try to get into an R-rated movie. If I wear a pleated skirt and Mary Janes, I can order off the children's menu. You want directions to the fountain of youth? A hyperactive metabolism, short stature, and freckles. As far as I can tell, I'll never be able to convince anyone to give me a senior citizen discount.

"Really. Any more questions?"

"Marital status?"

"Is that one of the questions?" Having a biological big brother, I tend to be wary of the governmental kind.

"Not officially, but another conservation officer and I are conducting an informal survey. We've documented a higher-than-normal call rate from unmarried women on Friday nights. Especially from those who've been drinking." He grinned at me again and I felt my Barbie fists curl and land on my hips.

"I think we're done here." I scurried to the door as quickly as my short legs allowed and popped it open, hoping a hungry mountain lion would pounce into the sugarhouse and consume one of us. I was embarrassed enough that I didn't even care which of us was eaten.

11

"It's your call." He pocketed the notebook and laid my pen and a business card on the bench next to the wine bottle. "Don't hesitate to contact me if you see anything else. I'll be working next Friday night, too." He flashed me a condescending smirk.

I stood there stunned into angry silence while he backed down the driveway. I slammed the door then opened it so I could slam it again. As soon as his taillights started to fade, I remembered I was several hundred yards from the main house and there was a mountain lion prowling nearby. Fueled by fear and anger, I ran all the way to the house. Just in time, too, because as soon as I'd snuggled myself under my quilt, the heat of anger finally dissipated in the chilly air of the drafty farmhouse, I heard the crunch of gravel in the driveway and my family's raised voices as they swarmed inside.

Two

Thanks to the efforts of the Sap Bucket Brigade, the grange hall looked festive and inviting when I arrived early the next morning hoping to make up for not helping the night before. Every table was decorated with a balloon bouquet and a maple leaf centerpiece. Each place setting at the contest table had a pint of Greener Pastures maple syrup centered on the plate. Members of the Brigade hurried around the hall, arguing over the number of expected attendees and when to start perking the coffee. As usual, Myra Phelps's voice rasped out over the rest and took charge. When not fielding calls at the police station, she served as the president of the auxiliary. With the clout of the police department behind her, she got her way the majority of the time. Rumor had it she had spent a portion of her youth working as a lady wrestler, and watching her bully the treasurer, Connie Wilson, into starting the coffee, it was easy to imagine.

I had just poured myself a cup of coffee when the door to the hall creaked open, sending the balloon bouquets dancing on their ribbon tethers. I looked up wondering if some hungry guests were trying to sneak in early. There stood Graham Paterson, turning a wool cap around and around in his hands. We locked eyes and he made straight for me. I looked around for somewhere to go and then, realizing the auxiliary women were all watching, decided to minimize any scene that might make for a good story as soon as anyone showed up to tell it to.

"I owe you an apology," Graham said, stopping in front of me.

"For what? Calling me drunk, calling me crazy, or for implying I was lonely and desperate enough to lie to get a man to my house?"

"All three. Some information has come my way that makes your call make a lot more sense and I should have taken it more seriously." I looked at him over the paper rim of my coffee cup.

"You look like you could use some coffee yourself." He nodded and followed me to the coffee station. I poured him a cup and watched as he carefully added cream but no sugar. No sweet tooth. After his attitude the night before, I should have known.

"I really am sorry. Could we sit for a minute? I've been up all night." I looked at his face a little more closely. His eyes were shadowed underneath, and his shoulders weren't quite as straight as they had been the night before.

Even his dark curls seemed to have lost some of their spring. I nodded and was surprised when he pulled out a chair at a long table and pointed at it for me to take a seat.

"So what's this new information?" People would be arriving in just a few minutes and we needed the seats. The pancake breakfast always runs to capacity, and this year they were expecting a bigger than usual turnout since the auxiliary decided to add home fries to the menu.

"The state police spotted an abandoned, empty tractor trailer truck on the side of the highway. A few miles up they found the driver on foot."

"So?"

"He'd been illegally transporting exotic animals for a friend who was selling them to another unauthorized collector."

"Did you say the truck was empty?"

"That's the heart of the matter. He pulled over and let all the animals loose."

"Why?" The thought of letting exotic animals loose to roam around someone else's town was completely unconscionable. And not just because of the danger to the people. Most exotic animals weren't built for New Hampshire winters and ours was almost here.

"He blamed it on the parrots."

"The parrots?"

"He ran out of room in the back so he strapped a cage with a pair of parrots into the passenger seat of the cab with him. At first he thought they were entertaining, the way they seemed like they were talking to each other."

"Skip to the part where he lets the animals loose."

"I'm getting there. As the miles wore on, he got better at piecing together what the birds were saying. By the time he got to Sugar Grove, they were repeating some choice bits of conversation between his wife and the friend he was helping." Graham's stubbly cheeks turned a bit red and he dropped his eyes to his coffee cup.

"What kind of choice bits?" Seeing him squirm was improving my morning.

"Endearments, passionate vocalizations, criticisms of the husband's bedroom performance." He picked at the rim of the paper cup with a rough thumbnail.

"So he decided to get back at the guy by turning the animals loose?"

"That's the gist of it."

"So what exactly did he let loose?" I could just feel the validation coming, could almost see it forming on his lips.

"Peacocks, a couple of cassowaries, several large snakes, a zebra, and a couple of kangaroos. A camel was mentioned along with lemurs, sloths, alligators, and a few squirrel monkeys."

"But no big cats?" I couldn't believe what I was hearing.

"There was a leopard tortoise."

"Have you ever heard of a tortoise with teeth?"

"No, but I've never heard of a mountain lion actually being in New Hampshire either. Maybe you saw a capybara. There was one of those, too."

"Aren't they the world's largest rodent? Those definitely don't have a swishy tail as long as their bodies." I could feel my anger rising again. "I really don't have time for this. The breakfast is due to start in just a few minutes and there are still some things I need to do." I shoved back my chair.

"I'm here not only to apologize but also to ask a favor."

"Hold on, now you want a favor? I already gave you a cup of coffee and somewhere to sit, not to mention time I don't really have to offer."

"I understand. I just want to make an announcement sometime during the breakfast to appeal to residents not to be alarmed if they also see unusual animals in the area."

"You're going to want to ask them not to take it upon themselves to remedy the situation while you're at it. Not everyone around here would think to call Fish and Game if there was an alligator in the backyard."

"So the Gila monster might be in more danger from the residents than from the cold snap in the forecast?"

"I think that's a safe bet. You can stick around and make your announcement but wait until after the pancake-eating contest. I don't want talk about a zebra stealing the limelight, at least not until it's necessary."

"Thanks. I'm sure it will help if I get to talk to everyone."

"Let's just hope you make a better impression on the pancake enthusiasts than you have on me." I stood up and lobbed my paper cup at the nearby trash can, making a neat basket, and then headed to the kitchen to see how I could help before the doors flew open and the crowds roared in.

"Who's the fella?" Myra lifted her voice over the sizzle of sausage and the clang of grill scrapers.

"The guy from Fish and Game. He wants to make a public service announcement."

"He's pretty easy on the eyes." She squinted through the smoke rising up off the griddle. A pair of ancient volunteers stood a couple of feet away beating pancake batter with a whisk. Several other women from the auxiliary raced to and fro with plates and pitchers of syrup. One carried a tray loaded with dishes of butter.

"I hadn't noticed." I kept my back deliberately turned on Graham, instead focusing on the river of fat leaking out of the sausage patties.

"Well, no wonder you're getting to be an old maid. When I was your age, I had a line of men stretching out the door." It was hard to imagine. Myra's year-round wardrobe consisted of stretch knit shorts and tank tops. Not to mention whenever she flipped a sausage patty, it set her flabby triceps swinging like a hammock in a hurricane.

"I guess I'm just picky."

"Well, I suppose with your youthful looks, you've got a little more time than most. Although if you go around telling eligible men you've seen a mountain lion, you'll die a spinster for sure. Wait 'til Mitch hears what you've been saying. He'll be glad you dumped him." Mitch, the police officer I'd been dating, had dumped me, but I wasn't about to correct her. "Do me a favor and open the doors." She pointed her spatula toward the entrance. Connie Wilson, the Sap Bucket Brigade's treasurer, hurried after me and stationed herself at the ticket table just inside the doorway. I heard the crowd and felt the tremors beneath my feet as I approached the threshold. A news report about a man killed in a Black Friday sale stampede flashed through my mind as I grabbed the door handle.

Within moments, tables were filled with people munching pancakes and sausage drenched in Greener Pastures syrup. My family entered with the rest of the guests and spread out to sit with friends at tables all around the hall. All except my grandparents, who headed for the contest table at the front like they had for more than fifty years. I poured them each a cup of coffee and picked my way through the throng to the front table. They both put on a good show, but their age was starting to creep up and I liked to make things easy on them whenever I could.

"So you're feeling better then?" Grandma asked. She used the same tone of voice she always had when asking if anyone knew who had been at the cookie jar. There was nothing left to do but confess.

"It was the sort of thing cured easily enough by a couple of hours left on your own."

"I find that particular virus gives me a bad bout of food poisoning. Your grandfather always has wondered how I'm the only one to get it." A smile spread over her ruby red lips. Grandma comes from a generation of women that always dress to go to town and she had outdone herself this morning. From her wool tweed skirt to her cashmere twin set and pearls, she was every inch a lady. Even in her seventies she favored strappy heels despite dire warnings from her physician about hip replacements.

"I won't be the one to tell him." I stretched up on tiptoe and planted a kiss on her papery cheek. "Doesn't Grampa look like he's in fine form this morning?" Grampa is as disheveled as Grandma is elegant. His long salt-and-pepper beard always drags in his soup and his socks never match. Making things even worse, he's colorblind but insists he isn't and won't ever ask for help. He caught us watching him and waggled his gnarled fingers flirtatiously in Grandma's direction. Despite their surface differences, they go together like pancakes and syrup. If I was picky about men, it was only because I knew what kind of marriage was possible after having them as an example all these years.

"He does love to be the center of attention." Grandma looked up and down the contest table. "Who's vying for the pewter syrup pitcher this year? Besides your grandfather, I mean."

"Roland Chick, Jill Hayes, Alanza Speedwell, and a couple of boys from the junior firefighters."

"That woman ought to know better than to show her face at a town function after the way she's ruined the property Lewis left her." Grandma scowled like she'd just found a gnat in her dentures. "And to imagine sitting at the table with Roland, outrageous."

"I've never noticed Alanza having a sensitive side. Besides, she is the secretary of the Sap Bucket Brigade. She's got to put in an appearance at their main fundraiser." I looked out at the sea of people, wondering when Alanza would arrive. I expected to hear a rumble go through the crowd when she did show.

Alanza inherited a valuable parcel of land covered in sugar bush three years earlier. The previous owner, Lewis Bett, had allowed townsfolk to tap the trees without a thought to charging them. The local snowmobile club was encouraged to establish trails through the property, and one of the area's best fishing holes could be accessed by cutting through the south corner of the eighty-acre spread. When Alanza first took ownership, she gave her blessing to all the activities the community was accustomed to, and Sugar Grove heaved a collective sigh of relief. She was welcomed with open arms into many town committees and clubs, including the Sap Bucket Brigade, despite her unorthodox appearance and flamboyant behavior. Things had cooled for her socially over the last year, once she decided to clear-cut pristine acreage in order to open a self-storage facility.

Suddenly, the happy rippling of a contented crowd vanished. A general sucking in of breath made it sound like the room had fallen into a hurricane. Roland Chick was on his bunion-burdened feet before Alanza could cross the room. His face was changing color as if his mother had been an octopus. First green then gray, then almost purple. Even the babies stopped crying. Alanza Speedwell headed toward us, her wispy eggplant-colored hair streaming behind her as she moved. Clacking from her thigh-high boots was the only sound echoing through the hall as she mounted the stage and found her place card at the contest table. She tugged at her zebra-striped miniskirt, which had migrated so far north it was threatening to become a cummerbund.

"Well, don't all stop eating on account of me," she said, dragging her chair back and settling herself, crossing one plump thigh over the other. Most women in New

Hampshire don't wear skirts on a daily basis. They certainly don't once the temperature at night drops below freezing. Just looking at hers dropped the temperature in the room by several degrees. Alanza was like a portable air-conditioning unit. I only wished it were July instead of November.

"I think your arrival has caused most people to lose their appetites," Roland said from the other end of the table. At least someone had enough sense not to seat them together.

"I can only hope that's true of the other competitors since I've got my eye on the pewter pitcher."

"Nobody puts me off my feed, especially not with my favorite cheerleader here to egg me on," Grampa said, blowing a kiss at Grandma. He took his spot between Alanza's seat and the one held for Jill Hayes, who had yet to appear, then nodded at the high school boys on the far side of Alanza. Myra took a break from flipping sausage to be sure the competitors were ready. It was already ten minutes past when the contest was scheduled to begin, and even though Jill still hadn't arrived, Myra announced we should get started. She signaled for the pancake servers to stream in from the kitchen. The official referee blew his whistle and the competition began.

Cheering erupted from the hall and children stood on their folding chairs to get a better view of adults eating in a way they'd be sent from the table for imitating. Roland held his own for the first three towering stacks of pancakes despite his heart troubles and his wife's admonishments to consider his health. The teenagers came on strong at the beginning but faded fast once the fourth and fifth stacks were placed in front of them. Only Alanza and Grampa remained by the sixth stack of steaming cakes.

Grampa shifted in his seat in just the way he did every year at Thanksgiving to make room for pie. Alanza seemed to favor saturating the pancakes with so much syrup they dissolved into a pile of mush and needed no chewing. Only slowing to swat his beard out of his plate, Grampa maintained a steady pace through his seventh stack. Alanza, however, began to slow down. Her shoulders slumped and her eyes became glazed. Squinting at her carefully, I noticed a bit of foam forming at the corners of her mouth. Before I could ask if she was all right, she swayed gently, let out a deep moan, and pitched face-first into her plate.

Three

I stood, stunned, unsure whether to cheer or to call for the ambulance. It looked like a win for Grampa, bringing his streak to thirty-seven in a row. The junior firefighters were on their feet attempting to administer first aid. One pulled Alanza's face out of her plate, the other felt her syrup-covered neck for a pulse. Grandma, a nurse before her marriage, stepped up to help him. After a couple of moments she looked at me and shook her head.

I looked out over the crowd, searching for Bob Sterling, the town's only full-time EMT. Graham materialized beside me.

"I guess now might not be the right time for my announcement," he said. I was distracted from answering him by Lowell Matthews, the police chief and my godfather, emerging from the kitchen, his business look on his face. It was the one he pulled out for speeding teenagers,

24

men attempting to get friendly with underaged girls, and drivers with boozy breath. I worked my way closer to Grandma once more. She placed her bony hand on my elbow and squeezed harder than I can remember her doing other than the time I started to tell Aunt Hazel what I really thought of the birthday present she sent me when I was six. Suddenly, she looked frail and not entirely like the grandmother I knew.

I felt a cold wash of fear pour over me, as if Alanza's death had suddenly made death real for us all and I wanted its cold fingers off my loved ones. I scanned the room for my mother and siblings but couldn't make them out in the chaos. Even though I stood on the stage area, many of the breakfast goers were still taller than me and blocked my view. At least Grampa was in sight. He bent over Alanza along with Lowell. They seemed to be conferring and I nodded at Grandma before sliding closer to them.

"Does it look like a heart attack?" Lowell asked Bob Sterling.

"Maybe. No outward signs of what happened. But then again, you never know." Bob raised an eyebrow like he had his doubts.

"Considering how popular she was and that she died eating something she didn't prepare, I'm going to play it safe on this one." Lowell said. Then he did something I'd never heard him do. He hollered. A deep, rumbling, frightening holler that stopped all noise in the grange, just as Alanza had when she traipsed through it earlier. Back when she still could move her body.

"I need everyone to remain here. I'm going to need to

ask a few questions and to take attendance of who was here this morning. But first, has anyone else here taken ill? Anyone who feels the least bit off?" Lowell scanned the room, as did everyone else. All heads rotated in unison, curious about their neighbors. "Please, don't eat anything else. I expect no one is in any danger but I don't want to take any chances. Please remain seated and an officer will be by to take your statement or collect your contact information just as quickly as possible." Grandma stretched to whisper something in Lowell's ear and I saw him nod. "Families with children will be spoken with first in order to let them get on home. Thanks for your patience."

He nodded at Mitch Reynolds, my tall, blond, and almost handsome ex-boyfriend, who headed for the the stage, an open notepad in his hand.

Lowell had a notepad of his own out and was jotting down things my grandparents were saying about timelines and consumption. Mostly, I heard Grampa evaluating Alanza's technique as a pancake-eating contestant until Grandma reminded him that Lowell was more interested in learning how she died. The two high school boys looked both scared and excited at the same time. This was going to be a really big deal at school on Monday.

I looked over the assembled group and thought about how a town that could be counted on to turn out for a firefighters' fund-raiser could also be one that would murder someone at the same event. Not that I was sure it was murder. Someone as rotten as Alanza might well be poisoned by her own spit. Considering the toxic things she said, it was a miracle it hadn't happened before now.

Mitch was dismissing families with small children at a surprisingly fast clip. The hall was steadily thinning out. He looked up from the Johnson family and noticed my gaze. He pointed at me and then at a seat at the table in front of him. I was tempted to ignore him and wait for Lowell to be available but decided that if everyone else was doing their best to behave like good citizens, I could, too. I plunked myself down in the chair he indicated.

"What were you doing up there with Alanza at the time of her unfortunate demise?" He towered over me, his notebook in one hand, a pencil with a freshly sharpened tip in the other.

"I was cheering my grandfather on, of course. Alanza just happened to be one of the other competitors."

"You aren't going out of town anytime soon, are you?"

"You know we never go anywhere for Thanksgiving. You know how the family is about all the decorating. After the effort that goes into gussying the place up, they want to stick around and soak in the sight of it. Why? Are you telling me I'm a suspect?"

"Of course you are. All the Greenes are suspects. Not only did she die while eating your syrup, you were standing right there when she died. For all I know, you slipped something into her food or drink when no one was paying attention."

"Why would any of us want to kill her?"

"The pewter pitcher, of course." Mitch shook his head and rolled his eyes at me.

I looked back over to the stage. Lowell was carefully placing Alanza's plate into one plastic bag, her jug of syrup into another, her coffee cup into a third. I tried to remember if I'd touched anything on the table, but the only thing I could think of was the coffee I'd handed to my grandparents. I wondered if they would check the surfaces of the items for fingerprints as well as the contents for poisons. There were so many people involved in an event like this, it seemed like fingerprints wouldn't be much help. Everyone on the kitchen staff could have touched the plates, cups, and flatware. The patrons could have touched anything, including plates they decided not to use. I'd noticed children being asked to stop touching things all morning long. Their fingerprints wouldn't make them murderers. Then there was my family. We had all helped handle the maple syrup jugs the night before. Who knew whose prints would be on each bottle? There was nothing special about Alanza's other than her name being on it to serve as a place marker at the table.

"You think one of us would kill over a pancake-eating competition?"

Every year Celadon takes a lot of care writing each contestant's name on a maple leaf shaped paper tag, which she then ties to a bottle of syrup. The tradition started years ago when Celadon wanted to show off that she had mastered cursive. Grandma even created a scrapbook with Grampa's tag from each year mounted next to a photo of him holding his pewter pitcher trophy. The trophy meant a lot to all of us since Grampa loves to win, but none of us would kill over it.

"I think if anyone thought they could get away with murder in this town, it's your family."

"There are plenty of other people in this room who are happy to see Alanza buttered side down. If I were you, I'd start talking to some of them." I stood and started to stomp away. It had been a rough few days, and the thought of being accused of murder was bringing on a headache that was much closer to a real migraine than I liked. Mitch grabbed my arm and held me in place.

"No matter what you say, I've got my eye on you. If you or any of your family had something to do with this, I'll go right over the chief's head to the state police if I think he can't be objective." Mitch shoved his pencil into his breast pocket so hard the tip punched through the fabric.

"I'll be sure to let him know you said that. It will do your career a world of good for him to know you are a man of such integrity." I wrenched my arm away. "And speaking of your career, don't you think you ought to hurry up and question the Shaws? You don't want to keep a seated selectman waiting longer than necessary." Mitch scurried over to the table where Kenneth was seated with his wife, Nicole. Kenneth checked his watch twice in the amount of time it took him to cross the twenty feet of the grange hall.

I found a spot in the corner to sit and let my eyes wander the room. Everywhere I looked, there were people who might celebrate Alanza's death. The snowmobile club had more members than the church; her neighbors Roland and Felicia Chick and even many syrup makers like the curiously absent Jill Hayes had good reason to celebrate her sudden demise. If she had been poisoned, suspects would be thicker on the ground than ticks in an unmown field. I sat wondering about how my family could stop being among them until Lowell came over to dismiss me about a half hour later.

"What do you think they'll do about the pewter pitcher?" Grampa asked as soon as I slid the minivan door into place.

"What do you mean, do about it?" Grandma asked.

"Well, I won, didn't I? I kept on eating after Alanza so I'm clearly the winner."

"I'm not sure it counts as a win if the competition dies," my grandmother said quietly. She isn't given to a lot of words like her husband and never has much to say that isn't worth hearing.

"I ate more than she did before she keeled over, too." Grampa leaned forward excitedly, causing his seat belt to cinch tightly across his belly.

"But no one can be sure she wouldn't have eaten more if she hadn't died."

"Ahh, but she did die, now didn't she? Making me the winner. I shouldn't think a thing like this should break my winning streak." Grampa pulled at his beard, stopping to inspect a bit of dried food stuck in the end of it.

"But Mitch already asked me if we poisoned her to make sure you won the pewter pitcher. I think you'd better lie low with this for a bit," I said, feeling a knot of worry tighten in my still empty stomach.

"Besides, Emerald, you know that is simply unseemly. You are absolutely without feeling carrying on like that." Grandma smoothed her skirt the way she always did when she felt the unusual need to rebuke Grampa.

"But, Olive—" Grampa said.

"Don't 'but, Olive' me. I will speak to Myra Phelps tomorrow after church but you will not, I repeat, not bring this up to anyone else. Dani is right. We don't need that sort of headache. If you insist on behaving like that, we'll all come down with one of Dani's migraines." Grandma skewered me with a knowing look that made me glad I had confessed earlier rather than having that to look forward to at the end of a long, hungry morning.

Grampa harrumphed and sank back against his seat, uncharacteristically quiet for the remainder of the five-mile journey. It was too early in the season for potholes and I was able to get a good smooth view off into the woods along the side of the road. Maples and hemlocks filled the woods with scatterings of beeches, their dried leaves clinging to the branches like old people wearing the hairstyles of their youth. Through the trees I spotted something moving oddly. After my encounter with the mountain lion the night before, my senses were on high alert. I leaned forward, pressing my snub nose to the tinted glass. I blinked, then blinked again. Last night the game warden had said wine was the culprit for my hallucinations. Now I was asking myself if it was low blood sugar.

Hustling between the trees, I was sure, sure enough to bet my bossy oldest sister Celadon's life on it, was a large donkey in a black-and-white-striped costume. I squinted and blinked some more. Sure enough, it was still there. No one I knew of in town had a donkey. The Spencer family had one in the past to keep predators away from their flock of chickens but it had unfortunately eaten some siding off its enclosure and died of internal bloating. Unless I was looking at the striped ghost of a gluttonous donkey, something else was up. Or I really was hallucinating. If I thought for sure I was seeing this apparition, was I still certain I had seen the mountain lion the night before? Could that obnoxious man from the state have actually been right about me seeing things? Then, I remembered what Graham had said about the escaped animals. Alanza's death had driven that bit of exciting news right out of my mind.

"Did you see that?" I asked Grandma, reaching toward her with my closest hand, not taking my eyes off the creature in the woods. But before she answered, the animal disappeared. I leaned back in my seat but continued to scan the trees for another glimpse of it. The road bends away from the woods, and before I knew it, we were out of sight.

"I'm sorry, Dani," Grandma said. "See what?"

"Never mind. I must have been imagining things. Besides, whatever it was is gone now." I didn't tell anyone about my mountain lion sighting, but they could find out down at the Stack or the general store or even the post office if the gossip about Alanza didn't manage to sink it deep enough under the feet of old news. I found myself hoping gossip would run amok and Myra wouldn't have any tidbits to share concerning me. Or that even if she did, no one would be interested. But since she was at the police department, it seemed like she would be the most favored conduit of information concerning the possible murder and that my secret was safe as long as the guy from the state didn't say anything.

Even if he did, it wasn't likely he'd say anything to anyone I knew. He could blab all he wanted to the other guys back at the Fish and Game station house, wherever that was, and tell them about the crazy woman who'd been drinking and thought a mountain lion was padding across her porch like a house cat. It probably gave him something fun to share with his coworkers, a good laugh, a deep rumbling chuckle, but nothing that affected my reputation as long as he didn't attach the name of the sugarhouse to the story.

Could he do that? Was there some sort of oath of office, some kind of professional code that would not permit him to disclose the names of people involved with a distress call? I didn't know whom I could ask, except maybe Knowlton Pringle, the local taxidermist. He spent a lot of time roaming the woods and encountered at least his fair share of game wardens. Maybe more than his fair share.

He looked a little disreputable and he'd been spoken to about keeping any flashlights pointed toward the ground on a few occasions when he tried explaining he was not out flashing deer, just trying to find roadkill in need of stuffing. At least that's what constitutes bragging in Knowlton's world, tall tales of deep woods encounters of the game warden kind. I'd rather stew in my own worry juice than approach Knowlton for information.

If I asked Myra about it, that would only serve to remind her about the incident in the first place and she would be sure to spread it round. If I asked anyone in the family, they'd want to know what I was doing in the sugarhouse when I had a migraine. No solution came to me and my spirits flagged. By the time we reached the house, I was ready to climb into bed and pull the covers over my head. Unfortunately, that wasn't on the schedule. We were already two hours later getting home than the worst-case scenario I had envisioned, and tonight was the monthly Griddle and Fiddle gathering at the Stack Shack.

I also knew I'd be dragooned into silver-polishing duty and all sorts of kitchen tasks in preparation for Thanksgiving creeping toward us on Thursday. Grandma was already drying a mountain of bread cubes for stuffing and had mentioned me whipping up a maple cranberry sauce. I was trialing a few new recipes at each holiday for possible inclusion at the shop and had even started tinkering with the idea of a Greener Pastures cookbook to sell there.

And I was still starving, having never gotten around to breakfast. I tucked my sneakers into one of the shoe cubbies lining a whole wall in the mudroom. For years the shoes from such a big family piled up helter-skelter and made us all crazy. One morning Loden woke us all with the sounds of a circular saw. By the end of the weekend we had a totally transformed mudroom thanks to his quiet way of taking on a project and solving a problem. I grabbed my pair of sheepskin-lined slippers from the wicker slipper basket and tugged them on as I headed for the savory smells floating out of the kitchen.

The wood-burning cookstove was lit, just as it had been since the middle of September. Grandma stood stirring a pot of stew she'd left on a cast iron burner to simmer while we were gone.

"Just as I'd hoped, not scorched in the least." She held out the tasting spoon toward me for a slurp.

"I'd eat it, even if it was." I swallowed the stew too eagerly and burned my tongue in the process. Damn. Now I wouldn't really taste a thing at the Stack tonight.

"Whoever heard of anyone not getting their fill at an all-you-can-eat pancake breakfast? Better not say that in front of Myra. She's sure to take offense." Grandma grabbed the saltshaker and added so little it seemed more like a habit than an actual correction of flavors.

"I meant to eat but Alanza's death sort of made everything a bit unappealing, safety-wise." Grandma nodded and reached for the ladle. I moved to a white-painted cupboard and reached up on tiptoe to pull down a stack of soup bowls. The ceilings in this part of the house are lower than those elsewhere but everything still seemed impossibly high. The original builders knew what they were doing in the kitchen. It was housed in the ell, attached to the barn, like so many other New England homes.

It wasn't built with a full basement underneath, more like a generous crawl space. I can stand up in it but no other adult I know can. Which has led to a lot of time spent down there fetching or placing things no one else can comfortably accomplish. The windows on the north side of the room were small, but they still let in the cold, so the low ceiling helped combat what could be considerable chill. With the stove working away all but three months of the year, the space managed to stay cozy.

I grabbed a handful of spoons and plunked them on

the counter next to the bowls. Grandma ladled stew into mine, and I dug into it with a will. I ate the first bowl standing over the sink then refilled it, and after thanking Grandma for her efforts, I took my second helping to the sugarhouse. I had a few things left to prepare for the state inspection scheduled for Tuesday morning. Besides, I was in no mood for the winks the battery-operated Santa my mother had positioned in the kitchen rocker kept sending my way. No matter how many times I snuck down in the night and removed his batteries, someone replaced them by the time I came down for coffee in the morning.

Four

No one else in the family was up for going to the Griddle and Fiddle evening. Mostly they were too worn out from the excitement of the day, but in Celadon's case, she couldn't stand the homegrown music. I grabbed the keys to the farm pickup truck and dashed out the door. I glanced down at my jeans and realized they were too dirty to wear out, even for me. I zipped back inside, dug a clean pair from the bottom drawer of my dresser, and tossed on a fresh T-shirt and wool pullover for good measure. I paused in front of the mirror to check that there were no burrs or twigs sticking out of my hair and twisted my head to check each ear.

Nestled tightly to each lobe was the only bit of finery I generally bother with, emerald earrings, given to me on my thirteenth birthday by my grandfather. All the Greene women had an almost identical pair with an emerald center and her own birthstone set around the outside. Mine had an outer ring of sapphires, and I wore them almost every day. The tradition started with Grampa's grandparents and had continued down through the generations. Oftentimes, a pair like mine had belonged to another woman in the family and had been saved to pass down. I swiped a quick layer of gloss over my lips and hurried back out the door.

On Griddle and Fiddle night, I always try to get to the Stack early to give my best friend, Piper Wynwood, a hand. She hates to ask the regular staff to come unless they volunteer, and she's always running around like a crazy person at the last minute. All the way over I thought about the buzz Alanza's death would cause at the gathering. Generally, the Griddle and Fiddle sessions were pure fun. I wondered if even Piper would be able to pull off the magical atmosphere that usually came so naturally to spaces where she appeared.

I pulled my car around behind the Stack and banged on the back door to be let in. Piper held it open while I carried in a slow cooker full of maple mustard glazed kielbasa bites. I loved the music at the Griddle and Fiddle, but it was also a great place to observe which foods were a real hit and which ones got a wishy-washy reception. Piper used the evenings to trial potential menu items for the restaurant, and I practiced on mixes and sauces we were considering retailing at the shop. Sometimes we combined the two. Piper would use my sauces on a menu item in the Stack and make a note in the menu that it was available at Greener Pastures. We did the same in the shop, mentioning that if you loved it in the jar, you'd love it the way Piper added it to her specialties in the Stack.

Piper lifted the dish out of my hand and set it on a gleaming stainless steel counter. Heat radiated off the grill like a pavement in summer. Enough batter to fill a washing machine drum sat mixed and ready in a container nearby. I smelled coffee brewing and suddenly realized how much I would need a couple of cups if I was going to last the evening.

"You look worn out. Knowlton dropped in straight from the breakfast this morning to tell me you were right there when the old bat keeled over." Piper never minced words. I wished I could be more like her, assertive without being mean.

"It was a shock. But that isn't the only thing going on." I filled her in on the mountain lion and the other loose animals. I didn't tell her the Fish and Game guy was nice looking. Some things are best kept to oneself. Not that that ever worked with Piper.

"So was he cute?"

"The mountain lion?" I asked.

"The Fish and Game guy." She scowled at me, which might have been intimidating if I hadn't known her since before she was old enough to cross the street alone.

"If you like his type, I guess he wasn't bad looking." I knew I was being evasive. I even knew it would cause her to dig like a badger into what happened last night. I just couldn't bring myself to admit I had made a fool of myself in front of a cute guy rather than scoring a date like Piper always managed to do.

"So he was cute. 'Check out his butt when he's bent over in frozen foods' cute? Or 'ram into his car in the parking lot in order to exchange insurance information so you can stalk him' cute?"

"He's not my type so I'm sure I couldn't say." I felt prim even saying it. I always sound prim when I lie. I hate that about myself. Lying turns me into a Victorian-era maiden aunt.

"Is he my type?" Piper leaned on the counter, propping her pointy little elfin chin on her fist. All down her forearm a Jack in the Beanstalk tattoo swirled and danced. Grimm's Fairy Tales were painted on all parts of her body; she was like a flesh-and-blood storyscape. My favorite was the one on her back of Sleeping Beauty at the spinning wheel.

"He might be a little clean-cut for you." Piper generally went for either similarly tattooed guys or ones in quirky vintage three-piece suits. Men with a normal appearance never seemed to register on her radar.

"Are you calling me a dirty girl?" Piper pouted and blew a giant pink bubble right in my face. I wasn't sure gum met health inspection regulations, but who was I going to tell?

"Of course not. He's just a bit pedestrian for your tastes. He was wearing a uniform."

"A uniform?"

"Yeah. Like a police officer."

"Nope. Not my type. I don't do uniforms. You can't tell anything about a man as an individual if he's wearing a uniform."

"I don't know about that. Clothes don't make the man."

"After what happened with Mitch, I can see why you said he wasn't your type if he showed up in a uniform." Piper slurped her gum back into her mouth and clicked on the fleet of waffle makers on a nearby counter.

"That was kind of a turnoff for the whole men-in-uniform thing," I said. Which was too bad since I didn't share Piper's view on that subject before Mitch. I mean really, most men aren't all that great at putting together a decent outfit. In the case of a uniform, a professional has designed it and all he has to do is put it on. I often wish I had a uniform of my own to wear that was a no-brainer and always looked great. The closest I had were jeans and a long-sleeved T-shirt. Not really the same caliber as a police uniform, but at least I could usually find something in my size.

"So was the whole Alanza thing as bad as people are saying?"

"What are they saying?"

"She foamed at the mouth. Turned turquoise then fell splat into her plate without so much as a moan."

"It wasn't quite like that. Who have you been talking to?"

"Who haven't I been talking to? Roland Chick is the one I've given the most credence to since he was at the competitors' table when it happened."

"Yes. He was. He wasn't sitting right next to her, but he had bowed out of the competition and was simply observing Alanza and Grampa by the time she keeled over. He was in a good position to see everything."

"So were you from the sounds of it."

"I was. I was standing right there, just to the side of the table. It was so strange, it almost looked fake. One minute she was cheesing people off and the next she was flopped over in the flapjacks. I can't believe I'm saying this, but it sort of put me off maple syrup."

"I wouldn't let it get to me that bad, sweetie. A good night's sleep ought to cure you of any bad memories and you'll be back to swilling the stuff by the gallon before you know it."

"I'm not so sure. It was pretty gruesome." I didn't like thinking about the way the syrup had clung to her face when Grandma had turned her head to keep her airways clear.

"You need to get right back on the horse." With that, Piper popped open a waffle iron and poured in some batter. Steam rose from the machine when she closed the lid, and the smell of crisp baking waffles filled the air. When the machine beeped, she pried it open and grabbed a plate. Placing a waffle on it, she reached for a syrup jug and uncapped it. "Here, do the honors yourself." She thrust the plate and jug into my hands and I noticed the Greener Pastures label on the jug. There was no way Alanza was going to turn me off my favorite food. Besides, with my hummingbird-like metabolism, I might just perish without a steady stream of the stuff.

I sat the plate on the counter, drizzled on a healthy slug of golden goodness, and hacked off a bite with the side of my fork. The deep, rich sweetness touched my tongue then filled my throat. The crunch of the waffle combined with the full flavor of the syrup took the edge off the memory of Alanza. Two bites later and I had forgotten I had any concerns about never eating syrup again.

Before I had finished my waffle, the doors opened and community members and people from surrounding towns poured into the Stack Shack like it was opening day at an amusement park. Stringed instruments were tuned, guitars were strummed, and a harmonica let out a few trial notes. Tansey Pringle motioned me over from a big booth in the corner. Unfortunately, her son Knowlton sat next to her, stroking his thin excuse for a mustache, which looked more like a chocolate milk stain than the pelt I imagined he fancied it. Maybe it actually grew quite well, but he had rubbed it off from too much patting.

I screwed up my courage and crossed the room, weaving between friends, neighbors, and acquaintances to slide in on Tansey's side of the booth. Knowlton lit up like a carnival midway, and I felt like a bad human because of how much I didn't return his interest.

"Dani, just the girl I wanted to see. Knowlton and I were wondering just what we should bring to your house for Thanksgiving dinner. Your grandmother invited us again this year and we couldn't be more pleased." Just one more reason I don't love the holidays. The family collects stray people like a pound collects dogs. And unfortunately the strays invariably include eligible men invited to free me from my prison of spinsterhood. Tansey is one of my grandmother's oldest friends and almost since my birth those two ladies have been plotting our nuptials.

"You'll have to speak to Grandma about that. I just

show up and peel potatoes." I'm a good cook but so are all the women in the family, even my mother, who'd rather snake drains than fix dinner. With so many capable cooks, our broth gets spoiled pretty fast if there isn't a clear leader. On all major holidays, that leader is Grandma. Celadon plays second in command at Thanksgiving, and Mother does at Christmas. I do it at Easter. My grandfather and Loden are in charge of the Fourth of July barbeque celebration. I could make a fair stab at what Grandma would be serving since a lot of the menu didn't change from year to year, but I wouldn't have dared step on her toes by speaking for her about what a guest should bring.

"You know, Knowlton's a wonderful cook. It's a wonder no lucky girl has snapped him up already. You'd be lucky to have someone like him around the house if all you can do is peel potatoes." Tansey leaned over and patted Knowlton's skinny arm. "Go on and tell her about your squirrel stew."

"I've got to run." I scootched to the edge of the bench seat, the vinyl squeaking under my jeans. Knowlton reached a long slim arm across the table and locked his slim fingers around my wrist.

"You ought to be careful, Dani. There's no telling what could happen to someone as small and helpless as you alone at night." His pale blue eyes, light as thick winter ice, fixed on mine. I always avoided Knowlton, always found him a little creepy and disconcerting, but never was frightened by him. Suddenly, I felt a leeriness that was as unpleasant as it was unfamiliar. Someone had probably murdered Alanza. I felt like I was in a strange land, not the place I was born and raised and eager to leave as a college student because it was so tame and benign. I was looking at everyone with new eyes and that included Knowlton. Was he really as harmless as he had always seemed? Or was he one of those kids who had been pulling the legs off frogs for years when no one was looking?

"I'll be fine, but thanks for your concern," I said, tugging my wrist away. He loosened his grip slowly and I hid my arm below the table before I rubbed it to soothe it. I didn't want him to realize how much he had scared and hurt me. It didn't seem prudent to appear vulnerable right now.

"Knowlton's right. A bitty little thing like you's got no business roaming the dark country roads alone under the circumstances." Tansey crossed her beefy arms over her droopy bustline. Her raw knuckles looked chapped and weathered from her lifestyle and what I expected was a total lack of moisturizing routine. I wouldn't want to run into her out in the dark either when it came down to it. She was staring at me in a way that made me uneasy, too. I slid farther out of the booth and popped onto my feet, ready to flee to another table or to a job I'm sure I could convince Piper to give me.

"I'll keep that in mind, but I'll get myself home under my own steam," I said. "Enjoy the music." I dashed away like a dog who'd caught sight of a squirrel. Or Knowlton, who saw one he wanted to add to his stew pot. Piper hollered my name above the sounds of music getting under way. When I looked, she pointed toward the area in front of the restrooms that served as a stage. Dean Hayes was blowing away on his oboe and Roland Chick was playing his bass. It suited Roland somehow with its sheen and its breadth. Roland was a tall, broad man with a gleaming bald head and a neat and tidy manner of dress that was out of sorts in the community but made him look trustworthy as an innkeeper. Ladies often cited Roland when either criticizing or trying to inspire more care in appearance in their own gentlemen.

Graham stood beside him, his uniform hat in one hand, a coffee mug in the other. After what had happened at the breakfast, he had never gotten to make his announcement about the loose animals. Most likely he was there to try again. I crossed the room, hoping to ask him if a mountain lion had turned up among the exotics gallivanting about the village.

Five

Before I could ask him, though, I experienced my third strange animal sighting in two days. This time, however, I knew I wasn't the only one to see it, judging by the gasps and the clumsy dying off of the music. There was an intake of breath best described as similar in timing to an elementary school concert. Someone had left the door open and a kangaroo jumped into view and headed to the stage area, its half-curled tail thumping against the black-and-white-checkerboard floor. A minuscule head poked out of its pouch, a pair of tiny ears pricked up above its neat head.

"Would now be the time to make your announcement?" I called out to Graham over the dying din of instruments and the silencing clatter of utensils against china.

Graham sprinted past me in the direction of the kangaroo. Everyone else instinctively pulled back then a few brave souls surged forward brandishing forks and coffee mugs. Knowlton sprang from his booth and flapped a dessert menu at the springing animal. It pounced toward him and landed an assertive paw on the sweets offerings. I found myself wishing I could ask her for some tips in dealing with Knowlton. That kangaroo was all right in my opinion. It was all I could do to keep from cheering her on. I wished I could take her out for a beer, but she obviously needed to keep a clear head with a joey on board.

Knowlton retreated to the safety of his booth and pulled his feet up on the bench. Tansey moved toward him and placed a hand on his shoulder, like he was still a joey himself. Graham disappeared into the kitchen and reappeared with a fifty-five-gallon gray plastic trash can in his hands. He held the lid like a shield and made a clucking, smooching sound at the kangaroo. She swiveled her ears in his direction but her eyes were focused on Roland's bass. She bounced toward it and the delicate underpinnings of the arthritic building trembled.

Roland scrunched his shoulders together like he was attempting to make himself disappear behind the instrument, but he did no better than a small child hiding under the covers to avoid monsters in the closet. His freckled knuckles clutched white on the neck of the bass. Sweat sprang up on his forehead like there was a sprinkler system tucked in behind his eyebrows.

Graham navigated the terrain well, considering how little space was available for a trash can between all the booths, tables, and music enthusiasts. The kangaroo hurtled forward into Roland and his instrument just as Graham attempted to upend the trash can over its head. The bass crashed against Roland and knocked him off balance. The kangaroo feinted right and Graham left, and the only thing Graham managed to slip his trash can on top of was the music stand Roland was using before the music had come to a crashing halt.

All hell broke loose. The inside of the Stack Shack erupted into a flurry of activity. It was as though a film crew had descended on Sugar Grove and asked adults to reenact a food fight from high school days. Waffles and sausages and a criminal waste of syrup littered the floor. Hash browns and home fries provided enough slipping hazards to support the need for a physical therapy clinic in town. Coffee flowed like spring snowmelt across the black-and-white-checkerboard tile. In among it all, the kangaroo and her baby dashed and darted and squeezed shrill shrieks from the most stalwart of New Hampshire countrymen. Men who from early childhood had accompanied their elders on journeys deep into the woods for hunting trips, camping trips, and firewood-cutting missions were laid low by this exotic creature running amok in their beloved breakfast establishment.

Emboldened braggarts hugged the walls whenever the kangaroo made a foray in their direction. Armed only with musical instruments and butter knives, they quivered like Chihuahuas in a New Hampshire winter. There would be much to talk about in the post office Monday morning. All tales of past glory were negated as men with bear heads mounted over their fireplaces leapt onto the countertop where they habitually enjoyed morning coffee to remove themselves from the dangerous clutches of a mother kangaroo and her tiny offspring. In a singular act of courage, Mindy Collins, the church organist and an experienced den mother, opened the main door to the Stack Shack. The kangaroo took the hint and bounced out through the opening. Graham followed in hot pursuit. My only sorrow was not having seen him do the same the night before when I informed him about the mountain lion.

I caught Piper's eye over the disheveled heads of the other Griddle and Fiddle participants. We had known each other since she taught me how to squirt milk through my nose the first day of third grade. We both got sent out from snack time into the hall in order to think about our behavior. We had enjoyed getting into trouble together ever since, but I don't think either of us had ever imagined trouble quite like this. I know I never had. If our third grade teacher could have gotten ahold of that kangaroo, something a whole lot more drastic than time-out in the hall would have been on her mind. I don't think that mammal would have gone out to recess for the whole school year.

Everywhere I looked, there were sticky spots and broken china. Flatware and ruined meals carpeted the floor. This did not even begin to address the condition of people's clothing or their stricken expressions. Anyone who had had the misfortune of holding a cup at the moment the kangaroo appeared was invariably wearing its contents of that cup. Grease and syrup and even ketchup spattered shirtfronts and sweaters. People who may not have ever been the snappiest of dressers but who never would appear in public with things sticking to their faces looked like kids in need of a hot bath.

Piper looked crazed. The Stack Shack was her life. Ever since we were kids, she had known she wanted to own the place. She had saved her birthday money, allowance, and even lunch money she chose not to waste on eating from the age of nine on. Many of her first customers at the Stack had been early supporters of her lemonade stand, the proceeds of which had also rolled into the Stack savings fund. By the time she graduated from high school, she was positioned to make an offer to the elderly owners. I'm sure they never would have envisioned this sort of crisis in their beloved restaurant either. Piper kept swiveling her head from side to side, shaking it in disbelief.

Tansey, always one to take charge, hoisted herself onto the top of the breakfast counter, the burnt orange laminate groaning under the strain. She dinged a spoon against a water glass and attracted even more attention than her attempt at athleticism had.

"All right, people, pull yourselves together. Does anyone have any idea where that animal came from or what it was doing here in the Stack?" People on all sides of me looked to others for an answer. As far as I could tell, I was the only one with anything close to an explanation.

I wasn't sure it was my place to pass along a message on behalf of the Fish and Game Department, but from the way that kangaroo had taken off, it didn't look like Graham would be available to do it anytime soon. And I was sure information about a loose kangaroo would whip through the town faster than a bout of the flu. I didn't want people going around saying out-of-control exotic animals were taking over the town. Someone would be sure to take matters into their own hands, and Knowlton would be posing an entirely new taxidermy exhibit.

"I do," I said, stepping toward the counter and scrambling up alongside Tansey, who wisely slid down to take a seat on a stool. Who knew how much strain the old counter could take? I may not weigh much, but who wanted to chance a collapse on top of everything else that had happened that day?

I went on to explain about the released animals and how Graham was hoping townspeople would help to round them up safely by reporting sightings and even corralling them when possible. "No one is in any danger here except the animals themselves. You know you wouldn't let your kids out in this weather in the evening without a jacket. So you can imagine what it must be like out there for a bunch of monkeys and a couple of parrots." People had a lot of questions and some expressed a desire to try lemur stew. But most were excited at the prospect of helping with something so out of the ordinary. Some people stuck around to help with the cleanup at the Stack, but most headed out the door as soon as I finished speaking, to follow tracks and to look for scat.

Piper got over her shock pretty quickly when she realized the animals were in a lot more trouble than she was. By the time we had righted the last overturned chair and mopped the last bit of sticky from the floor, she was all for joining the hunt.

"What about leaving some food out near the back door of the Stack? We could wait behind the Dumpster and then throw a net over them or something." Piper rubbed her hands together excitedly then clapped them like a little child.

"Do you even know what kangaroos eat? Do you have a net big enough for that thing?" I didn't want to show it, but I was feeling a little intimidated by the idea of trying to corner that creature in a darkened back alley. Not that the space behind the Stack was really at all like the average idea of an alley—gray and dark and narrow with more shadows being cast than light by the streetlamps overhead. No, the space behind the Stack, just like most other stores in Sugar Grove, looked out onto some bushes and a generous parking area. In sight of which were dense stands of trees. More leaves littered the ground than trash ever did. No one in my life had ever been assaulted in an alley in Sugar Grove. But then, kangaroos never roamed here either. Nor had anyone died under suspicious circumstances at a public function. Or any other way for that matter.

Wallace Coombs was thought to have bopped off his wife and hidden her body under the floor of an old icehouse back in the twenties, but that was before my time. And she turned up alive and kicking a couple of years later, having sown her wild oats by running away with a food vendor she met at the county fair. People had gossiped about Wallace when she left and even more when she came back.

But today had been different. Alanza was well and truly dead. She wasn't going to show up two years later, whatever had ailed her worked off by many moons spent slaving away as a fried dough maker or lemonade squeezer. She wasn't going to see any more kangaroos, and I was worried about either Piper or I sharing her fate.

"They're herbivores, I know that much. Maybe a big bowl of tossed salad would do the trick. I'd hate for that little joey to go hungry. He was awfully cute with his dark eyes and pert ears."

"Joeys only require milk, so long as they still fit in their mother's pouch." I said this with a lot more authority than I felt. I had no idea if they were like human babies and supplemented their caloric intake by hopping out now and again and having a nibble of some shoots or leaves. I wasn't even sure she was right about the herbivore thing. From the way the mother kangaroo thrashed the Stack to pieces, I had no doubt she could hunt down a bit of meat for her baby's dinner if she set her mind to it.

"So salad for the mother and a saucer of milk for the baby." Piper yanked on the door to the walk-in and fetched a glass bottle of milk from a local dairy. Rummaging around on a shelf under the counter, she found a metal mixing bowl and filled it with vegetables. The salad looked like something fresh from the farmer's market. Even when she was serving wildlife, Piper was a food artist first. If someone told me she baited rat traps with triple-cream Brie, I'd believe it. Before I could complain any more, she hurried out the back door. I followed her—there's safety in numbers—and watched while she placed her offerings carefully on the ground in front of the Dumpster.

"You know the frost is just going to reduce that to a soggy mess by morning, don't you?" I pointed at the heaping serving of mesclun, grated carrots, and ruby-colored grape tomatoes.

"With any luck, it won't last until morning."

"We won't last 'til morning. It's already near freezing and there are hours and hours 'til dawn. I'm not planning to spend all night out here."

"Be a sport. Where's your sense of adventure?"

"That still leaves you with the problem of a net," I said, hoping to knock her off track.

"I know just what to use." Piper hurried back inside and headed for the employee bathroom. I followed her and watched her grab at a rope dangling from the ceiling. The tugging swelled the outlines of her beanstalk tattoo and made the plant look like it had received a hearty helping of fertilizer. Down came the ladder to the creepy Stack attic.

When the Stack was built, it was meant only to serve as a summer eatery. There was no original attic since there was no need for insulation if the pipes were properly drained before cold weather. The restaurant was open all the way to the curved underside of the roof. The people Piper had bought the place from had converted it to a year-round business by dropping in a ceiling and adding insulation. The townspeople got a year-round eatery, and Piper got a place to store everything that didn't fit in her camper. I mounted the creaking stairs behind her, wondering what she could possibly have up there that could be used.

She pulled on a string that looked like the malnourished younger brother of the rope hanging from the stairs and tugged on the light. The bulb was as pikerish as Scrooge with his piggy bank.

"Aren't you worried about mice or even squirrels?"

"What do you think all those boxes of Mouse Be Gone are for?" Piper gestured impatiently around the attic at some paper cartons and then reached for a large, card-board box.

"Here it is. Just what we need." She spun around, clutching a ropy mass.

"What is it?" I asked, not sure I wanted to know the answer.

"My hammock. You know the one I hang out in front of the camper all summer and tell myself I'll get to use one day when things slow down around here?"

"I love that thing. I go over to your place and use it when I know you're working a double shift and won't be able to."

"Well, now I will be able to finally get some use out of it myself. It's perfect, don't you think?" Piper's gleaming white gigantic smile glowed even in the low light.

"I guess if that's what you want to do with it, it is your hammock." I was a bit worried about my leisure time in the upcoming summer. What if by some miracle Piper managed to net the kangaroo with it and it struggled free, tearing a huge hole right through the side? Somehow I didn't think it would be right to take it back to L.L.Bean and ask to use the money-back guarantee under the cir-cumstances. And I didn't think Piper would be inclined to lay out the cash for a new one since she never got time to use the original. All in all, the hammock seemed like it might be in danger, and there was little I could do to stop it. I felt the warm summer breezes and gentle swaying slipping away from me with each step she took toward the ladder and the back door of the Stack.

"Don't you want to leave this to the professionals? The

guy from Fish and Game seems like he knows what he's doing. I think we should let him handle it."

"I noticed you going over to talk to him just before the kangaroo stirred things up. He is pretty cute." Piper winked one of her false-eyelashed eyes at me and blew me an air kiss so loud it filled the air between us with vibrations that would have rung a bell if there were one up in the attic.

"I hadn't really noticed." This lying thing was starting to get out of hand. If I kept it up, untruths would begin to cling to me like a second skin. I'd need to get one of those little voice-activated tape recorders to make memos of all the stories I was telling in order to keep them straight.

"Fortunately, I care about you enough to know when you just want me to coax something out of you. He was cute. You did notice. I saw you do your thing." Piper tossed the hammock through the opening and began descending after it. "Turn off the light, would you?" Piper was scooping the hammock up and rushing toward the back door before I even hit the floor.

"What thing?" I wasn't being coy. I had no idea what she was talking about. Piper is a great cardplayer, and every time she says someone does something unconsciously, I've noticed she's right.

"You tip your head to one side so hard you scrape your ear on your shoulder. You've been doing it ever since the day Brice Dayton moved to town."

"That was almost twenty years ago." Why hadn't she ever mentioned it before? Had anyone else ever noticed?

"At least you are consistent. Besides, it's adorable. You look vulnerable and sweet."

"Vulnerable and sweet?"

"Yeah, like a Pomeranian with an itchy ear." A cold blast of air drove a ribbon of leaves and sand across the pavement toward us, but I was feeling heated up by my burning cheeks.

"A Pomeranian? With ear mites? And you never told me? In all these years you never told me? No wonder I'm still single."

"I didn't say ear mites. You said ear mites. I said itchy. Lots of things can cause ears to itch. You should ask the Fish and Game guy. He might know." Piper placed the hammock on the closed lid of the Dumpster and squeezed in behind the metal bin. She slid in easily with room to spare. It must be the long hardworking hours at the Stack because she eats like a teenage boy and considers exercise to be filling in a sudoku puzzle.

"I'm not asking Graham to check me for ear mites."

"His name is Graham?"

"That's right."

"Like the cracker? I bet he'd be good with chocolate and marshmallows. Like a big cuddly s'more." Or butter. I loved my graham crackers slathered in butter, and I nibbled them a tiny bite at a time. What was I thinking? Piper needed to stop and I needed to go home and get some sleep. Maybe I was just hungry after all the excitement. The fluttering in my stomach didn't mean I thought a guy who specialized in insulting the public he was supposed to be serving was at all attractive. No, it certainly did not. I probably wouldn't even see him ever again, and I could go back to eating graham crackers any which way I liked without feeling naughty about it in the least.

"Exactly like a cracker. What were his parents thinking? Did he have a sister named Saltine?" Not that I was one to judge with a name like mine. Dani got me by but it wasn't the whole story and it was unlikely Mr. Fish and Game was destined to hear it. No matter how much he looked like the man of my dreams, he was here for a short, busy visit, punctuated by rudeness and aggravation.

"Maybe he has a brother named Animal and we could double date." Piper nudged me in the ribs with a bony elbow.

"I think you mean single date. I never expressed any interest in the first cracker in the barrel." I rubbed my side where she had poked me and tried to remember why we were friends. Being called a dog and then being shoved around was not dredging up any positive memories of our friendship.

"You like him, teacup doggie, I know you do. Would you rather have coffee or hot chocolate while we wait for the kangaroo to pick up her dinner?" Now I remembered why we were friends through thick and thin. She may be insulting but her hot chocolate is worth a five-mile trudge on your knees through sleet-covered pucker bush. World peace could be achieved if only someone had the sense to express flasks of the stuff to any warring regions of the world. Heads of state would take one sip, develop a swooning rosy glow of good humor, and commence slapping each other on the back. I've seen it work at budget committee meetings. I am certain it is the real reason our teachers have gotten a new contract and the fire department received funding for its new ambulance.

"Do you have to ask?" I followed her inside and waited more or less as patiently as any other grown-up as she slowly and carefully heated a pan of the magical concoction over a low flame on the stove. The smell of it was driving me over the brink by the time she poured us each a mug. We reached the back alley once more just in time to see the outline of something small and furtive dragging away the bowl of salad.

"Grab the net." Piper dropped her cup in the excitement. I liked to have cried at the waste of hot chocolate but, as I still had a grip on mine, was able to hold off the waterworks. And I wasn't about to lose it scrambling to put my favorite hammock in harm's way either. Piper could become an exotic animal wrangler all on her own. I was just here to make sure nothing made off with my friend.

"I think it's gone," I said, blowing on my mug. The clattering of the metal bowl against the ground faded away into the other night sounds. Whatever had started dragging off the salad had done so. And the hammock sat safe and unused on the top of the Dumpster. It looked like next summer could proceed much like the past had, swinging and swaying, lost in a book.

"Well, that's just great. I try to help and end up out one large salad bowl. Now what? I'm not sure I want to lose another one tonight." Piper stood there, her fists balled up on her slim hips, booted foot tapping impatiently.

"We should head home for tonight. Whatever took that salad will have gotten something to eat and won't likely be back before early tomorrow. You can send one of the weekend kids out to tromp round the countryside looking for your bowl if you like. For all you know, there won't be anything for them to do other than chase down salad bowls. Once word gets out that the Stack is popular with wildlife, people may be a bit leery about eating here."

"No way. Anyone who wasn't here tonight to see the kangaroo will be hoping it returns tomorrow or at least will want to see with their own eyes where it all went down. I'll be lucky not to run out of supplies."

"Then we best get home so you can get a full night's sleep if you expect that sort of a run tomorrow. I'll help you lock up." I placed a steering hand under her elbow and propelled her toward the door. She threw a long last look toward the underbrush, where her salad bowl had been dragged away to die, and then turned her attention to closing down for the night.

By the time we had locked everything and said our good-byes, it was ten at night. I dragged my exhausted carcass to the car and hauled myself inside. It started without any trouble, a credit to the loving care Grampa lavishes on it and all the other geriatric vehicles parked around the farm. One thing about the Greenes, we may have more money than New England farms have rocks, but we don't throw it away on a bunch of foolishness.

My mother, even though she's only a Greene by marriage, took to being a cheapskate like a hypochondriac takes to an ambulance. I never wore a pair of jeans not first worn by my older sister until it became obvious Celadon was going to keep growing and I wasn't. I had to wear through the ones she passed down until it was becoming what my grandmother described as vulgar before we could go buy new ones in my size. Even then my mother just clucked and hissed at the waste of it. She just couldn't imagine what had gone wrong to leave me unable to take advantage of all the hand-me-down bounty.

It wasn't until Grandma reminded her of how much the church thrift shop appreciated gently worn children's clothing that she calmed down and took me to a discount chain for a couple of pairs from the clearance rack. Fortunately for me, there are always some great bargains to be had in the smallest sizes.

I steered down the lumpy road out of town and kept my eyes peeled. Between suspicious deaths and wild animals, I was pretty spooked about being a ways from home. I felt like I was on one of those television shows where a solitary individual sets off minding her own business and is confronted by Bigfoot. I kept expecting at least a mountain lion to make an appearance. Every so often I was sure I caught sight of something slinking through the woods, but like it is with distant stars, as soon as I tried to look straight at it, whatever it was faded away. I welcomed the sound of gravel crunching under the tires as I turned into the driveway at Greener Pastures Tree Farm.

The porch light glowed wanly in the gloomy fall night. I was grateful for any kind of welcome. The distance between the truck and the kitchen door looked farther than usual. I grabbed my purse and scooted off the seat, breaking into a dead run as soon as I shoved the door shut behind me. I sprinted to the kitchen door, popped it open, and launched through it as though the hounds of hell were on my tiny heels. Loden looked up from the rocking chair near the cookstove. He paused in the peeling of his apple, the long curl of skin dangling in midair.

"Feeling kind of jittery, are you?" he asked, resuming his careful removal. You'd think he was a colonial young woman hoping to reveal the name of her beloved with a complete apple peel under her pillow on the night of a full moon.

"You might, too, if you'd seen a woman topple over into her stack of hot cakes at breakfast then a kangaroo take out your best friend's eatery in five minutes flat." I plopped into a creaking wooden chair at the well-worn kitchen table and helped myself to an apple from the bowl in the center. I didn't remove the peel. From an early age, I learned to eat everything put in front of me in a serious attempt to sneak up on a growth spurt. I was still hoping it would work.

"Roland stopped in to tell us about it on his way home from the Stack. How's Piper?" Loden asked. If I had to guess, he kept hoping the peel under his pillow would take the form of the letter *P*. Neither of them said anything about it but everyone else knew they would be perfect together. Both of them pooh-poohed the idea whenever it came up, but secretly I think it would do each of them a world of good. Loden loves his work and doesn't make demands on others. Piper is the same way. And I'd love for her to be a part of the family officially instead of almost officially.

"She took it pretty well. She even tried to lure in a lost

creature with a big bowl of salad in order to capture it with her hammock."

"Did it work?" Loden finished with the peel and sliced off a thin piece of Cortland apple, then popped it into his mouth.

"Whatever beast it was made off with the salad as well as the bowl. But no, we didn't manage to catch anything." I leaned back in my chair, but I wasn't tall enough to tiddle back on the two back legs. No one had ever asked me to keep four on the floor.

"We could add her bowl to the list of things to be on the lookout for while tooling around town. Or I could go out personally tomorrow and see if I could find it."

"I'm sure she would appreciate it. Of all the mess the situation caused, that was the only thing to really faze her."

"Maybe it was the last straw. I'll run by in the morning before church."

"Sounds good. I'm turning in or I'll not be warming a pew myself tomorrow." I patted him on his flannel-shirted shoulder as I went by and noticed a little thin spot developing on the crown of his head. If he was interested in Piper or any other woman, he'd better get on it. Bald may be beautiful but the process of getting from here to there certainly is not.

Six

As usual, some members of the family were up and ready for church the next morning, and some were not. Grampa and Grandma were waiting by the door. Loden sat at the kitchen table sipping coffee and listening to the weather report on the old radio with tinfoil wrapped around the antenna. Mom rarely went to church, and Celadon was already there with her kids since she believed in the power of Sunday school. I attended about one week in four, and despite the fact I was bone tired and behind on my work, I wasn't up to the idea of explaining to Grampa why my soul would be still saved if I missed this particular Sunday. I would have to also admit to being a bit curious about the gossip floating around town about Alanza and even if there were any animal sightings in the night. Sad to say, gossip, not God, was my motivation for pulling myself out of a warm cozy bed, but there it was.

The Congregtional church was just exactly what you would expect in a small New Hampshire town. The clapboards were white, the windows large and stained glass. A bell sat in a high steeple, and a narrow path led to the stairs. Grampa parked and Grandma and I headed for the church kitchen in the basement to drop off the maple Bundt ring she had prepared at the crack of dawn. Everyone always looked forward to her cakes. She used maple sugar for the sweetener and iced the top with a maple syrup glaze. As a final touch, she sprinkled maple-sugared chopped pecans on top.

At home, Grandma wouldn't let her cakes be seen on anything but a glass-footed plate with a dome, but for church, she preferred for God to be the glory and settled for a sensible, if unattractive, plastic carrier. I thought God must have more good taste than anyone else, but my opinion on ostentation in church was not a popular one with anyone except my mother. Things like the plastic cake carrier were reasons why my mother never went to the church if she could help it. While my mother is as thrifty as anyone else when it comes to bargain shopping and wasting electricity, she simply cannot abide ugly. Even the mismatched paper cups and plastic spoons drove her bananas. Offerings of gelatin salads in reused margarine tubs were not something she could reconcile with the concept of God.

We stuck the coffee cake with the rest of the offerings along a long folding table in the center of the room. Service hadn't even started yet, but the coffee already smelled scorched. I reminded myself to drop by the Stack later for a cup of something worth slurping. Piper wouldn't let coffee like that down her sink drain, let alone into anyone's cup. That was just one of the many reasons she stayed in business. The smell dissipated a bit as we climbed the narrow stairs to the sanctuary.

The church was better attended than usual. That is to say that instead of the usual seventy or so faithful souls, the count was closer to a hundred. There were only two ways I could explain the upsurge in attendance. Either everyone was looking to get right with their maker, or people wanted to be in the loop for the latest on Alanza and the gallivanting wildlife. Looking around at the heads bent together and whispering, I was jaded enough to think it was the latter.

I slid into the pew near the back in which all the Greenes always sat. Celadon, dressed in a starched navy shirtdress, every shiny brown hair in place, strode down the aisle. With a look of extreme exasperation on her face, she herded her children, Spring and Hunter, in next to me just as the opening hymn rattled to a stop. No one came to service to listen to Mindy Collins thump out her version of what God might consider to be a joyful noise. With considerably more enthusiasm than skill, she faithfully fulfilled her duties as the church organist no matter how many times others had told her she did too much for her own good. If only she weren't so sincere herself, she might have taken the hint by now and let the local music teacher take over. As it was, the congregation was reconciled to helping her unemployed husband find a job that would require relocation. Either that, or praying for some sort of accident that would rob Mindy of the use of her hands despite the risk to their immortal souls.

Celadon looked at risk of her soul as well. From the way she yanked at the hymnal in front of her and snapped it open to the correct page, you'd think it had done her a personal affront. My best guess was that the children in her Sunday school class had been worked up about all the loose animals. It was either that or she had finally managed to miss her husband, Clarke. Usually, she's just as happy for him to be away on business, like he had been for the past three weeks, as she is for him to be home. But eventually she feels the lack of him and her mood takes a turn for the worse. She leaned toward me, squashing Spring and Hunter's heads together in the process, completely oblivious to their discomfort.

"The kids were a bunch of little heathens this morning. Preaching the word to those outside the fold is one thing, but acting as a babysitter for parents who wouldn't know a sin if you baked it in a biscuit and fed it to them for breakfast is another matter entirely. All they want to do is gossip about Alanza and talk about a loose circus act or some such a thing." Celadon shook her head.

"Maybe the offering baskets will see the benefit of it," I said, trying to find a bright side to remove the crazy eyes from my sister's face. The last time I saw her with that look, she had threatened to drive our mother to the state mental hospital and leave her on the doorstep. She wasn't old enough at the time to drive anything other than the lawn tractor, but the threat was still plenty motivating. Mom immediately stopped using Celadon's dolls to hold séances.

"Don't count on it. I expect with the way those kids were acting, we'll be lucky if the adults don't take it as an opportunity to filch a few bucks to buy lottery tickets on their way home." I waited for a second to see if God was going to strike her dead. When he didn't, I tried another tack.

"Did you at least get in a lesson that took advantage of the situation and helped bring light into the darkness of their little lives?" Celadon was always sending money to charity groups that helped little children in other countries to hear our version of what God should be. I thought that might be the way to get through to her.

"I thought it was going to, but I was wrong. I gave the Noah story as the lesson."

"Good plan. Current events make it relevant."

"You'd think so but the whole thing got reduced to a birds and the bees lesson instead of a lesson in God's mercy."

"Birds and the bees?"

"Some little freckled thing with curly hair made a point to tell everyone, in vivid detail, just exactly why Noah needed two of every animal. He even acted out the part of a horse with a volunteer from the class."

"Yikes. What did you do?"

"The only thing I could do. I peeled him off her and outshouted him by talking about snack time."

"Did you tell his parents?" I turned over in my mind just exactly what that conversation would sound like. Celadon is forthright but a bit prudish. I wasn't sure she'd be able to convey the exact nature of the incident beyond mistake. She really ought to have had Mom there to help her. Although come to think of it, our mother might have paired up all the kids and had them pantomiming a pagan ceremony more suited to adults. She never was good at boundaries or judging age appropriateness.

"I did my best to explain what had happened, and instead of taking his rotten son to task, the father just clapped him on the back and said, 'Go get 'em, tiger.'"

"He did not."

"He did indeed. His mother didn't even have the good grace to blush. It makes me wish one of the animals running around town was inclined to swallow human families down whole. They'd be top on my list." Celadon leaned away from me, and a look of relief flooded over both her children's faces. I edged a bit farther away to give them a little room if she got going again. Fortunately, Pastor Gifford took the pulpit and led us in a prayer. Even at her angriest, Celadon wouldn't talk over anyone praying. It was almost like a safe spot to run for while playing a childhood game of tag. Anytime Celadon was about to pitch a fit, the rest of us knew we could drop to our knees, hands steepled together, and remain that way until she gave up and went away. I'm still not sure she has caught on. I've even shared the secret with Hunter. He's a great kid, I love to spoil him, and I know he'll never tattle on me to his mother because then the trick would no longer work and he's a bright boy.

I didn't talk while others were praying either, but I wasn't above peeking around a bit. There is something so conspiratorial and even uncomfortable about catching the eye of another transgressor while you are doing it, though. And you are always surprised by who it will be. The church elders, the pastor's wife, the guest missionary speaker, or even your own grandmother. I never quite know what to do when I meet someone else's eye. I tend to dart my gaze away and then glance back apologetically, but I wish I had the guts to wink. I usually don't, though. Maybe I will when I am an old lady. I've got a mental checklist of things to do when I'm an old lady and that's definitely on it. When I catch a kid's eye, I already wink or even start a small game of peekaboo. By the time I'm an old lady, most everyone will seem like a kid to me, and I think the situation will resolve itself.

The rest of the service went smoothly, and by the time the offering plate went round, Celadon was breathing normally, and while she did keep an eagle eye on whether funds were going into the silver platter or coming back out of it, she kept to her seat and appeared not to have discovered any wrongdoing. As soon as the final hymn hiccupped to an ungainly finish, I grabbed Hunter by the hand and did a good imitation of a sprint out of the sanctuary. I paused briefly at the door to congratulate the pastor on a well-delivered sermon, fibbed, and said Hunter desperately needed to use the gents, then took the steps two at a time. I hadn't had any breakfast, and after what had happened the day before, I wasn't taking any more chances.

I busied myself with a flimsy paper plate decorated with a Fourth of July motif. I wasn't a bit bashful about taking the first slice or scoop of anything that looked worth sampling. First of all, of course, was Grandma's coffee cake. I only took a small slice because I can have it at home, too, but I couldn't resist just a bit. Then on to the cheese and crackers, the fruit plate where I speared a succulent bit of pineapple, and then a piece of maple blondie bar. I took a bite of that before leaving the table and resolved to discover who made it. It was exactly the sort of thing I'd love to offer at the shop to people while they were browsing. Barely cooked through and almost caramelly in texture, the rich maple flavor mingled with the buttery richness of it, making me pluck a second off the plate before even trying anything else.

To make up for my low-nutrition, high-calorie choices, I also lifted a maple granola bar onto my plate. I knew who made these. The pastor's wife was famous for them. They were oaty and chewy and studded with dried dates. You certainly couldn't tell they were good for you when one crossed your lips.

The basement steadily filled with congregants, old and new. I heard snatches of conversation about Alanza and about the Griddle and Fiddle. I even heard a few people joking that if we couldn't get Piper to start attending church, we could at least buy a couple of urns of coffee from her to replace the stuff we were serving, which tasted like it was what was left of mud season. A lull in conversation fell on the gathering the way it often does when people are enjoying their food. Generally, when this happens, someone is trying to make themselves heard concerning a private matter to someone nearby and their voice unexpectedly travels across the room. This time it was a freckle-faced redheaded kid on Celadon's animal chow wish list who made himself the center of attention.

"What the heck is that?" All eyes turned toward him then followed his pointing arm to the generous basement windows, which doubled as escape routes in event of a fire and extreme athleticism on the part of our overweight and aging congregation. Framed by the window, four knobby kneecaps and some furry underbits sure to make Celadon curse under her breath clearly showed. Half the assembly shrank back toward the kitchen. The other half surged forward, eager to get a better look at the strange sight. Hunter and I surged, Celadon and Grandma shrank back. Grampa offered an opinion.

"Looks like the chassis of a camel. Anybody got some rope in their vehicle?" All around me, men and children shoved plates at their wives and mothers. There was no shortage of sexism in the church that morning. The few surging mothers heaped their foisted-upon plates onto chairs, counter edges, and even the women who shrank back. Within a minute I was faced with deciding if I wanted to view a live camel or to snarf down a couple more maple granola bars with a clear conscience. I split the difference by grabbing a couple along with a napkin and tucking them in my shirt pocket. I sailed out the door and into the fray, where I wiggled between the other people in the group, something not so hard to manage when you are my size, and found myself with a front row seat.

Camels are big. Scary big. With just a bit of bad posture, I could almost walk right under it. The attitude of the shrinking-back crowd looked more and more sensible. Especially when the camel swung its head with its big flapping lips in my direction. It blinked a long-lashed eye at me and flared its nostrils. I was momentarily reminded of Celadon before she calmed down in the church pew.

I tried to take a step backward, but the crowd was like a living wall of lurid interest. Everything slowed down in front of me, the way it does in movies or when you are having an out-of-body experience. The camel waggled its jaw, exposing domino-sized teeth. I tried again to back up but no luck. The camel stepped deliberately, painstakingly closer. Out of the corner of my eye I caught sight of my grandfather's red-and-orange-checked sport jacket. Someone in a much more subdued color palette was next to him. I didn't dare take my eyes off the giant creature. It continued its course and came to a stop right in front of me, so close its breath warmed the top of my head. I felt sweat spring from my armpits like a massaging shower head in a five-star hotel.

The camel lowered its head and snuffled my chest. I couldn't have moved if I had been on fire. I think I tried to whimper, but even my voice was so scared, it went and hid. The camel nibbled its lips along my collar and then onto my neck. When it licked my face, I could only be grateful I didn't wet myself in full view of the congregation.

Now the crowd backed up and I backed up, too. One step at a time, like an experienced ballroom dancer, that camel backed me all the way to the peeling white clapboards of the church. I rummaged through my brain for camel facts but could only see cigarette packets in my mind's eye. I didn't think camels ate meat, but with the size of its teeth, I wasn't sure the swallowing was what really mattered to me. Tearing off a hunk of my neck would be just as bad for me whether or not he spit the undesirable bits out.

He lowered his head once more and dropped from investigating my collar to my waist and then my sides. With even more vigorous interest, he began probing my pocket. The one with the maple granola bars. A special on an educational channel blipped through my mind about some women and their cross-desert quest for specialty dates. Camels were their companions. My heart squeezed around in my chest like my great-aunt Hazel squeezed a buck—long, hard, and thoroughly.

If only Piper had known to use the granola bars instead of the salad the night before, she might have had better results from her rescue mission. I held stock-still, barely breathing through my nose as the camel's head jostled around under my armpit. It's fur pricked through my thin shirt and made me glad I had resisted the urge to dress for service that day. Truth be told, I'd grabbed the least wrinkled things in the closet because my grandparents so hate to be late for church. With the way the camel was behaving, I was glad the shirt wasn't one of my favorites.

It seemed like it was one of his, though. Snickers and guffaws rippled across the church parking lot. I would have been embarrassed if I wasn't so concerned about being operated on by a camel not qualified to perform breast reduction surgery. I was in no position to have a bit to spare in that department. Celadon had gotten most of whatever there was to receive genetically when it came to bustlines. Which was horribly unfair as far as Celadon was concerned since she was very clear about how vulgar it was to run around looking like a dairy maid.

I, on the other hand, was grateful for whatever little anything I could pile in and push up, and there was no way I was about to surrender a gram of it to a wayward camel. Just as I was reaching up to risk my hand being bitten off instead, a whole other sort of Graham entered the picture.

My hand froze in midair as I realized who the green-garbed person speaking to Grampa had been. I should have recognized the outline of his uniform hat, a rather dashing and distinct piece of headgear, I had to admit. But the camel had filled the foreground of my thoughts and it hadn't seemed to bear scrutiny. Now I could see him inching closer, a pole with a loop on the end of it in his hands. The camel stuck out its tongue and lapped the front of my shirt, wetting it sufficiently to render it transparent. It was more like some sort of exotic dance show at a strip club involving animals than it was an assembly of worshippers. And the camel didn't even have the decency to stuff my clothing with dollar bills for my trouble.

Graham worked his way to the left of the camel and Grampa moved in on the right. Grampa made a clucking sound, similar to the ones he makes to call horses. The camel made a noise back, best described as a cross between a rumbling stomach and a roaring belch. I felt my knees get all wonky, and I started to slide down the wall. The camel chomped down on my pocket, favored bits of me protected only by granola bars, and ripped it from the shirt. In a flash, Graham slipped the loop at the end of his pole over the camel's head and then did something that cinched it closed.

The camel whipped its head toward Grampa, pulling Graham nearly off his feet. It made more gurgling growling sounds then spluttered blubbering spittle into my favorite geezer's bearded face. I dove downward and scooped up the spilled granola bars. I waved them frantically above my head, hoping the smell would get through to the angry beast. I got my wish and then some. The camel whipped its head back toward me, its flapping lips dripping onto my head. I tossed the granola bars toward Graham. The camel rushed after them, dragging Graham and his looped pole after him.

I pushed through the crowd and raced back inside. The rest of the granola bars sat mostly untouched. I grabbed them then snatched a tray piled high with cereal treats for good measure. If camels liked one grain-based breakfast item, maybe they would enjoy another. I raced back out the door and skidded to a stop in front of the camel, who was trying to blow a bit of napkin from his gluey bottom lip. I wish I could say I had it in me to reach up and help him, but I didn't. The best I could manage was to toss another bar on the ground in front of him.

He snarfed it so fast I felt a pang at how hungry he must have been. The freckled kid's father appeared out of nowhere with a piece of pink nylon rope in his hands.

"If we could get this looped over his neck, we could hitch him to the tie-downs on your truck until we get a trailer for him," he said, pointing at Graham's state-issued vehicle.

"Great. If someone would fish my keys out of my pocket, we could back it over here." Graham panted a little when he spoke. I assumed it was from wrestling with the camel, not from gazing on my sublime beauty, slobbered shirt, goopy camel spit hair, and pit stains the size of reservoirs.

"What about this instead?" I asked, dropping another piece of granola bar a few feet closer to the truck. The camel pounced, if that is a word that can be used with camels. The bit of bar was down the hatch and he was swinging his head scanning for more before Graham could regain his balance. I tossed another piece and another until I ran out of bars and had to switch to cereal treats. From the look on the camel's face, I wasn't sure how well he liked them at first, but he got over his aversion, and got all the way to the truck before the batch was gone. Freckle boy's father slipped the rope over the camel's neck. Graham tied it to the truck.

After all that work, I felt the need for a cereal treat myself. But minding my manners, I offered one to Graham first. I would have included freckle guy, but he was already back with the others bragging and laughing about something I hoped was not me and the frisky way the camel had behaved.

"No thanks. I'll pass."

"Not much of a sweet tooth?" I asked, hoping to confirm he was a disaster of a human being.

"Not a fan of a camel's leftovers." Graham pulled off

his hat and wiped his sweaty forehead with the back of his arm. "You must be all right if you're tearing into a snack. Or are you a stress eater?" He squinted at me, as if the secrets of my mental health were splayed across my face like a milk mustache.

"I don't discuss my interior life with complete strangers." I crossed my arms across my chest, suddenly aware I didn't stand around in wet blouses in front of them either.

"Interior life? And how do you define strangers? I introduced myself to you two nights ago." He crossed his own arms across his chest, but the way he did it looked expansive and strangely appealing, not huddled and defensive.

"I acknowledge you are an embodiment of an establishment with which I have familiarity. That does not make us confidants." What was I doing? Channeling Celadon? Or a long-dead Victorian spinster? I suddenly wondered if my mother had dosed me with some strange potion in my morning java.

"I just saved you from being mauled by a camel." Now he untucked his arms and jacked his thumb at the humpbacked beast standing quietly behind the truck.

"Oh, he's a real killer, that one." I pointed, too, as the camel let off what appeared to be an enormous yawn before sagging to its knees on the parking lot.

"At least that animal isn't a figment of your imagination."

"At least he wasn't endangering anything. Well, at least anything besides your pride. I seem to remember him dragging you off your feet until someone thought to lead him along quietly with food."

"Maybe he's a stress eater, too." Graham clapped his hat back onto his head with a little more vim than was good for something made of fabric.

"I'm sure you have better things to do on a Sunday afternoon than to ask me about my eating habits."

"I suppose they aren't strictly under the purview of the Fish and Game Department."

"But all those animals still roaming around are, so I won't take up any more of your time." Behind me I heard footsteps and a hacking, throat-clearing cough. Grampa stood there, sticking out a gnarled paw in Graham's direction.

"Nice job, young man. Quick thinking. I've called my grandson, Loden, Dani here's brother. He'll be along with a horse trailer in just a few minutes if he doesn't get stopped for speeding by Dani's former beau. Laser gun Lenny." Grampa pumped up and down on Graham's arm with enough enthusiasm to bring up water from a well. I was enjoying contemplating how sore his arm was going to be tomorrow morning between the camel and Grampa.

"His name's Mitch, not Lenny. And you know he doesn't use the laser gun. He prefers to eyeball speeders."

"He prefers to eyeball the ladies." Grampa pulled on Graham's arm to draw him closer. "That's what broke them up. A speedy, roving eye. But Dani doesn't like to talk about it." Graham grinned at me, a beguiling, boyish grin, one of his top front teeth overlapping the other just enough to keep him from being pretty. Darn. I didn't want to notice something like that.

"Dani doesn't seem to want to talk about much, does

she? Not her ex–gentlemen friends, not her eating habits, and if I remember correctly from the other night, not even her given name."

"Well, I'd feel a bit funny giving out any more details of her love life or even talking about what she eats." Grampa drew even closer and dropped his voice. "Women can be awful funny about that sort of thing. But her given name is a matter of public record so she can't be sore about that, now can she?" I couldn't believe it. I was going to turn into a stress eater at this rate. Between the mountain lion, Alanza's death, a pat-down performed by a camel, and now the outing of a closely held secret by my own relative—it was enough to send a swimsuit model to a fudge factory.

Rumbling on the road drowned out what my grandfather had to say. Gravel sprayed into the air and the camel sprang to its feet. A truck rattled to a stop and Loden popped open the driver's door, leapt to the ground, and towered over me before Grampa could squeak out another word.

"Here it is. And that must be the new guy in Dani's life." For a heart-hammering second, I thought he meant Graham, and my cheeks got so hot I thought they'd blister for sure. Then I realized, only a little less embarrassingly, he was referring to the camel. As the only brother in the family, he got away with a lot and expected we would all forgive him no matter how mercilessly he teased. Usually he was right, but I was ready to spit nails dipped in camel slobber. Without a word, I turned my back and headed for the church basement.

I found Grandma at the sink up to her elbows in soapy water and the spirit of Christian helpfulness. I ignored all the stares and giggling and asked if we could head home.

"Well, of course we can, Dani, love. You look completely done in." She wiped her hands on a faded apron she'd never allow in her own kitchen, then slipped it off and handed it to Mindy, the organist, saying the hot water would help keep her finger joints nimble. I grabbed another maple blondie off the church table. I must have looked even worse than I felt because Grandma didn't say a thing about how unladylike it was to be gluttonous, and she didn't even take the time to collect her ugly plastic cake tote. Anything that separates a New Hampshire woman from her Tupperware is serious business indeed. I'm not sure if it is inherent cheapness in our culture or if it is a collective consciousness about the fact that a New Hampshire native invented Tupperware. You can expect a lot from a mother or grandmother here, but don't expect to come home to a smile and a cookie when you tell them you've lost their Tupperware. Women here wash and reuse aluminum foil. You can just imagine what happens with stackable matching bowl sets with burpable lids.

Seven

I spent most of Sunday afternoon pacing in the sugarhouse and trying to convince myself not to stick my nose into police business. Unfortunately, I'm not that persuasive. By the time the sun was thinking about packing it in for the day, I was in my father's old MG Midget tooling along toward Jill's house to ask a bunch of questions that were none of my concern.

Sugar Grove is like most towns in New Hampshire. The roads are narrow and they twist and turn around natural obstructions like rock formations and stream beds. Jill's property wasn't very large and she didn't own that many trees of her own, which was why she borrowed trees from Alanza for her sugaring operation. But their properties did touch even though the public road didn't connect them. I wondered if there was some sort of logging road or cart track that did. If I didn't want to let Jill know that

I was curious about her relationship with Alanza, I could ask Knowlton. He knew all the back roads, paths, and underbrush in the area. I'd have to see if there was a better way to find out, though, because owing Knowlton a favor was always on my not-to-do list.

I slowed down, scanning the side of the road for the hidden entrance to Jill's property. Her driveway blended in perfectly with the ground, completely covered in beech and maple leaves. A large boulder flanked one side and a weathered signpost with no sign hanging on it marked the other. I turned in and puttered up the long stretch of dirt to the tiny cape-style house, glad the ground was starting to freeze instead of it being mud season. Their place is impossible to access in mud season without a four-wheel-drive truck and hip boots.

I decided my best tack to take would be of concerned breakfast attendee. That way I could ask questions without feeling so nosy. What I really wanted to know was why she missed the breakfast and whether or not she had reason to harm Alanza. I wondered what she was going to do to replace the loss of income from the trees they could no longer tap.

I pulled in alongside Jill's little white jeep and a dirty, pockmarked gray truck. The truck looked familiar but I couldn't place it since it really wasn't at all interesting. I yanked on the emergency brake to be sure I didn't need to chase my ride down the side of the hill and made my way to the front door. A twig wreath with plastic eggs tucked into it, left over, I assumed, from Easter, slapped up and down in my face as I knocked on the door.

The door was yanked open and Hanley Wilson stood in the entrance looking for all the world like he owned the place.

"You need something?" He took a tug on a can of beer, then let out an echoing belch.

"I was hoping to speak with Jill. This is her house, isn't it?" I was surprised to hear myself even asking that question. I knew it was Jill's place. I'd been here off and on over the years for syrup-making things and community events as well. What I couldn't understand was what Hanley would be doing there.

"It is." He turned his face away from the door and yelled inside, "Jill, you've got company." He drained the can, crumpled it, and tossed it past my head and into the lawn before pushing past me, leaving the door hanging open. I stood on the threshold waiting for Jill to appear to invite me in. I felt the warm air from the house streaming past me and decided the neighborly thing would be to enter and close the door, invitation or no invitation.

"Jill, are you in here? It's Dani Greene." I heard some rustling in the room to the left of the central hall and followed the noise. Smoky woodstove smells filled the air, and a log popped and hissed. Despite the warmth in the room, a figure huddled beneath a brown and orange afghan on the sofa. A bit of deep brown hair peeked up above the blanket. "Jill, are you okay?" I asked.

"I'm a bit under the weather." Jill's voice sounded weak. I stepped just a little closer. I sure didn't want to catch whatever she had. I might not want to challenge Grampa for the pewter pitcher but I could hold my own at

Thanksgiving dinner and a brush with the stomach flu would ruin all that.

"I thought you might be. Is that why you missed the pancake-eating competition?" It was hard to imagine the effects of all those pancakes on a stomach wrestling with a bug. I felt a rush of wind beside my leg, then a flying ball of fur landed on Jill's body. A tiger cat with a crumpled ear stared at me. Jill lurched upright in surprise and the blanket slid away from her face. My jaw dropped at the sight of her. A fist-sized purple mark marred her usually pale skin. One brown eye was swollen shut and her top lip was cracked open in two places. Even her nose looked inflated.

"Please don't say anything." Jill burst into tears but it looked like the act of speaking and crying was causing her even more pain. I slid a pile of magazines aside and sat on the trunk in front of the sofa.

"How could I not? Is this why you weren't at the competition?" I dug in my pocket and found a crumpled napkin, probably from the Stack. It didn't look used so I handed it to her. She dabbed her eyes so slowly I knew she was still trying to hide. She nodded just enough to let me know I was right but even that looked like it hurt from the wince on her face.

"Who did this to you?" I asked. "Was it Hanley?" I waited for an answer that took its time coming.

"Yes." Jill's voice came out muffled through her tear-clogged throat and inflated lips. "It was Hanley."

"What in the world did he do a thing like that for?"

"He gets drinking sometimes and he doesn't think."

"But you hardly know him."

"We've been seeing each other for several months."

"But he's married to Connie." And even if he wasn't, I couldn't imagine what Jill saw in him. Hanley was such a loud, obnoxious kind of guy and Jill was so pleasant and soft-spoken. I would have thought someone like him would have turned her off completely.

"He says he doesn't love her. Not like he loves me."

"This doesn't look like love to me."

"This is the first time it's been like this." Jill snaked a slim hand out from under the blanket and rubbed the cat behind the ears.

"Has he ever hit you before?"

"No. He's grabbed me and shaken me once or twice. Sometimes he holds on to my wrist or arm too tightly and leaves a bit of a mark. He had too much to drink up at his camp on Friday night and he let loose on me, that's all." That's all. Not really a healthy standard.

"How did you meet him?" Not that everyone in town didn't know the guy. It's just that most tried to steer clear of him whenever possible. Considering he is the most experienced forester in Sugar Grove, and Greener Pastures is a tree farm, that isn't a luxury I've had.

"We got to know each other up at Alanza's last spring when I was tapping her trees. Hanley takes care of the trees on the property so he was always around. One thing led to another." And he wasn't working at Alanza's anymore since there wasn't any Alanza. I wondered if Jill had heard about her death.

"Jill, did he tell you what happened to Alanza?"

"No. He hasn't said anything besides 'Is there any

more beer?' to me since he did this." Jill gestured at her face.

"Alanza's dead. She keeled over in her stack of pancakes at the competition yesterday morning." I watched her face, looking for surprise or worry, but it was hard to make anything out with all the bruising and swelling.

"That's terrible. Did she have a heart attack or something?" Jill pulled the afghan up closer to her chin like she was warding off the bad news.

"Not exactly." I wasn't sure how much Lowell wanted the public to hear yet so I felt like I was on slippery ground. "The police are treating it as a suspicious death."

"Oh my God." Jill slumped back, clutching the afghan even higher up on her chest, so high, in fact, her chin and lower lip disappeared behind it. "Do they have a suspect?"

"I don't think anything is certain yet, not even exactly how she died. It looks like it could have been poison."

"Poison. That's terrible. How did she take it?"

"Badly."

"That's not what I meant and it's not something to joke around about either." I think Jill was glaring at me but I couldn't be sure with the way her eye was swelled shut.

"It looks like it may have been in the syrup bottle at her place setting."

"Didn't your sugarhouse donate the syrup?"

"We did."

"You must be frantic. What if the whole batch was tampered with?" Jill sat up again and loosened her grip on the blanket in her distracted state. "You'll have to recall everything sold since the last year. Or even before that if the syrup wasn't from this year's batch."

"We sold out last year. It was definitely this year's batch." That got my dander up. Selling out is something I pride myself on. Sometimes we have so many orders we have to dip into the family's private stock just to not have to disappoint customers before we can put the sold out announcement on the website or up in the store.

"Well, that's good. Still, I wouldn't want to be in your shoes. It's going to do a lot of damage to your business if people think they'll get poisoned using your products." If I hadn't known better, I would have sworn Jill was trying to hide a smirk. I wanted to hit her myself, but of course, that would be the wrong thing to do. I decided it was time to go.

"Is there anything I can get you before I leave?" I thought she needed some soup or maybe a stiff drink.

"Just promise me you won't tell anyone about this, Dani. Things will only get worse if Connie finds out." Jill looked at me cockeyed.

"I can't promise I won't say something to the police if I see this again. But I won't go around telling anyone else. It isn't anyone else's business. But if something happened to you and I hadn't said anything to Lowell, I'd never forgive myself. That's the best I can do."

"Then I guess I'll have to accept that."

"I make a mean maple martini. Would you like one?" I had to at least offer.

"Drinking's what got me into this mess in the first place. I think I'll pass." Jill twisted her puffy lips into a smile. "But thanks for offering. Maybe some other time when I have something to celebrate."

"Are you going to be all right here alone? What if Hanley comes back? He didn't seem like he was in a good mood."

"My brother will be here any minute. He'll be staying overnight."

"It sounds like you're all set then." I waved good-bye and let myself out, making sure the cat didn't slip out with me. With a mountain lion on the loose, Sugar Grove was no place for a house kitty.

Nothing starts the day right like a walk through the sugar bush. Any time of year the trees and the quiet and the fresh air make me glad to be alive. Which is why my early morning wanderings so often take me to the spot on the property where my father died.

I had just reached the spot, the one I had made my brother take me to after I got home from the funeral and needed to see just where it had happened, when I heard the kind of crackling underfoot that meant someone wanted to be noticed.

"Good morning, Dani." Knowlton stood a few feet away holding a bulging backpack. This was not a favorite part of my mornings. Often when I was out taking my early, early morning walks, Knowlton was finishing up his night of wanderings and we ran into each other. Grampa always let him make himself comfortable on our property, and in my opinion Knowlton took advantage of that fact. He could wander anywhere he chose to look for dead things, but he preferred to lurk around here in hopes of catching sight of a live Greene girl.

"Still out, I see."

"It was a great night. I saw all sorts of things out roaming around."

"You didn't see anything large, did you?" If I was forced to run into Knowlton, the least I could get out of it was a report on mountain lions. Maybe one would eat him.

"I think I saw a couple of the escaped lemurs. And I picked up a couple of feathers that look like they belong to parrots. Do you know if there were any escaped parrots?" Knowlton will stuff anything dead enough to hold still, but his specialty is birds. Maybe it's his beaky nose but he is nutty about birds. From the chickens he raised for 4-H fairs as a kid to the bird sanctuary he tried to get Lewis Bett to establish on his property before he died, Knowlton was a hardcore birdaholic. Which got me thinking about Alanza's death.

"I heard a couple of them were instrumental in the escape of the other animals." Not that I was going to tell him how. Any opening to talk about amorousness was not something I was planning to ever give Knowlton.

"I knew parrots were smart but I wouldn't have thought they could plan and orchestrate an escape other than out of their own cage."

"Let's just say they were more the catalysts than the masterminds and leave it at that. I wouldn't want to go gossiping."

"That's one of the things I love about you, Dani. You're

always thinking about the right thing to do." I can't stand being around Knowlton. Every time I'm with him, he says something sweet and goofy like that, and it is so hard to brush him off. My only strategy was to hold him at arm's length until he found a girl of his dreams that reciprocated. Questions about his proposed bird sanctuary always distracted him.

"So now that Alanza is no longer in the picture, do you think the bird sanctuary has a better chance of going ahead?"

"I hadn't thought about it." Knowlton shifted his bag on his shoulder and the tips of his ears pinked as if the temperature had dropped by a good twenty degrees.

"You hadn't thought about it? The guy who once told me he wanted to name his kids Chickadee, Oriole, and Tanager?" I surprised myself by taking an unprecedented step closer to him.

"Well, maybe I did have a passing thought that since the plans she hatched for the property weren't going to go forward, the sanctuary might have a chance of happening. But Mother said the property will be going to a conservation land trust group."

Tansey wasn't one to gossip and what she did share was usually very accurate. If she went so far as to say something, it was almost guaranteed to be true. Quite possibly embellished and embroidered beyond the easily recognizable, but true at its core. If she mentioned a land trust, there was sure to be something to it. Especially since she and old Lewis Bett had been neighbors and friends of a sort for almost forty years.

"Did she say which land trust?"

"No. I didn't really pay any attention to that. Once she said she thought the land was going to be protected, I just went back to thinking about the birds. Why do you care anyway? You never pay any attention to birds no matter how much I've tried to interest you."

"It's not that I don't care about wildlife. I mean, I was the one who figured out what to do with that camel at church, now wasn't I?" I had enough problems with the local Fish and Game official without it getting around that I didn't like animals. And besides, I did like birds. Especially the kind slowly baked in a maple mustard glaze.

"I heard you let that camel get to first base."

"I didn't know you were a sports fan."

"Generally, I'm not, but I'd be willing to play a few rounds of baseball with you, Dani." His eyes got all moony and he closed the gap between us.

"They're called innings, Knowlton, not rounds. Golf is rounds." I stepped back so quickly I tripped and ended up on my backside, completely knocking the wind out of myself. He stood over me as I gasped, and that panicky feeling that comes from not being able to breathe filled my entire being. I scrambled to my feet and hurried away as fast as I could go. There was no way, if I was going to drop dead in the woods like my father, Knowlton was going to be the one to find my body. He'd stuff me for sure. I flew out of the woods, leaving Knowlton calling after me about ordering a cable sports channel when he made it home. I had gotten back to the sugarhouse before I realized I still didn't know any more about the bird sanctuary than I had when I ran into Knowlton in the first place.

The back of the shop area houses a small office, and it was there that I spent a lot of my time since it was built the previous year. We always used to do the books in the main house den, but as the business has grown, I said I wanted to keep things separate for tax purposes but really it was so people would stop using up all the sticky notes. Besides, once something was on a sticky note, I wanted to be able to find it again, and in a shared office, peopled by family members, my notes kept getting stuck to the inside of a wastepaper basket more often than not. No one else liked the shop office as much as I did, and I was putting my own stamp on it.

I paused on the porch of the sugarhouse, looking carefully at the floorboards for any sign of a large cat. A bit of hair, a claw mark in the wood. Even a bit of dried-on feline drool. Zip. I pushed open the door and entered the familiar space. The rough wooden walls and long workbenches were worn smooth in places by generations of Greenes boiling down sap. Down under the bench in the corner my great-great-grandfather had carved his initials in the wall, and when I was six, I found them one summer day playing hide-and-seek with my siblings. When I bragged about discovering them, they said they already knew about them. That's the thing about being the youngest in a family with a long history in one spot. There's no new territory to explore unless you make it up yourself or find a new way to look at a place already traveled.

Which was exactly why I was so committed to making the sugaring operation a success. Everyone else had filled a niche in the community. Grandma and Grampa endowed scholarships and funded the building of a new high school. My parents created a summer artist colony in a back parcel of land. Celadon was the driving force behind the historic preservation of the local opera house as well as many other neglected buildings. Loden used his law degree to offer pro bono services to community members in need. What I wanted, more than anything, was to put my own stamp on the community. Building the sugaring business using organic and sustainable methods was my way of doing just that. Our website played an important part in making that happen. Once a week I posted a new recipe or article on green living on our blog attached to the site. I even started selling green products such as stainless steel water bottles and cloth shopping bags with the Greener Pastures logo on them.

I wandered through the shop, running my hand over the stock and checking for dust. Not many people came to the sugarhouse in late fall, but we still did get the odd customer looking for a gift. At this time of year, between fall foliage and skiing, most people who stopped by were locals, but I still wanted to make a good impression. I had made a good case for Internet sales a couple of years before, and their success was one of the reasons I was listened to when I made the suggestion to add a shop onto the sugarhouse. Even Celadon had to stop complaining about crass commercialism sullying the family name when I reported on sales figures and reminded her we were donating all post-tax profits to environmental causes.

I heard creaking on the wide maple floorboards and looked up to see my mother standing in the sugarhouse doorway. Her finger was stuck as a place marker in a book. I squinted at the spine and noticed the title, *The Casting Out of Evil Spirits from About One's Person*. I had to assume she was looking up what to do about Alanza. God forbid Alanza should cling to any of us in this life or any other.

My mother considers herself to be psychically gifted. She reads tarot cards, dowses, and sees auras. She uses Ouija boards for information the way most people use the Internet. I'm not saying I believe she can do all the things she believes she can, or that such things are even possible, but she is right about enough stuff that I can't help but try to be open-minded.

She wandered through the sugarhouse, pausing near the evaporator, her peasant skirt swirling and her brace-lets jangling as she walked. Everywhere she goes, she swishes and jingles. With her around, it's like Halloween an extra 364 days each year. She stopped in front of a bench we use to hold jugs.

"Why do I want to bring in a love potion and sprinkle it everywhere in this room?"

"Because you always want to bring in a love potion. Did you need me for something?" I hoped an abrupt topic change would keep her from talking to me about my love life. The last few days had been hard enough without that. She had been following me around all week telling me my aura looked a bit tarnished and plying me with herbal teas designed to realign my chakras.

"Your grandmother was hoping you would run over to Felicia's to drop off the pickles for the swap." My mother placed her hand on the bench and squeezed her eyes shut. Grandma and several other women in town had swapped jars of homemade pickles for holiday tables for years. Each of them had a specialty, and the swap allowed all of them to enjoy a variety of excellent choices for no extra effort.

"I'll be sure to take care of it just as soon as I can."

"Outdoorsy, a little above average height. Dark hair. Confident. Nice sense of humor. Unmarried." She'd just described the guy from Fish and Game if his lack of a ring meant anything about marital status. "I'm getting a strong sense of someone like that in here."

"Are you sure? Do you remember that time when Celadon was in high school and you were sure she was pregnant? You even called the school nurse about it, but it ended up that Celadon's supposedly male guinea pig was actually an expectant female."

"That was before I had honed my gift. I've improved so much with time."

"Last month you convinced Martha Rollins to spend her all her disposable income on lottery tickets because you told her you could see an end to all her material concerns."

"I was right, wasn't I?"

"She was struck and killed by a log truck as soon as she left the store with her lottery tickets."

"She had no more material concerns, though, did she?" That's the thing with Mom's impressions. If she didn't try to interpret them, they might actually be spot-on. It was always the reading into them that made a hash of things. You had to take what she said with an ocean's worth of salt.

"I'd best go tell your grandmother the pickles will be all set before she puts it on her own to-do list," she said. I followed her out the door and onto the porch, where she came to a dead stop.

"I'm sensing a large presence here." She pointed to the spot where the mountain lion had made himself at home. I didn't want to tell her about it, though, because knowing Mom, she'd have a team of investigators, complete with video crew, swarming the place. "I'm picking up on curiosity, and stealth. And doubt mixed with derision. Strange. Not at all in alignment with sugar making." It looked more than ever like that guy from the state thought my report was laughable despite his apologies.

"Maybe you should come by and do some sort of cleansing ritual." That ought to distract her from any further interest in big cats or single men. "I wouldn't want any derision-flavored syrup."

"What this place needs more than anything is some holiday cheer." Mom looked around the porch and shook her head sadly at the faded mums and tattered ornamental cabbages. "I'll take care of it while you're off on your pickle errand."

Eight

I intended to set off right away to deliver the pickles but I spotted Hanley in back of the barn with Grampa. Grampa pointed at the trail leading into the north part of the property, and Hanley nodded and started off on his own. Grampa wandered off toward the lower field where he turns out his cows if the weather is decent. I hung back so he wouldn't spot me following Hanley. Talking about extramarital affairs is not something I wanted to do in front of my grandfather, no matter how much I preferred not to deal with Hanley on my own. Besides, I thought he might be more inclined to tell the truth to just one person instead of a group.

Hanley wasn't in much of a hurry so it was easy enough to catch up even factoring in the wait for Grampa to disappear from view. I hustled up behind him just as he was coming to a stop in front of a large sugar maple with a broken limb that flopped like a hangnail.

"I see Grampa sent you to one of our neediest." I hadn't been trying to be quiet but I must have been doing a pretty good job because he jumped up off the ground like I'd dropped a sledgehammer on his foot. It made me wonder if he had a guilty conscience.

"Dani, you snuck up on me real quiet like. What're you doing here?"

"Well, I may not be making syrup at this time of year, but I try to walk the property and check on trees every day. I can't get to all the property every day, but in the course of a week or so, I can get my eyes on most of the trees." Now to figure out how to insert his affair with Jill into the conversation. "When I was talking to Jill Hayes yesterday, she said she can do hers every day in one short trip." I kept my eyes pealed on Hanley's face. He squirmed a bit at her name, tracing a circle with the toe of his boot in the leaf litter at the base of the tree. Gotcha.

"Her property is a lot smaller than this one."

"Do you service her, too?" I asked. He looked up, startled. "Her trees, I mean."

"I tend out on her trees. Hers isn't the biggest account I have, not by a long poke, but every client's important."

"Jill said she gets a bit of extra service from you that might not be on the books with Connie." I felt a little sick and a whole lot embarrassed even letting those words leak out between my lips.

"Are you flirting with me?" Hanley looked like he'd swallowed down one of Grandma's hot biscuits slathered with butter and drizzled with maple syrup. "Are you asking if you can sign up for extra services, too?" He took a step back from the tree and a step closer to me.

"Was the big bruise on Jill's face one of the extra services?"

"Did she say I did that to her?"

"She said you'd had a bit too much to drink while the two of you were up at the camp on Friday night and that you let loose on her."

"I don't remember things going just exactly like that."

"But you might not remember if you'd been drinking as much as she said you had, would you?"

"Maybe not."

"Do remember being with Jill?" I wondered how credible a witness he was. If he didn't remember hitting her, would he remember her even being around? And even if he did, could his memory be trusted?

"Jill is very memorable, if you follow my meaning." Hanley winked at me and, even worse, licked his lips. I could do without that picture being seared into my brain, but I guess I had asked for it by poking my nose into police business.

"So she was with you on Friday night?"

"Why do you care? I'm not your husband."

"Jill wasn't at the pancake breakfast like she was supposed to be. When I asked her why, she said it was because of the bruise you gave her."

"Why is it your business?"

"Because it is my business that is being impacted by Alanza's death. If Jill knew not to go to the breakfast, that looks like she had something to do with what happened to Alanza."

"Jill was with me on Friday night. But I wished I hadn't been away from home."

"Why not? If Jill was so memorable, I would have thought you'd be glad of all the time you can spend together."

"Because of the goats. I came back to a hell of a mess. Something got into the goat pen and tore things up good on Friday night while I was away. Connie was all shook up about it. She couldn't get me on the cell phone since the coverage up there ain't too good."

"What do you think did it?"

"It's hard to say. The fencing was damaged; one goat was cut up pretty bad but'll recover. Another one is just missing, like it was spirited off. It makes me wonder if that Fish and Game guy is really telling all he knows or if there is something more dangerous on the loose around here than he is admitting." I considered the possibility that Graham was holding something back. Or maybe he wasn't aware there was a big cat in the group of animals released because the guy who let him out hadn't admitted it. Next stop, Connie's, I was hoping to spot evidence of a mountain lion.

Connie waved me into the hallway of her antique cape, a phone clamped tightly between her ear and shoulder. I stood in the cramped space trying to shove down my feelings of claustrophobia. Old farm tools with pointy ends and hooks covered the walls and made the hall feel like an inside-out cheese grater. There might have been a hall table in there, too, but it was hard to tell because of the mounds of unopened mail, library books, and firewood stacked every which way. Connie's dog, Profiterole, curled up in his basket, which mostly blocked the entrance to the kitchen. I wondered what Hanley's camp looked like inside and if he liked to go there to get away from all the mess that surrounded him at home.

"Sorry about that, Dani. One of my bookkeeping clients needed me to clarify something. So what brings you by?" Connie ran her rough hand through her curly graying hair. She looked more like a farmer than an office worker with her weathered complexion, well-muscled hands, and rugged, earth mother clothing.

"Hanley was up checking our trees today and he told me about the trouble with your goats. I wondered if I could take a look."

"Well, sure you can, but why would you want to?"

"Let's just say I have a bet going with the local Fish and Game officer about what might have done it."

"That sure is a mess with all those animals running around. Do you think this had something to do with all that?"

"I don't know but it seems strange that the same night a bunch of exotic animals get loose, you end up with your goats getting attacked."

"If it turns out it was that truck driver's fault, I don't know what I'm gonna do. Whatever could that guy have been thinking when he let those animals out?"

"I think he was thinking about how his wife was being unfaithful to him with someone else he trusted." I tried gauging Connie's reaction to the topic of infidelity without being too obvious. The lines between her eyebrows scrunched down deeper, whatever that meant.

"That would be disheartening, but even so, you know how I feel about my goats."

"I do. Hanley said you were all alone when it happened, too."

"I was. I was too angry and worried for the goats to be scared, so it could have been worse." Connie pried the closet door open as far as she could, given the stack of newspapers on the floor in front of it. Wrapping herself in a canvas jacket that looked like it belonged to Hanley, she led the way out to the goat enclosure.

The fence was indeed damaged like Hanley had said. Some of the heavy wire sagged out of shape and was distended in several places. The ground inside the enclosure looked torn up like there had been an altercation of some sort. There wasn't much else to see until we went inside the barn at the end of the enclosure. Connie entered the building and motioned for me to follow. At first it was difficult to see, the light levels were low, and the colors were mostly drab browns and wood tones. As my eyes adjusted, I could make out several animals huddled together at the far end of the barn in one of the old horse stalls.

"Clementine was the one scraped up in the fray," Connie said, pointing at a white female with a crooked horn. She had a nasty gash along her haunch and someone had covered it with ointment, which glistened against her matted fur. All the goats, except Clementine, took a few tentative steps toward Connie as she clucked at them.

"She seems like she's still afraid," I said, noting the way she hung back from the others, cowering against the back wall.

"She must be. Clementine usually runs right over me with her displays of affection."

"What about the one Hanley said went missing?"

"It was her sister, Susannah. The two were very close. Clementine must be heartbroken." I wondered if one of them behaved like Celadon. I'm not sure I could see myself feeling as heartbroken if Celadon simply went missing one evening. I might even be the tiniest bit relieved.

"Do you have any idea what might have done this?" I had my own, of course, but there was no way I was going to be the one to mention the mountain lion to her if she hadn't heard it through the grapevine already.

"Well, I heard you thought you saw a mountain lion, and until this happened, I agreed with the rest of the folks in town that you had finally cracked from all the Christmas hoopla your family puts together. But now, I'm not so sure."

"So you think it could have been a mountain lion?"

"I don't know what else could have come in here and then jumped back out with a full-grown goat in tow. Do you?"

"I don't need to be convinced. I saw the thing with my own eyes."

"What did Fish and Game say?"

"There is no such thing in New Hampshire anymore."

"Well, then, maybe it was a yeti."

"Maybe you had a yeti here messing with your goats, but there was a mountain lion at my sugarhouse and I hope we can prove it."

"Well, whatever you do, make sure you tell your grandfather to fortify the situation in your own barn. I'd hate for his cows to meet a similar fate."

"I'll be sure to tell him. And please let me know if you have any more trouble. I know the Fish and Game guy's number and would be happy to ask him to give a look around."

"I'll do that. And if you see Hanley when you get home be sure to tell him I'm making a tuna noodle casserole for dinner. There's nothing like making a man's favorite meal to keep him happy at home." Maybe Hanley had lied about his favorite meal. Or else Jill was an even better cook than Connie.

I always loved the ride over to Roland's place even if the reason was a mundane errand like a pickle delivery. The road wound through some of the prettiest parts of town, with peeks at the mountains and even a glimpse of the lake along one stretch. I'd been there many times delivering syrup for the inn. Roland and his wife, Felicia, had been kind enough to offer to use only Greener Pastures syrup on their guests' breakfast tables and even to sell bottles of it at the front desk.

Roland and Felicia Chick had waited until their kids were grown and then set about realizing their lifelong dream of running an inn. Everything about the place spoke of how much care they had lavished on it. The windows gleamed, the paint dazzled, the gardens lulled. Even the birds frolicked in a way that was almost magically cheerful. Every bit of it was enchanting except for the view.

From the gracious, wraparound porch with its gingerbread trim and lush hanging baskets of hyperactively blooming petunias, you used to be able to look out over the gentle rolling hills in the distance covered in dense trees and shrubs. Now, standing out like a cockroach on a wedding cake, a mini storage facility blighted the view. The property line lay just beyond a carefully planted border of flowering quince, lilac, and weigela the Chicks had installed several years earlier. A road leading into Alanza's property cut right behind the border and some of the heavy equipment used to construct it had demolished some prized specimens and enabled an unobstructed view of the metal shacks. The machines were still there, poised and threatening like an enemy army just beyond a city wall.

Roland had developed angina and a nervous twitch. His wife had taken on the new hobby of constantly monitoring his blood pressure. It was a wonder Roland had outlasted Alanza. With the breakfast rush over, Roland leaned against the front desk looking like he had nothing on his mind but time.

"Hey there, Dani. What brings you by? Lowell was

already here confiscating your syrup for testing." I hadn't even considered that could happen. He hadn't mentioned it to me. But maybe I wasn't his first priority while handling a murder investigation. I wasn't so overwhelmed with a sense of my own importance that I couldn't see that without being told. Still, it was a bit of a blow to realize my syrup was being treated like a public health hazard.

"Actually, I'm here for the pickles. Only three days 'til Thanksgiving." I reached into my tote bag and dug out two jars of Grandma's famous maple syrup bread-and-butter pickles. "But I wish I were here delivering syrup. I don't know when I'll be back in business."

"I'm so sorry. I know what it means to have a business you've worked so hard to establish turn to a pile of horse dung right in front of your eyes."

"That view of the storage facility is pretty bad." Even in the daylight it was easy to see Alanza's custom-ordered, very pricey, neon sign, flashing on and off with enough wattage to kill bugs from a distance. It looked like Santa had put his head together with a Las Vegas casino owner to design the thing. When she had first turned it on, panicked calls had come into the police station from all over the area saying Sugar Grove was being visited by alien crafts.

"And it was only going to get worse with her deciding to scalp Bett's Knob."

"She was planning to do what?" I was horrified. Bett's Knob lay within the confines of Alanza's property, but the whole community felt it belonged to us all. It wasn't a large part of the property, but it had a view that went on for miles. It rose up above the surrounding land enough to be visible from most of the town and boasted some of the finest displays of fall foliage in the area. As a matter of fact, after years of lobbying, the Chamber of Commerce had convinced the select board to approve plans for one of those oversized View-Masters alongside the turnpike to attract more business to town during leaf-peeping season.

The Chamber fund-raised and solicited donations from people all over the community and had even held an unveiling ceremony for the oversized View-Master. Myra Bett Phelps, one of the members of the family after whom the lumpy foothill formation was named, had the honor of yanking the red, white, and blue vinyl tablecloth off the thing and leading the crowd, such as it was, in an ear-thrumming rendition of the National Anthem.

"You hadn't heard? Alanza announced at the last Chamber of Commerce meeting that she was going to start up a sugaring operation. When I asked her how much more she was planning to impact my inn, she told me about Bett's Knob." Why Alanza would choose to tap her own trees was entirely beyond me. I loved the business myself but I couldn't imagine just deciding one day to go into it without any prior experience. It wasn't as if she was even a country girl at heart. I'd never even seen her in a pair of shoes with a less than two-inch heel. I tried to picture her standing in a pair of snowshoes, wearing a miniskirt, drilling holes in a maple to place a spile. I couldn't even picture her figuring out how to hold the drill, let alone tap the tree. The only thing I could imagine her tapping was her pointy-toed pumps to a lively beat at a dance club.

"She'd never have been allowed to clear Bett's Knob, would she? What about filing an 'intent to cut' form with the town?"

"She didn't need to file an intent to cut if the timber was being used to boil sap down for syrup." He was right, of course. Alanza could have cut as much timber as she wanted if she used the wood for her own sugaring operation. And she had enough trees on the property to produce a lot of firewood and a lot of sap. As long as she didn't confuse the maples for the firewood. If someone had killed Alanza, they had done the town an even bigger favor than I had thought.

"So just like the rest of us, I bet you weren't too upset to see her face plant in the pancakes then." It seemed like as good an opening as any. And it wasn't like I was questioning him. We were just chatting about neighbors like anyone does from time to time. I had to keep it light. Alienating any potential business at this point would be disastrous. The last thing I needed was more ill will.

"The worst thing about that whole situation was that it didn't happen before that God-awful shanty town sprang up." Roland's face was beginning to flush like an ice pop. Maybe he wasn't going to be too long following Alanza off to wherever she went on the other side. Not that I'm saying I'd expect them to end up in the same place.

"Well, at least the construction on her property should

110

grind to a halt. That should be good news for you and Felicia, shouldn't it?"

"It's great that nothing more is likely straightaway, but I don't know what whoever gets the property now will do with it."

"So you don't know who will be getting the property then?"

"No idea. I didn't know Alanza until she had settled into the house over there and started introducing herself around town as the owner. If I had known how things were going to go, I would have sold the business and headed south like all the rest of the geezers."

"You're not a geezer and you know it." Felicia Chick, Roland's wife of thirty-something years, emerged through the doorway, her arms full of folded table linen. "Are those from your grandmother?" She nodded toward the pickles.

"They are. She wanted me to bring them by so you'd be sure to have them for Thanksgiving. And she said to tell you she was sorry to have missed the quilting group Friday evening."

"Tell her we missed her, too. Come on back to the kitchen. I've got the ones to trade on the counter." Felicia thrust the stack of tablecloths and napkins into Roland's outstretched arms. "Be a love and spread these round while I tend to Dani. And try to think of something pleasant. Your face looks like a blood sausage." I followed Felicia's slim frame to the back of the house, where the kitchen stood, warm and smelling of cinnamon and yeasted bread.

"I tried something a bit different this year. I hope your family will like it." Felicia handed me a jar of crabapple pickles. I turned it around in my hand admiring the color as the fruit swirled gently in the rosy pickling liquid.

"Whatever made you think of these?" I asked.

"My mother used to make them and I was feeling nostalgic. You're probably still too young to get that way, but someday once you've gotten older, those things your parents used to do will mean a great deal to you."

"They already do. That's why I'm so committed to making a success of Greener Pastures." Making my father's favorite thing, maple syrup, let me feel closer to him even though he was gone.

"How insensitive of me. I'm getting old and run at the mouth sometimes. Forgive me?" Felicia's warm brown eyes crinkled with concern. She might have been ten years older than my mother but you couldn't guess it looking at her.

"No need. I understand. So why did your mother make these?"

"She competed religiously at the local county fair, and Millicent Marcotte used to beat her for the blue ribbon every year. Finally, she had had enough and decided to go all out with something different."

"Crabapple pickles?"

"We always had a bumper crop and she thought they were so pretty. She decided to tinker with them a bit at a time until she got the flavor just right. I'll bet you can guess the secret ingredient."

"Maple syrup?"

"You got it. She went to a neighbor who tapped his trees and got a gallon of it. Then she set to work in earnest."

"How long did it take her to come up with something?"

"We ate a version of the darn things every night for at least a month."

"But the crabapples wouldn't have come ripe until after the fair, would they?"

"Well, that was the worst of it, waiting almost a whole year to enter them into the fair. Mother started picking fruit about a week after the fair was all over."

"Did she enter anything at all that year?"

"No. She didn't get around to it since she was so busy putting up trials of the new recipe. Millicent told everyone Mother had finally given up because she realized she just couldn't win."

"Please tell me she got back at her."

"In spades. Mother won the blue ribbon, best in show, prettiest, and they even made a new category for most creative. After Mother died, they named the prize the Norinda Bett Folsom Ingenuity Award."

"So your mother was a Bett, too, before she married?" There were more Betts coming out of the woodwork in Sugar Grove than carpenter ants.

"She was indeed. Between the Betts and the Greenes, we make up the majority of the population. When it comes down to it, Myra and I are cousins of a sort."

"Speaking of Greenes, if I don't get these pickles back to the house and start giving my grandmother a hand with the Thanksgiving preparations, I am going to be in big trouble." Felicia walked me to the door, and in no time I was zipping along the road, headed for home and all the whirlwind of preparations for the upcoming holiday the family was stirring up.

Nine

I was up before Grampa on Tuesday morning and that took some doing. Despite the fact the man never had to earn his living, all his life he had kept the hours of a dairy farmer. No one cared more about their herd than Grampa. But this morning I cared even more about my state inspection. My stomach was a mess, and I kept vacillating between feeling half starved and certain I'd lose anything I tried to choke down. I pulled three different almost identical outfits from the drawers and ended up choosing the one with the jeans that needed rolling up the least. Sometimes my hems are turned up so many times they look like my ankles are members of an Olympic snow-tubing team.

I had turned in the organic application to the state a while ago and I hoped my business was a shoe-in for certification. We didn't have any diseases in our sugar bush, and we had been using an organically certified cleaner for the spiles and hoses as well as the buckets and jugs for years. My grandfather always said it didn't honor the land to take something good and give back something bad so he never allowed it. Green practices were second nature at Greener Pastures, and it made the whole thing a lot easier. It also helped that we produced all our own sap. For the people like Jill Hayes, who tapped trees on property belonging to other people, the process was a whole lot more complicated. Not only did they have to run through all the fertilizers, pesticides, and cleaners used on their own property, they had to verify and document the ones used anywhere they tapped. Some sugar makers tapped sources all over the area so the organic certification could feel a bit overwhelming.

I wondered again how the tapping situation was going to affect Jill. I knew from the grapevine, and by that I mean Myra Phelps's flapping jaws, that she relied heavily on the sap from the trees on Alanza's property to stay in business.

Even though I felt good about my application, I was at the sugarhouse for a last round of tidying and pacing an hour before the inspector was due to arrive. Not that I was enjoying being in the sugarhouse all that much. My mother had made good on her threat of gussying the place up with a bit of Christmas cheer. Which meant everywhere I looked things twinkled, sparkled and glittered. She had even added a fake tree in the corner with blinking lights and a tinsel garland. I wondered if all that fake greenery would disqualify Greener Pastures for organic status. At least she hadn't hidden the coffeemaker I had installed for the customers to enjoy. I busied myself making a pot to pass the final few minutes of my wait. By the time I'd located a couple of clean mugs and poured myself a steaming cup, I heard the clattering of heavy feet on the sugarhouse porch. This guy was never going to be mistaken for a mountain lion.

I took a breath that reached all the way to my thick-cuffed ankles and pulled open the door. Standing in the threshold was a real live garden gnome, complete with a drooping red hat and round rosy cheeks. The little old man standing in front of me was short enough that he looked me straight in the eye. Granted, my work boots had a very thick sole, which boosted me up by a couple of inches, but this was a first for me. I took a step back and wondered if my mental health was finally as eroded as a dirt road running down a mountain. I'd watched a couple of children's movies with Hunter and Spring lately, but I didn't think that could explain it.

"Are you Dani Greene?" the gnome asked. I nodded, stunned to hear that the voice was not mechanized or quavery. "Good, good. It's nice to meet you. Yep, very nice to meet you. I'm Brantley Sims. We have an appointment." He held out a firm, small hand and grasped mine with bone-pulverizing vigor.

"Come on in." I tugged a little at my hand, hoping he would relinquish it quickly since it felt like I'd caught it in a car door. Maybe he noticed my sharp intake of breath because he dropped my hand and opened a notebook. "I hope you found the place easily enough."

"You bet I did. I've been roaming these hills long before there was such a thing as a GPS and I haven't got lost yet. Now let's get a jump on this. I've got a bunch of meetings today and I promised the wife I'd be home in time to help her greet my family when they roll in this evening for the holiday." Lord forgive me, all I could envision was Snow White standing at a window twitching back the curtain and clucking her tongue as six white-haired little men made their way across her drive.

"Just tell me what you need. I'm eager to get this out of the way, too."

"Why? Are you nervous? Trying to hide something? Got some kind of a guilty conscious?" He fixed a bright blue eye on me and poised his pen above his notebook like he was going to add my response to my permanent record. I gulped. And from his vantage point, I'm sure he could see it.

"No sir. I'm just eager to hear the good news that I can be certified organic. I'm just itching to update my website and let the customers know they can feel even better about our products." And my prices could move up the scale a bit, too.

"And your prices will go up a good bit, too, if you pass, now won't they?" I gulped again. "I'm just teasing. Don't get yourself so worked up. You won't live to be my age if you never develop a sense of humor." He walked over to the evaporator and started poking around. For the next forty-five minutes he looked everywhere, rummaged around in cupboards, cabinets, and closets. He asked questions, wrote the names of cleaners in his notebook, and even snapped a few photos on a camera that looked like it took actual film. As the moments passed, I felt myself relax and even thought we were developing a rapport of a sort. We made our way into the shop area, where he made a beeline for the coffeepot.

"Is this organic?" I was gulping so much I wondered if it was possible to get an extended warranty on my Adam's apple. I looked at the gnome and scrutinized his face for signs of mirth, humor, anything to get me off the hook.

"I'm not sure. I serve organic coffee during the high season when there are tourists in the shop, but I'm afraid this might be some my sister brought in from the house the last time she deigned to visit. Will that count against me?"

"I'm just joking. You really do need to lighten up." He was right, though. I tried my best to walk the walk and those little things all mattered. My grandparents still made the majority of the decisions about the groceries, and I hadn't been able to convince them coffee drinking had changed a bit since they bought their first can of Chock full o'Nuts. They like to think they are keeping up with the times in a lot of ways, but shade-grown and sustainable cups of joe weren't even on the list.

"Well, then, would you like a cup?"

"I never touch the hard stuff when I'm working. It goes straight to my head." And he elbowed me in the ribs. "You're looking kinda peaky. Why don't we take the air while you show me your sugar bush?" I nodded and opened the door leading out of the shop and to the parking lot, where customers had crowded onto the grassy verges in the height of leaf-peeping season. We picked our way across the semifrozen ground and entered the sugar bush at one of my favorite points on the property. An old, tumbled-down stone wall runs for a ways and then peters out at a beech tree, which looks like the one used in every fairy tale illustration. Its leaves rattled and quaked in the slight breeze. As the trees grew denser and larger, the carpet of crackling leaves beneath my feet grew more luxuriant. Acre after acre of the stately trees stretched above my head, some so close their branches touched and made it feel like a sanctuary in the woods.

"Your application says you don't buy sap from any other producers."

"That's right. We make our syrup exclusively from our own sap. We tap the trees and boil it down right in the shack using wood from our own property."

"So you've got a fairly good-sized setup here. You're pretty young for such an ambitious project."

"I'm not as young as I look."

"And I'm not as old as I look, but that doesn't change how much effort it takes to make a go of something as big as this."

"No disrespect, sir, but my family has been making syrup for four generations. I don't remember a time when I didn't go out with my father to check the buckets or watch him fill the evaporator pan with sap. I may be young but I have over twenty years' experience."

"But do you have it in running a business?"

"No. But I want to. And I'm hoping organic certification is going to help me to get there."

"From the looks of things, I think you stand a decent chance of that. Let's finish touring the sugar bush then we'll see if I have any more questions."

For the next hour or so we moved across the property in much the same way he had moved about the sugarhouse. He was observant, methodical, and thorough. But by the time we'd worked our way back to the shop, I felt pretty good about my chances.

"Well, now that the work's all done, I'd be delighted to accept that cup of coffee if you're still offering, organic or not." He winked at me, dipping an overgrown eyebrow down under his spectacles, where it got tangled up in the frame. He yanked it out with a gnarled finger and accepted the beverage. We were making small talk about the likelihood of favorable weather in spring for a decent sugaring season when I heard more clomping on the front porch.

I looked up at Lowell coming through the door. Thinking back, it seems he must not have spotted Brantley, not that I can blame him since he was almost completely hidden by a stack of crates displaying maple leaf printed dish towels, place mats, and napkins.

"Dani, we need to talk right away." His voice was forceful and worried, two things I never associate with Lowell. He is always calm in any crisis. Tell him you lopped off an arm and he'd be tying a dog leash around what's left while speaking with quiet authority to 911. I almost dropped my coffee cup at his tone.

"Can it wait?" Whatever it was, I knew I didn't want to know it. No one is ever happy to know what will be said by someone who sounds like he did.

"No, it can't. I got the results from the state lab. Alanza Speedwell was poisoned by ingesting Greener Pastures syrup. Something called Compound 1080 or sodium fluoroacetate. It's a highly toxic pesticide that's been off the market for quite some time." My Adam's apple froze in mid-bob. I should have been thinking of something else, I'm sure, but for some reason all I could focus on was whether or not an Adam's apple could actually get stuck like an elevator trapped between floors. I was starting to feel a wave of panic crashing down on me when the gnome snapped me out of it and reminded me of what was important. Brantley stepped out to a spot where Lowell could see him.

"Did you say the syrup from this establishment killed someone?"

"Who are you?" Lowell looked a little like I must have when I spotted Brantley on my porch.

"I'm the state ag inspector here to review an application for organic certification, which no longer seems necessary." He looked me over from head to foot. "No wonder you were so jumpy this morning. I should have put things together a little faster. The pancake breakfast incident on Saturday. That's where I had heard the name *Sugar Grove* recently."

"I'm afraid so. And I'd appreciate it if you wouldn't go telling all you know to anyone," Lowell said.

"All I'm gonna say is this inspection is over. And I think you've got bigger problems than organic. This place is gonna be shut down completely."

Lowell and I watched as the gnome fled as fast as his

short little legs would carry him. He was out the door and down the drive in less time than it took a camel to swallow a homemade granola bar.

"I need to let the family know what is going on."

"Yes, you do. But I wouldn't be too worried. We tested all the other jugs at the breakfast and hers was the only one that had been tampered with. I will need to check out your supply, though." Lowell clapped a gentle hand down on my shoulder.

"What a nightmare. Can you imagine what it will do to business if any more syrup is found to be poisoned?"

"Try not to think about it too much. You've got all kinds of things to worry about, like surviving the holidays and finding a husband."

"Don't you start in on my love life. I've got enough trouble between Knowlton and Mitch."

"And don't forget about the camel who sounds like quite the kisser."

"You heard about that?"

"Of course."

"You will tell the family about it gently, right? You know how Grampa looks like a strong blustery guy but something like this is really going to throw him for a loop."

"I'll be careful. And I'll reassure them we only found poison in the syrup at Alanza's place setting."

"I'm not entirely sure that will help."

"You know I'm going to have to ask some uncomfortable questions to eliminate you as suspects, right?" Lowell looked at his uniform shoes and I thought I saw the faintest bit of a blush spread under his cheeks. I had never considered how a crime might worm its way between Lowell and my family. He had always seemed like one of us more than not. I often forget about Lowell having any family other than us. His parents died in a house fire along with the family dog while Lowell was away in the service. He came back to Sugar Grove at the end of his hitch and my family tried to fill his loss.

My father had been his best friend since early childhood, and he had spent as much time in our house as his own for years. The same could be said in reverse for my father, and the loss of the elder Matthews had hit him hard. The death of the Matthewses was one of the reasons the Sap Bucket Brigade's fund-raiser was such a popular cause. My first thought was to realize what a terrible position Lowell was in. My second was to feel even angrier at whoever had done this thing and had brought this sort of mess to our community.

"I wouldn't respect you as much if you didn't. It can't always be easy to do your job, and everyone appreciates that you do it anyway. Besides, I wouldn't want it said that you were showing us favoritism because of your relationship to the family. It would make people wonder if there really was something to worry about when they bought our syrup if the investigation wasn't proper. Fire away." I patted his hand and he gave me a half smile that didn't really light up his face like it usually did.

"Tell me about the syrup and how it got to the grange from your place."

"Well, as you, and everyone else in town, probably

know, we donate the syrup for the contest every year. We actually put up twenty-five special glass bottles shaped like New Hampshire as a souvenir for the participants since Grampa always wins."

"People were saying Alanza was giving him a run for his money until she keeled over."

"People can say whatever they want. Grampa will be winning until he's eating loaves and fishes with Jesus. Besides, Alanza slowed down a couple of plates before she dropped out of the race entirely."

"But witnesses said she was starting to look dazed and disoriented before she actually fell face-first into her short stack. The poison could account for the slowdown. I've heard a number of people mention she could have taken the pewter pitcher from Emerald this year."

"No one's said that in front of me." I was stunned and felt heat prickling under my collar. After everything Grampa and Grandma had done for the town, did anyone actually believe he would kill someone to keep winning a trophy?

"Well, they wouldn't, now would they? But that doesn't stop them from saying it when your back is turned or when they think they are trying to help the police find out who did it. But back to the subject. Who handled the syrup?"

"We all did. It was part of this year's batch, of course. We filled the bottles and set them aside until they would be needed months later. They go into one of the cupboards in the sugarhouse. Then, we pulled them out along with all the larger plastic jugs that get used on the tables for the regular fund-raiser participants. Everybody helped load up the jugs and then all the rest of the family went over in the minivan to help set up the tables, put out the jugs, and to generally be helpful."

"When was this?"

"Friday night. We always do it the night before, because that way, if there is a problem at the grange, like not enough tables or dirty chairs, there is plenty of time to resolve it."

"So you didn't go to the grange?"

"No. I told everyone I had a migraine, but really they were all just driving me nuts with Christmas cheer. I wanted to hear myself think without someone humming carols in my ears."

"So you didn't actually see what happened with all the jugs and such."

"No. You'll have to ask someone who was there. But it would be the same as always, I'm sure."

"So the jugs just get left out on the tables unattended overnight?"

"Sure. Why wouldn't they? No one steals them and there has never been a problem before."

"But if someone could get into the grange, they could have accessed the jugs?"

"Definitely. They are just left sitting out."

"How would the poisoner know which one was Alanza's?"

"That's easy. Her name was one it. All the names were on them. The bottles have a ribbon with a paper maple leaf attached to it with the contestant's name written on it. They served as a place holder."

"So, clearly labeled. And no one switched them?"

"I don't see why they would. The ribbons were tied off short so as not to leave a dangling piece to drag into someone's pancake plate. And all the jugs were identical so it wasn't like a contestant would have wanted to swap for some reason. All of them were grade B amber syrup."

"So the best time to take care of adding the poison was after the jugs were put in position and before the event started in the morning."

"I'd say so. The family got home around nine thirty, quarter to ten, I think." I remembered huddling under the cold covers in the dark and having a hard time drifting off to sleep, but I hadn't consulted the time.

"What about safety caps or something? Wouldn't Alanza have noticed if her bottle had been opened?" Lowell looked thoughtful and I had to think for a second about it, too, but then it came to me how easy it would be to pull it off.

"We do use caps with those twist-off lower rings that show the cap has been opened. But we don't use an inner seal on the syrup. Maybe we should but it has never been an issue before now and the extra steps never seemed necessary."

"So no inner seal like those pieces of plastic film covering the opening but under the cap itself."

"That's right. All someone would need to do would be to twist open the cap, cut off the lower ring left behind, and replace it with a new cap that matched the others. Alanza would never have noticed a thing." Creepy. Now there was something else I was going to need to consider when it came to modernizing the operation. I really resented how evil made so much more work and cost for the rest of us. When I thought about all those little plastic pieces of film degrading and turning into pollutants because some people wanted to hurt others, I just wanted to screech.

"So who would know that?" Lowell asked.

"I suppose anyone who had ever participated in the contest or had been the one to open a jug for the first time at the fund-raiser or had ever bought our syrup would know there was no inner film. I'm not sure the average person would remember, though."

"But someone who wanted to kill Alanza might have noticed."

"Or someone who makes syrup. None of us use the film. It just doesn't seem worth it." Or it hadn't until now.

"Other sugar makers had reasons not to like Alanza, too, didn't they?"

"Some did. She didn't make anyone happy when she stopped allowing some of the smaller operations to tap her trees."

"Didn't Jill Hayes and her brother have permission to tap there?" Lowell asked.

"I believe they did but so did quite a number of other people."

"We don't know if any of the stored syrup has been tainted. I suggest you suspend sales until we can get to the bottom of this," Lowell said. "I need you to show me where the syrup is stored so I can get Mitch to start rounding it up for testing." Great, more reasons for Mitch to be relieved he had broken up with me. But if it was the only way to stay in business, then I had to act more mature than I felt and get on with it.

"Follow me."

I walked back to the storage area, knelt before the cupboard, and retrieved a contest bottle. These special bottles were made of clear glass and shaped like the state of New Hampshire. The caps were always a deep green as a nod to the family name. Grampa never worried about the expense of anything; he worried about the value. He had the bottles custom-made as a consolation prize for all the other contestants.

I dug around in the back of the bottom shelf and felt a ruffle-ridged side of another New Hampshire bottle. I pulled it toward me and saw exactly what I'd expected. I bent even farther into the cupboard and pulled all of them out. When we bottle syrup in early spring, we don't know how many people will sign up for the pancake contest in November. It varies wildly from year to year with the only consistent contestant being Grampa. So, to be better safe than sorry, we fill twenty-five glass bottles every year. They are all the same. Every year.

Most of the time we have around six to eight contestants, but a few times we've needed all twenty-five. One year we even had to dig into the leftovers from the year before but that was because there was a family of twenty-six competitive eaters who happened to be staying at Roland's inn just in time for the competition. Grampa didn't eat for three days after that year's contest, and truth be told, he didn't eat pancakes for over a month. Grandma was a little insulted, then worried, that it took him so long to get back in the game.

I ran my eyes over the bottles. All had identical dark green plastic caps. I ducked back down for plastic jugs of the sort we donated for the larger tables. These were brown plastic, with dark brown caps. We donate the grade B because most people enjoy the pronounced maple flavor. Besides, there's a lot more of it to be had, so it makes good business sense to donate what's not in short supply.

Every one of the jugs was consistent with its type. I explained all of it to Lowell and he made a bunch of notes. We put it off as long as we could, but finally we both ran out of reasons we weren't ready to head to the house to deliver the bad news to the family.

Ten

Lowell had them all go through their versions of the syrup delivery. Everyone said just about what I would have expected. They placed the syrup on the tables, locked up the grange hall, and returned home. Everyone was in bed by just past ten since the next day needed an early start. By the time they were done telling what they knew, my family looked grim.

Grampa slouched in a chair, one of his bandanna handkerchiefs draped over his knee, which meant he was choked up. I guess it must have been the Greener Pastures involvement that did it since he certainly wasn't keen on Alanza when she'd been sucking down breath and spewing out vitriol.

Grandma stood behind his wingback chair, a firm hand squeezing his shoulder. In our family it was not an unusual event to see tenderhearted Grampa's eyes tear up. Grandma's, on the other hand, never did. I didn't like to give any thought to the sorts of things that would crack her stoic exterior. She looked like she had bitten down on a lemon, and a moldy one at that. My mother sat on the antique camelback sofa I couldn't bring myself to sit on since the incident at church on Sunday, fingering the dowsing pendulum she wears around her neck.

Loden paced near the long window facing the oak tree with the swing and the most perfect sledding hill on the property. His hands were stuffed into his pockets, but I could see the outline of them clenching and unclenching. Celadon looked like she'd had a portion of Grandma's lemon but had dunked her bite in vinegar before she popped it into her mouth. Fortunately, the children were not in the room. I expected Celadon had sent them out when she heard the syrup might be involved. Little pitchers have big ears, and while the children aren't inclined to be naughty, they might not be able to resist mentioning what had happened. It was sure to be all over Sugar Grove before the end of the next day, but still, we didn't need to blow wind in the gossip ship's sails.

"We don't know if any of the stored syrup has been tainted. I suggest you suspend sales until we can get to the bottom of this," Lowell said.

"You don't really think we've sold something poisoned, do you? Could anyone else be hurt?" Grampa crumpled his handkerchief in his gnarled hand.

"Emerald, I don't. I think Alanza was deliberately poisoned, and Dani has come up with a good way to determine if the bottle was tampered with. Why don't you tell them?" Lowell gestured, giving me the stage. I suddenly felt a bit shy, as if I were nine years old again giving an impromptu piano recital to a group of my parents' friends at a dinner party. But it was a good idea and would put everyone's mind at ease.

"Lowell is going to check the syrup bottle Alanza had at the breakfast and check the ring around the neck for color and style. If it isn't the same as all the others, we'll know it was tampered with individually." Everyone nodded in understanding since they were all familiar with the way the bottles were capped.

"But what if it is the same as the others?" Mom asked, rubbing her pendant a bit faster.

"Then we'll have to start testing everything. We'll need to recall the syrup sold online and at the shop," I said, hating to hear the words come out of my own mouth.

"We may need to contact media outlets," Celadon added, practical as usual.

"We're hoping it won't come to that. The best thing we can do now is to check the evidence. I'll drive over to the state lab tomorrow as soon as they open to check the ring on Alanza's bottle with the other ones. Hopefully, there won't be any worries about your stock after that."

"What about actual access to the grange itself?" Loden asked. "Was there any sign of a break-in?"

"No, there wasn't. As a matter of fact, that was one of the first things Mitch checked for once we suspected her syrup had been tampered with," Lowell said.

"So it may come down to who else had access to a key?" Celadon asked. The family has a key, which of course they would since Grampa and Grandma have been on the grange facilities committee since my father was a toddler. But they would have locked up when they finished.

"It looks like it. Any idea who did?' Lowell asked.

"Easier to ask who didn't. Not only have the locks never been changed, I'd be willing to bet it was the most copied set of keys in town. We have at least three sets to the place at our house alone," Grampa said. The grange was one of many buildings in town where keys were handed out like beads at a Mardi Gras parade.

"Each board member always has a set, and most people stay members for life. No one thinks to ask their loved ones after they die for their keys back, so sets go missing from time to time. It's not like there is anything worth stealing in there so no one seems to care," Grandma said.

"Just about everybody in town either has a set or is related to someone who does. Myra, Hanley, Roland, Jill, even Alanza herself would have had a set somewhere in her house since Lewis Bett was a key holder. Just about anyone in the fire department could have used the set they have at the station," Grampa said.

"Don't forget, Mindy Collins has one because she uses the hall for Scout meetings," my mother added, shaking her head.

"That doesn't exactly make things easier." Lowell let out a long sigh.

"No, I'm afraid it doesn't. There could easily be fifty or more sets of keys rattling around Sugar Grove," I said.

Any of those people could have let themselves in to tamper with the syrup.

"There must be some way to narrow it down," Loden said.

"Considering the tamper-resistant seal angle, I'll start with grange members who also make syrup." Lowell said his good-byes and my mother walked him out. I walked myself to the kitchen for a snack.

Celadon followed me to the kitchen and scowled as I started to fix myself a plate of ham with all the trimmings. "How can you eat at a time like this?"

"I'm hungry." I put two biscuits instead of my usual one onto my plate to make my point. "Besides, starving myself isn't going to fix the problem."

"There wouldn't be a problem to fix if you hadn't decided to take it upon yourself to open the business in the first place." Celadon began yanking dishes out of the drainer and slamming them into place in their cupboards.

"Are you saying I'm responsible for Alanza's death?" I put down the biscuit I'd been slathering with maple butter.

"I'm saying Grampa looks like he's on the verge of a stroke, Grandma's about to spit nails, and Mom hasn't stopped talking about bad luck and curses since Saturday."

"But we've always donated syrup, even before I started selling it."

"But selling it is the point. Now there may be poisoned syrup all over the country. And that is definitely your fault."

"But you heard Lowell. He thinks it was just Alanza's

bottle that was messed with." I pushed my plate away, suddenly feeling more queasy than hungry.

"I heard Lowell trying to be reassuring once he saw how distressed Grampa was. I also heard him tell you to suspend sales until he figures out what is going on."

"What I'm hearing is a big 'I told you so.'"

"I did tell you. But I guess it was too much to expect you to listen to reason."

"Just because you don't approve of something doesn't make it a bad idea."

"Tell me how it was a good idea for someone with an environmental science degree to start a business."

"People from all walks of life start businesses every day."

"People with experience start businesses."

"I have experience."

"You can't count selling Girl Scout cookies."

"Don't forget my lemonade stand."

"That's great, make jokes while you drag our name through the mud. You only started the business because you felt guilty about Dad's heart attack." Celadon smacked a wooden spoon down on the counter so hard the bowl snapped off. Then she stomped out of the room with footfalls so heavy she rattled the glasses in the cupboard. And to think, back in the sugarhouse when Lowell delivered the news about the poison, I thought the day had gotten about as bad as it could. The house felt too small to be in at the same time as Celadon. I grabbed my keys and headed for the Stack.

* * *

I was a couple of miles from home when I noticed Graham's state-issued vehicle pulled over to the side of the road. I slowed to a roll that would have come in second in a walker race at a hip replacement facility. I had just about given up looking for the driver when I saw a leg thrashing about from above. I came to a complete halt and craned my neck up into the limbs of an apple tree that had sprouted up alongside a tumbledown stone wall. All through New Hampshire it is possible to spot the remains of long abandoned farms. From bits of wall that no longer mark out boundaries to apple trees on the edge of dense woods, you can read the signs and imagine what life was like before refrigerator trucks brought produce from warmer climates, before people bought all their clothing ready-made at the mall.

Graham's right arm wrapped around a limb that didn't look up to bearing his weight while his left reached toward something that looked like a teddy bear that had been run through a laundry wringer. If that teddy had claws like a garden rake. The creature was moving slowly enough that the entire race between them looked like it was being replayed in slow motion by a sportscaster with a sense of the absurd. Graham inched out farther and farther on the steadily narrowing limb, but with each inch, he moved forward, the furry guy moved, too, and remained just out of reach.

I hopped out of the car just in time for Graham to fall

at my feet, sprawled on his back, blue eyes looking up at me. I don't know who was more surprised, Graham or myself. I reached out a hand to help him up and then reassessed. The last thing I wanted was to be pulled down on top of him when he overbalanced me. Well, maybe not the actual last thing, but since it had been hours since I'd brushed my teeth, it was pretty far down on the list. I stuffed my hand down into my jacket pocket and willed it to stay there. He scrambled to his feet with no need for my assistance whatsoever.

"What is that thing?" I asked, politely not mentioning his fall.

"A three-toed sloth." Graham brushed at a twig sticking out of the loops of his navy sweater. The twig left a snagging hole, which would surely have upset the knitter if it had been seen. I had to conclude Graham had not knitted it himself nor had he ever disrespected a hand knit in front of the knitter. A grandmother, perhaps who was only too happy to tell him how many hours were involved in creating something to supply his comfort. No one made that mistake with my grandmother's hand knits. I still had pristine sweaters, mittens, and hats from childhood in my closet because of just the same sort of behavior when I was still a preschooler.

"Three toes, huh. Per foot or all together?"

"According to the Internet, they've got three per foot." I looked up and tried to do a count of my own. You can't believe everything you read on the Internet. The creature looked like it had gotten its neck tangled up in a taffy-pulling machine. The reason for the sloth's tree selection became clear as it reached its neck slowly toward a withered apple barely clinging to the far end of the branch. I held my breath, hoping it wouldn't end up like Graham, flat on its back, a dazed look in its eyes.

"Well, no matter how many toes it has, it seems to have beaten you hands down."

"Apparently, I am too heavy for that tree."

"It looked like that tree actually bucked you off like you were in a bronco-riding contest."

"I don't think of tree farmers as the sort of people who attribute animation to their crops."

"You have a lot of experience with sugar makers?"

"I've known a few."

"It doesn't look like you've had much experience with trees, though. And yes, I am certain there is a lot more going on in the natural world than human beings like to believe. It would make it harder for us to make the choices we do if we gave trees and plants credit for having some sort of consciousness." I felt my collar getting hot. I didn't usually spout off my convictions to others. I preferred to offer information in a way that was palatable to the average modern person. I darted a look up at Graham, checking to see if he was likely to call in the guys with the white coats. Instead, he just nodded and looked thoughtful.

"You'll have to tell me more about how you reconcile your beliefs with a willingness to puncture trees and draw off their vital fluids for your own profit when I'm not up to my gun holster in runaway critters." He sounded a little snarky. I wondered if he was just embarrassed I'd seen him fall or if I had been too combative in all our previous encounters. Maybe it was just because he hadn't gotten enough sleep and still had too many animals to round up and not enough help in doing so.

"At the rate you're going, that's a conversation you'll have to anticipate for a long time to come."

"Not if you do your part and help out an officer in distress."

"Help out how?" My eyes were drawn to the claws at the ends of each of the three toes. Any desire I'd ever possessed to be a good citizen abandoned me as fast as it did whenever the church nursery was looking for volunteers.

"You are a lot lighter than I am. You could follow this guy up into that tree a lot further than I can without falling."

"You want me to shimmy up the tree and pry a sloth out of it?"

"That's right. Nothing to it."

"Is it even legal for you to ask me to risk my life in the line of your duties?"

"There's no risk. Look, I'll stand right below the tree and catch you if you fall." He stretched out two long arms that looked capable of wrapping tightly around just about anything he'd like. Except a sloth.

"I live on a tree farm. I haven't fallen out of a tree since I was knee-high."

"So, last year?"

"Is this really how you ask for a favor?"

"Sorry. Point taken."

"It's more the claws that worry me. They look pretty big. As big as maybe . . ."

"A mountain lion's?"

"I never said I saw its claws. I was too busy noticing its teeth."

"And its swishy tail."

"You remember that?"

"I remember that call quite distinctly. Most often our damsels in distress are nowhere near as cute as you." I felt myself turning hot and simultaneously pleased and nauseated. Most of the time when a guy around here gives me a compliment, he isn't the one I wish was delivering it. As a matter of fact, all the time. The dating pool has a crack in it the size of the Grand Canyon, and all the juices leaked out about three weeks after high school graduation. Given my track record with men, scampering up the tree seemed a lot less dangerous than standing on the ground making small talk.

"Have you got something to put him in once I fetch him down?" I changed the subject with all the smoothness of a country road at the end of March.

"I've got a whole assortment of pet carriers, trash cans, and plastic storage tubs with holes punched in the top to allow for breathing. Does this mean you'll help?" Instead of answering, I grabbed a low-hanging limb and began pulling myself toward the shaggy, drooping creature. It had finished the first apple and had moved on to a second, which dangled even farther out on the narrow branch.

Sooner than I wanted to, I reached the limb it was on. I sat, my legs dangling to either side of the branch, observing the creature, paying the most attention to its claws. I was surprised to see the way its fur parted along its belly like another animal's would along its back. I guess that said something about its time spent hanging upside down compared with upright on its feet. Although, strictly speaking, I guessed it couldn't be considered upside down if that was the way it preferred being most of the time.

"I think it's still hungry. Have you got any sloth treats in your weapons arsenal?" Graham's truck looked like it could hold a zoo's worth of food with room left over for take-out Chinese.

"I haven't brought anything specifically for sloths. What do you think it will eat?"

"It seems to like fruit. Where's it from?"

"Central and South America. Maybe it would like a cup of coffee."

"How about something leafy?" Graham nodded and hurried to the truck. He came back with a bag filled with produce. I flipped around and hung upside down to grab a head of romaine and a sleeve of celery from the bag. Without loosening my grip on the groceries, I righted myself on the branch once more, broke off a stalk of celery, and crushed the leaves just a bit. I hoped the scent would appeal to the poor hungry creeper. With excruciating slowness, the sloth turned its face toward the celery. I wasn't sure if it was trying to make up its mind about how appealing it was or if it just required that long to get going in a new direction.

"Where did you learn to do that?" Graham asked.

"Do what?" The sloth began making its move. Inch by inch it oozed its way along the branch toward me.

"That crazy bat-swooping thing." The look of awe on

his face was priceless. It probably mirrored the one I had been wearing when I spotted the mountain lion peering in the sugarhouse window. Maybe I should tell him he was the one who was now imagining things. I resisted my childish side.

"I told you I knew how to climb trees." I hadn't told him about the years of gymnastics.

"Climb, yes, turn them into apparatus for an Olympic event, you did not." He looked cute when he was startled, like a small child awakened from a dead sleep.

"He seems to like the celery." I held the stalk out tentatively and scooched closer. The sloth was doing his part, but I figured the whole rescue operation would take a lot less time if I met him more than halfway. What I was planning to do once I got him within arm's reach, I had no idea, but his interest in the celery felt like progress. "I think you ought to get a container. I've got a good feeling about this." Graham hustled off again, this time returning with a pink plastic box with a matching lid. Just as advertised, it had jagged holes the size of half-dollars punched into the lid, making a grid of breathable space.

As the sloth came closer and took a first tentative nibble of the leafy end of the celery, I assessed my options. While his claws were intimidatingly long, he looked too complacent to pose a real threat to my safety. My jeans were thick enough to protect me and so was my jacket. As to size, he looked like a medium-sized dog. I never had problems picking up the family dogs even when I was much smaller than I was now. I bent my arm and pulled the celery closer to myself as the sloth reached for a second bite. He followed, and little by little I coaxed him right into my lap. He clung to my arm as if it were a tree branch. I tried to keep my attention on his flat, appealing face instead of his claws.

The stalk of celery was diminishing in my hand, an inch at a time. I felt panic start to rise. What would happen when it got right down to the end near my fingers? Should I have laid it flat in my hand like I was feeding a horse? I shifted the celery and felt it begin to fall. Without thinking, I lunged for it. I lost my grip on the tree, but the sloth never lost its grip on me. It clung like a baby monkey to its mother as I fell ass over teakettle from the branch into Graham's outstretched arms with a thump.

"Now I know where I had heard your name before," Graham said, staring at me with wide-open eyes. "Knowlton mentioned you at the USM." I began to struggle, realizing I'd survived my fall. I'd never been too interested in being swept off my feet, and certainly any notions of that kind I may have briefly entertained never included a sloth, three-toed or otherwise.

"What do you mean, Knowlton mentioned me?" I asked as Graham stood me on my feet in one swift motion.

"At the Underground Swap Meat, he mentioned your talents." Amazingly, the sloth still clung to me and was attempting to pull itself higher by grabbing fistfuls of my hair. "Here, let's get him into this before he creates a bald spot." Graham pried the lid off the container and began gently tugging on the sloth.

"The what?" I asked.

"The Underground Swap Meat. It's a semiannual event

where taxidermy enthusiasts get together and swap supplies."

"And by supplies, you mean carcasses?"

"Basically, although sometimes tools and even business supplies get exchanged. I think someone even traded vehicles once."

"How do you know about this?"

"The state used to hold a roadkill auction before rabies became such a worry and we had to shut it down. When the USM sprang up after the closure, we decided to investigate as a matter of public safety."

"And everything was aboveboard?"

"It was all very clean. As a matter of fact, after the first time we showed up, the organizers sent us an invitation every year. Taxidermists aren't fans of disease any more than the rest of us." Graham held out another stalk of celery toward the sloth.

"That still doesn't clear things up for me. Why was Knowlton talking about me?"

"Oh, it wasn't just me he was talking to. He bragged about you to anyone standing still. None of us understood how a guy like that ended up engaged to a woman like he described."

"Engaged?" I felt my voice climbing the scales more than I heard it. Maybe because it had gone up into dog whistle range.

"Right. He would go on and on about his fiancée's acrobatic talents and how entertaining that could be under certain circumstances."

"What sort of circumstances are you talking about?"

I was starting to feel a boil in my stomach that spread up into my chest and threatened to pop my eyes straight out of my head.

"I don't think I know you well enough to go into the details. It might embarrass you to no end. I know it would make me uncomfortable."

"You didn't know me well enough to listen either." Graham kept tugging on the sloth, attempting to pry it off me. I was beginning to think the thing was part octopus the way it stuck to my torso.

"You've got me there. It was disrespectful and it was none of my business. For the record, he made it sound very flattering."

"He made it all up."

"It did sound like he was exaggerating a bit. After all, how could anyone really manage to . . ." Graham tapered off, turning red and staring at the ground instead of meeting my eyes.

"He wasn't exaggerating, he was lying."

"I don't see how you can be so sure if you weren't ever there."

"That's what I'm saying to you, I wasn't ever there. And neither was he. Knowlton and I have never been more intimately enmeshed than sharing a seat on the school bus."

"So you're one of those old-fashioned girls who's saving herself for the wedding night?"

"We aren't engaged either. We never have been."

"Well, that's disappointing."

"What?"

"Knowlton was describing every man's dream girl,

and now you burst my bubble and tell me he made it all up?"

"I didn't say I wasn't a dream girl. I just said he had no way of knowing if I was or if I wasn't."

"There are going to be a lot of disappointed guys when I tell them Dani Greene isn't as advertised."

"What do you mean by a lot?"

"I mean all across the state. Guys came from everywhere to attend the USM. By about the third year I started wondering how many of the men showing up were more interested in hearing the next installment of the Dani escapades than swapping critters."

"That doesn't seem flattering."

"They do love their carcasses, so it might be saying more than you think."

"Too much has already been said. This has been one of the worst days of my life."

"Come on, it can't be that bad." Graham wrapped one hand around the sloth's arm right where its wrist would be and managed to detach it from me. For a moment the animal dangled between us like a child swinging from its two parents' hands while out on a walk.

"It is that bad. My business is headed for ruin and now I find out my reputation has been destroyed for years and I never even knew it."

"Then that's not so bad, now is it? If you didn't know, it didn't affect you." Graham tossed the rest of the celery into the box then gently dangled the sloth in after it and snapped on the lid. He hoisted the box into the back of his truck, all set to go.

"You must be an optimist."

"I guess maybe I am. I'm the guy who always stops people thinking their bags are too full, not that they've been taking fish that are too small."

"So what's the silver lining to finding out my syrup is responsible for a death and that my business needs shutting down?"

"Did you like the person who died?"

"No. I definitely did not."

"There you go, a very shiny silver lining if you ask me."

"My business is in the tank, my reputation's shot both professionally and personally."

"At least you've got someone who wants to marry you."

"And that's a good thing in your opinion?"

"Sure. I've always wanted a family of my own. Haven't you?"

"I've got more than enough family already, and they do enough worrying about my marriage prospects so I don't have to do it myself."

"You come from a family of incurable romantics?"

"Consummate meddlers."

"You're lucky they care enough to butt in."

"You'd be singing a different tune if they kept trying to set you up every time you turn around."

"Maybe I could use the help." I had noticed Graham didn't wear a wedding band, but he didn't look like someone who would need help finding a date. He had excellent posture, a decent job, and all of his teeth. That was a whole lot more than I could say for most of the guys Celadon tried setting me up with.

"I'll let them know. I'm sure they'd love to expand their hunting grounds."

"I'd appreciate it."

"Although you'll be too busy for a while chasing all those exotics to spend time running around after any women."

"For the right woman, I'd find the time." Graham leaned a bit closer and looked me directly in the eyes. I felt flustered and broke off eye contact. Just through the trees an equine shape slipped through the woods. "Did you see that?" he asked and dashed off in pursuit. I guess I must not have been the right woman.

Eleven

After that, there was nothing for it but to keep heading over to the Stack and drown my sorrows in a flood of some nontoxic maple syrup and whatever fatty carbohydrate Piper was serving to go with it. Piper gave me a hurried smile over a plume of steam rising from a row of freshly filled coffee mugs. I couldn't find it in myself to smile back so I just nodded and slid into a booth near the back. If I sit in them just right, my size allows me to be completely hidden in a booth. Not a bad thing when what you want is food, not company.

Before long, Piper arrived carrying a plate piled high. She slid into the seat across from me and plunked the plate down in front of me.

"What's that?" I asked, eyeing the plate.

"The special. It's called the Who'd a Thunk It. With a

side of sweet potato fries, so crispy they're almost burnt. Just the way you like them."

"I don't know if I'm up for anything new."

"You'll be up for this. It's really just a gussied-up toasted cheese sandwich."

"It looks like waffles."

"I sandwiched maple cheddar cheese, caramelized apples, and crispy bacon strips between two whole-grain waffles then toasted the whole thing on the griddle. It's best drizzled with syrup so eat it with a fork." Piper plucked the syrup pitcher from its spot snuggled against the wall and sozzled my sandwich with a heavy hand.

"I think you mean drizzled with death."

"Myra stopped by earlier. She blabbed about the lab results."

"I just hope I haven't poisoned anyone else."

"You haven't poisoned anyone at all. Someone else tampered with Alanza's portion. As soon as the lab results on the rest of the jugs come in, you'll be back in business."

"Bad news spreads faster and sticks longer than good. I don't know if the business will survive this sort of thing. Especially if Celadon has anything to say about it." I poured syrup over everything on the plate.

"As soon as you reopen, we'll put the stock we have here on sale. Buy one, get one free, or some such thing. People will be so happy with the price they'll forget all about anything else, and you'll be back at the top of your game."

"What about the people who buy online?"

"I'm telling you, it isn't going to matter before you

know it. So cheer up and clean your plate. You're still looking a little frazzled." I told her about my run-in with Graham and all the things Knowlton had said about me at the auctions.

"You know what the most surprising thing about all of this is? That Knowlton knew enough about sex to make up something interesting. That guy has hidden depths." Piper got the kind of look in her eyes she always did before announcing some new delicious idea she had for the restaurant.

"Don't even think about it."

"About what?" She batted her baby blues my way, like she did at flirtatious geezers who said more than they should. Like she did when we were kids and the teacher thought she'd been stirring up trouble.

"About Knowlton. You know how you are about hidden depths. If you start trying to plumb his, or worse, let him get round to measuring yours, I will lose my anchor in the sea of reality." And I would, too. Some things a person can count on. Mosquitoes will bite, paper cuts will sting, and Knowlton will not be of romantic interest. These things were as immutable as the laws governing the moon's trip around the earth. It was bad enough Knowlton had invented some escapades for me. Watching Piper contemplate stirring some up with him for real was enough to drive me away from my fries. And nothing ever drove me from my fries.

"I don't know what you are talking about."

"Good. See that it remains that way. I may be young but there is only so much my ticker can take in one week."

And just as always happens, the Stack filled up all at once, like a basement after a sudden storm. Piper hurried back behind the counter to welcome the newcomers and Mitch took the opportunity to fill her spot.

"So I hear not only have you been bopping off the locals, you're hallucinating, too." Mitch reached across the table and plucked one of my fries off my plate like we were in the habit of companionably sharing food. I was pleased to see a big blob of syrup land in the middle of his uniform shirt. If the angle was just right, you could see a bit of softening across his midriff. The syrup landed just about where a spare tire was thinking of inflating.

"I must be because I could swear I just saw an officer of the law steal some of my meal." I yanked my plate closer and wrapped my arm around it like a pirate guarding his rations.

"Yup. You surely are seeing things then. You know how upright our police officers are."

"I seem to remember you trying to convince me to join you in being anything but upright." I speared a forkful of outrageously delicious sandwich and bit down on it with more force than I had intended. Mitch blushed a bit under his baby-smooth shave. He probably would never be able to grow a beard like Grampa's.

"I heard you were hallucinating about mountain lions out at your property the other night." Mitch always did know how to change a subject.

"Now where'd you hear a thing like that?" Myra was the only one I could think of who knew about my call. Honestly, I was surprised she hadn't gotten on the horn and spread the news before she even put in the call to Fish and Game.

"From that game warden." Unbelievable. And to think I had maligned Myra in my mind.

"I think you mean conservation officer. And why would he tell you a thing like that?"

"We're both law enforcement officials, and I think he wanted my expert opinion on the reliability of the person who claimed to have witnessed the big cat."

"I see." If Graham didn't hurry up and finish his business in Sugar Grove, I was going to be tempted to move out.

"Don't worry. I didn't tell him anything he didn't already know." His hand crept across the Formica table-top at about the same rate Graham's sloth would have.

"Which was?" I grabbed a sticky menu from the rack at the table and whacked the back of his hand with it.

"That you're a crazy pipsqueak with a taste for the grape."

"He said that?"

"Not in those exact words but that's what it boiled down to in the end. He stopped by the station after he got done at your place. Asked if you had ever been picked up for DWI or public drunkenness. Wondered if you were legally blind or affected poorly by the full moon. That sort of thing."

"All of which you confirmed, apparently."

"Well, I felt duty bound to reveal it was you who spiked the punch at the post-prom party."

"I added a container of iced tea mix because it wasn't sweet enough."

"And that you suffered from eye strain."

"How do you figure that?"

"You were voted class bookworm. That had to lead to some permanent damage."

"Dare I ask about the moon?"

"Remember in the fifth grade how you jumped on Andy Peals and started hitting him with your lunch box when he mooned the pastor's wife from the school bus?"

"Are you really allowed to take down witness statements?"

"He seemed pretty interested in what I had to say. And now with the way things look about Alanza dropping from eating your syrup, I'll be surprised if you don't get hauled off to the loony bin in Concord."

"The syrup is not my fault. There are all sorts of people with great reasons for poisoning her."

"Like who?"

"Like Roland. Like Knowlton." Although knowing Piper's taste in men, if Knowlton landed in jail on a murder charge, she was sure to become even more interested in him.

"Don't forget Myra."

"Myra had a problem with Alanza, too?"

"Of course she did. Myra was a Bett before she married a Phelps. Alanza got her mitts on the property bearing the family name and then set about destroying it. You can bet Myra was angry."

"I didn't realize Alanza and Myra were related."

"Only distantly, to hear Myra tell it."

"But how did someone from out of town like Alanza inherit when Myra didn't?"

"That I don't know. Myra likes to yak but she decides what about, and she wasn't mentioning anything about the terms of the inheritance."

"Did you try to pry it out of her?"

"Of course not. It was none of my business."

"Well, it might be now. It sounds like it could be a motive. And Myra has access to the grange hall."

"So does everybody and his brother," Mitch reminded me.

"That doesn't mean she shouldn't be asked about it."

"That's something best left to Lowell. I have no intention of tangling with her." Mitch slid toward the edge of the booth. "As a matter of fact, I think I'm going to leave it to you to mention it to Lowell. Something as potentially explosive as accusing an employee of murder might be best coming from you."

"Why me? You're the professional, remember?"

"But you're the do-no-wrong goddaughter, remember? Have you forgotten the crossing guard incident?" Mitch stood next to the table and managed to snitch one last fry.

"You steal my food again and I will be sure to speak to Lowell about your proclivity for crime."

"That's to get you back for the radar gun details Lowell put me on after I dumped you." Mitch walked off, wiping sausage grease from his fingers on his pant leg. Just another reason things would never have worked out between us. If my grandmother had ever seen that at her dinner table, she would have given him some poisoned syrup on purpose.

*   *   *

I meant to keep out of things and simply wait for the call from Lowell letting us know someone had tampered with Alanza's syrup bottle. But by nine the next morning, I had bottomed out my e-mail in-box, polished silver service for thirty-six, and scorched three different batches of caramel sauce for Thanksgiving dinner. I could hardly refuse when Grandma suggested I leave her kitchen in peace by heading for town to do some early Christmas shopping. I decided to use Christmas shopping as an excuse to ask Tansey Pringle a few questions about Alanza.

Tansey had her feet up on an overturned plastic milk crate when I pulled up into her driveway. I'm sure she was surprised to see me since generally I am doing my best to elude her efforts to hook me up with her son, Knowlton. She knocked over the crate and sprang to her feet, an impressive feat considering her age, sixty-six, and her arthritis, rheumatoid. Neither of which stopped her from serving as president of the local snowmobile club or running her small family farm.

Tansey liked to complain but never about her health or her work. She was happy to complain about town politics, other people's decisions, and the weather but not about herself and certainly never about Knowlton. He could do no wrong in her eyes, and she just could not comprehend why it was that he was still single. I don't know that it had occurred to her that having her as a mother-in-law might be a part of the problem. She spat a huge gob of tobacco on the ground next to her before speaking. A little trickle of the juice strayed down from the corner of her mouth, and I resisted the urge either to stare or point it out to her. If her mother had never gotten basic niceties into her head, there was no way it would be worth my time to try to do it. Besides, my grandmother would take me over her knee if Tansey reported I had been sassing my elders.

"Knowlton's not up yet. But if you wait a bit, he'll be moving around. He had a long night out in the woods."

"Actually, I wanted to talk to you about the snowmobile club." I didn't want to come right out and ask her about how the club would have been affected by Alanza's plans to close the property for use. She might take offense and clam up entirely. But given any sort of opening, she was sure to let it all out. If I was careful, there was no way she could resist. Now for a good excuse as to why I was asking. I hated to do it to him, but I was about to sacrifice my own brother to the snowmobile gods.

"Were you thinking about joining?" Tansey leaned toward me like she always did when she got excited about something. Usually she was bragging about Knowlton and the latest thing he had dragged home and stuffed, but talk about snowmobiles ran a close second.

"Oh, not me, Loden. I'm having a hard time deciding what to get **him** for Christmas this year, and I thought a membership **to the** snowmobile association would be just the thing."

"I didn't know he was interested in snowmobiles." Tansey looked up into the sky like she was checking her file on potential in-laws for Knowlton and then brought her eyes back down to my face like she came up empty. Which went to show that despite her advancing years, there was nothing wrong with her memory. Loden had never in all his life expressed an interest in snowmobiles. He had expressed plenty of disgust, but never any interest. He hated their noise and the stink of the exhaust.

"Well, that's why it would make such a great surprise. He could really use something new to do in the winter, and this might be right up his alley. What can you tell me about the club?" I tried not to shift from one foot to the other like a little kid needing to pee, but that's what lying did to me. It made me have to pee.

"Well, we've got a strong club established. We have over two hundred members and miles and miles of trails we maintain every year."

"I heard Alanza's decision to stop use on her land impacted the trail system. He's not going to be disappointed, is he?"

"Now that she's dead, I don't expect that to continue to be an issue, do you?" Tansey leaned in a little closer and looked me straight in the eye like a human lie detector. I could tell she thought there was something fishy about my interest but couldn't quite put her finger on it. I needed to tread carefully or Tansey would stick her lips together like the blades on some pruning shears left outside to rust all winter.

"I hadn't heard how any of that would play out. I was just worried maybe Loden would get all excited about tearing around with all of you across the frozen wilderness and then have to come to a screeching halt with nowhere to go. That sounds awfully disappointing to me. Not the sort of gift I'd want to give him at all." I shook my head with it hanging down a little, hoping the gloom was contagious.

"Nope. She hadn't finalized anything before her fortunate face plant. I couldn't be happier your syrup did her in. I'm tempted to give you a hefty discount on the membership for a job well done." Tansey nodded up and down, her gray hair waggling as much as it could considering how short she wore it.

"We didn't poison her. Someone else used our syrup as a vehicle for the poison."

"I don't give a half-rotted cow flap who helped her into permanent hibernation. But I'd love for them to know how happy we all are at the snowmobile club."

"So it really was a big deal?" But was it big enough to kill over?

"It was. Alanza's parcel separated two major trails a lot of people used to get to their camps. The main trails lead to smaller trails and even serve as the main roads into other towns during the winter. There are people who would have had to add at least a couple of hours' driving time to their camps if she'd had time to implement this. And then there were the people who couldn't have gotten to their properties at all."

"I didn't know snowmobiles were that important as transportation." This time I wasn't lying. I really had no idea since my family didn't go in for snowmobiling at all.

"They are indeed. There are plenty of people with

camps in places where there are no actual roads. If you go to them in summer, you hike in or ride an ATV. But in the winter you can enjoy skimming over the snow, not a care in the world."

"Like who?" I was curious not only for the case but also because I wondered which of my neighbors had a camp somewhere so remote. After all, Sugar Grove is already pretty far into the sticks and I wondered who would want to go even deeper into undeveloped territory.

"Hanley Wilson is one. My own Knowlton is another."

"Knowlton owns a property up north?" I was stunned. I had never thought of Knowlton as being able to detach from his mother long enough to go away overnight.

"Sure. He inherited it from my brother when he passed away a few years ago. Knowlton loves it up there. He spends some time each fall up there as a base for his business ventures." By that I could only assume she meant he went up to the cabin by himself and located creatures to stuff.

"So Hanley and Knowlton both must be pretty glad she's out of the way then." I tried to sound casual but held my breath.

"Well, you can say that again. I heard Hanley went directly to the Stack Shack after the police finished questioning him at the breakfast and bought everyone there a round of coffee. Piper had to start several new pots just to keep up with the demand."

"Sounds like a pretty enthusiastic reaction to her death."

"It certainly was, considering what all has been going

on between those two." Tansey gave me an exaggerated wink that took so long on the recoil I wondered if she'd managed to glue her eyelid shut.

"Are you implying he was up to no good with Alanza in the way I think you mean?" I was shocked from the crown of my head to the tips of my toes. Granted this was not as big a deal as it would have been for someone of a more normal height, but it was all I could do. Tansey nodded.

"Where did you hear that?"

"From Myra, of course. Who else says such things?" Tansey winked again and I wondered if she had always done it and I had never been old enough to be a recipient of her winks or if this was a new thing for her.

Myra was known for flapping her lips whenever a tasty tidbit landed in her ears. As outrageous as the things she passed on generally were, she wasn't often wrong even if she was known for exaggerating. The trick with Myra was sifting out the reality from the embroidery of any situation. Time for a bit of digging.

"What did she say exactly? Coffee together at the Stack? Sharing a hymnal at church?" Any bit of anything could be read into especially as the winter was starting to gather around the town. Winter sports included snowmobiling, skiing, ice fishing, local politics, and dissecting the rumors passed on by Myra.

"Coffee isn't drunk on your back. And whatever they were sharing wasn't sanctified by the church. But it's nice to meet a girl in this day and age still so innocent. No wonder my Knowlton is smitten." Tansey looked my small frame up and down and I suddenly felt the need for a shower. With borax.

"An affair between Hanley and Alanza? Do you think Connie knew about it?" I wasn't sure whether or not to believe it. Before Jill told me she was having an affair with him, I wouldn't have thought Hanley could have seduced even one woman, let alone caught two in addition to his wife.

"If Myra knew, then most everybody else in town did, too. She isn't exactly known for her discretion, now is she?" That was an understatement. Every embarrassing love affair, case of venereal disease, or arrest for DWI was something Myra shared with everyone in earshot.

"And what about Knowlton? He must have told you how he felt."

"Well, you know Knowlton, never a bad word to say about anybody. He did say he wasn't looking forward to coming back with a load of animals for stuffing an extra two hours out of his way. Even in the cold air, some of them can give off a powerful stink." Tansey spat again like she was punctuating her thoughts.

"I can only imagine. So he can't be mourning her loss, can he?"

"Well, of course not. No one is."

"So why would Alanza want to shut down the access through her property for the snowmobile trails? Did someone do something to tick her off?"

"That's no secret. Alanza wanted to be elected president of the club."

"She didn't seem like the outdoorsy type." I'd never

seen Alanza wearing anything that looked like it was built for the cold weather. She favored clingy silky tops and bottoms that wouldn't be allowed in most public high schools even today, despite the fact her figure wasn't up for such indignities.

"Everyone was shocked when she showed up at our first meeting of the season last year but we welcomed her, of course. She had a huge parcel of land and we wanted her to keep the status quo."

"But no one wanted to curry favor enough to vote for her at the election?"

"There were some. I know I don't have the easiest temperament." That was news to me. Not the temperament part, the self-awareness. Tansey always seemed oblivious to how her actions and statements were affecting others. It never occurred to me she recognized what was happening and simply went on as she pleased anyway. "I argue for what I believe in no matter who says otherwise, and I've made my share of enemies over the years." Tansey nodded to herself like she was thinking over a specific incident or two. "In the end, more people voted for me than they did Alanza. I'd like to think it was because they believed I'm a good president, but it may have been because she'd only been riding since she moved here and wasn't what anyone would call an expert."

"What I don't understand is why Alanza was interested in the presidency in the first place."

"Alanza started in joining things before she finished unpacking her moving van. She hadn't been here a month before she had joined the Sap Bucket Brigade, the friends

of the library, and the women's club. She was the record-
ing secretary for two boards and volunteered in the
church thrift shop."

"So you think she was just one of those people who
love to volunteer?"

"Good Lord, no; she was solidifying a power base. I
think she wanted to be elected to a lot more than the
snowmobile club. My guess is she had designs on the
select board."

"Are you sure?"

"As sure as I am cows give milk, not mayonnaise. She
had already been recommended for appointment to the
spot on the planning board Connie was vacating and said
she was planning to run for the zoning board of adjust-
ment." Both of those boards were powerful and pertained
to land. Alanza had a lot of it and had planned to change
the way she was handling the land she owned. Could those
things be connected? Did she have plans for her land she
wanted to get through that might require power in town to
make happen? It wouldn't be the first time someone had
set themselves up as a public servant for some private gain.
A good dietary recommendation for Alanza would have
included increasing her daily intake of moral fiber.

"But now what? Does Alanza's death stop the closure
of the trails just in time for an uninterrupted snowmobiling
season?" How convenient the breakfast had taken place a
few weeks before snow could reasonably be expected to
start stacking up in the area. About fifty percent of the
time, Sugar Grove experienced a white Christmas.

"Well, I'm not quite sure what happens. I am sure the

new owner will be delayed in making any decisions that will affect us this year. When my parents died, the whole probate thing took quite some time. I imagine with the circumstances of her death being what they are, the property won't be released to the inheritor anytime too soon."

"That's a lucky break for all of you snowmobile enthusiasts then, isn't it?"

"And for you."

"How do you figure that?"

"Because that Christmas gift you wanted to give your brother is much more valuable with all the miles of uninterrupted trails. Or was your interest just a cover to ask me questions that weren't any of your business?" She had me there.

"How much do I owe you?"

Twelve

 After my chat with Tansey, I decided to talk with cabin owners. Since I am always interested in putting off talking to Knowlton, I decided to start with Hanley. I drove over to his place of business and found him just turning down the driveway. In order to avoid arguments with his wife, Hanley had rented a place off Tinkham Road to house his business just as soon as they could afford to do so. Connie complained about the noisy equipment bothering her goats and the crews of day laborers showing up in her dooryard. Since the Wilsons had no children, her goats took on an importance the average couple might not assign them.

I bumped to a stop as his truck threw gravel up on my windshield. Hanley hitched himself out a few inches at a time and hopped to the ground. Over time he'd gotten a bit shorter as well as wider and I think it contributed to his surly attitude with most people. Unlike the other night over at Jill's and the other day at the farm, he was usually pretty decent with me, and it may have been on account of my height. Even so, I did my best to leave interactions with him to someone else in the family. Grampa was his usual point of contact, which suited the rest of us just fine. Grampa could charm the horns off the devil if he took a notion to do so. Hanley was a bit of a devil himself, but he must have left his horns at home because all I could see was a bit of a bald spot glowing through his wavy, sandy hair.

Hanley wore the same red-and-black hunter's plaid wool jacket he always wore whenever the temperature dipped below sixty. It matched his florid face and I imagined he thought it enhanced his image as a traditional forester. What he probably didn't imagine was how much it emphasized his beer gut when he strained the buttons closing it on the coldest days. Hanley had been wearing that jacket the day he lost his footing while up in a tree and had gotten snagged by the fabric. The fabric held without a tear and he was able to wrap his arms around a thick limb on his way down. He's worn it as a good luck charm, despite the thirty pounds and six inches he's added to his waistline, since the incident.

Connie's way around a stove accounted for the weight gain. Piper has been telling Connie for years she'd love to have her come on at the Stack if she ever gets tired of her bookkeeping business. For the longest time Connie refused, insisting she needed to devote her time to a number of local businesses she serviced, including Hanley's.

Recently, however, she agreed to help out for a special event and ended up enjoying herself so much she decided to join the staff part-time.

"I never get over pretty young things following me back to my place." Hanley leaned against his truck, one leg propped up on his running board like he needed to air something out.

"What would Connie say if she heard something like that?" That was another reason I preferred for Grampa to deal with Hanley. He had the nickname *Handsey Hanley* around town for a reason. Despite my close call back at Greener Pastures, he never had got his hands on me and I intended to keep it that way.

"Connie's a good sport. She knows not to take my sense of humor to heart. Sounds like you didn't intend this to be a social call, though."

"I stopped by to ask you about checking some trees for me as soon as you can. Yesterday, I noticed a few trees that could use some attention before they get covered in snow load." I wanted to ask him about his property but easing into it in a friendly fashion seemed more comfortable than acting like a terrier at a woodchuck hole.

"Sure. I'll check my calendar and let you know. Or we could go into the office right now and set something up." He grinned at me, his too full, too red lips stretching away from teeth scaled for the big bad wolf. No way was I going into a dark office alone with Handsey Hanley.

"So you wouldn't have time this evening to stop by?"

"Nope. I'm already booked for tonight." He widened his grin to car salesman proportions. Now was the time to get to the subject and head for home before things dragged on or dragged me into unpleasant territory.

"Oh, are you having a boys' night out up at your camp or something?"

"Now how did you hear about my camp?" His grin slacked off a bit.

"Tansey told me you, Knowlton, and a bunch of other people like to head up to your camps on your snowmobiles. I thought you might be getting ready for hunting season."

"Tansey's big mouth was one of the reasons she had to fight Alanza for snowmobile club president."

"Tansey said the election results were the reasons the club was going to lose access to Alanza's land. She said people were really upset."

"Uh-huh." Hanley crossed his arms across his barrel chest. "She say who was all riled up? She mention any more names while you two hens was yakking away?"

"She said Knowlton was worried it was going to put his camp out of reach for him to be practical about it if she persisted in closing the trail. She didn't say anything about your thoughts on the matter since I don't expect you shared them with her."

"And are you hoping I'll share them with you?"

"I don't expect you to do anything but check on the trees at Greener Pastures as soon as possible." Hanley wasn't just known for being free with his hands. He ran his mouth like a man runs a brand-new snowblower—loudly and even when it isn't strictly necessary. If I just waited long enough, he wouldn't be able to pass up the opportunity to sing about it if he felt Alanza had maligned him.

"Good, 'cause I'm sure not one of those guys who runs around howling about his troubles at the top of his lungs."

"Never said you were."

"I wouldn't go around letting everybody and his brother know that Alanza closed off her property just for spite."

"Certainly you wouldn't." Hanley's mouth had a little spit building up in the corner like a Shakespearean actor's.

"I wouldn't mention to anyone within earshot that a hardworking man who just wants to spend a few precious hours relaxing with friends, hunting down all the animals God sees fit to toss in his path, would be denied the opportunity to do so by the vindictiveness of a high-handed woman."

"I'd hate to be the sort of person who would have that kind of complaint to share."

"Darn right you'd hate it."

"Sounds like a cantankerous lunatic."

"Spiteful's more like it. It's not like she didn't know about people with the camps using her portion of the trail. When I first went to work for her, I told her all about it."

"What kind of work did you do for Alanza?"

"Oh, just the regular stuff, checking trees and such, just like I do up at your place."

"That makes sense. So when was the election?"

"About a month ago. The elections are always held early enough for the president to get a handle on things before snow's likely. Tansey squeaked in a win in the end, but it was close for quite a while. If she hadn't busted out gifts of her famous maple bacon fudge for every voting member, I'm not sure she would have kept her seat." Tansey's fudge had been known through the years to sway a lot of elections, but I had never known her to use its power on her own behalf. She must have been concerned about the outcome. It made me wonder if she hadn't been satisfied with just beating Alanza at the election. Perhaps she poisoned her, too, just to be sure she never had to face her at voting time again.

"So when did Alanza announce the trails through her property would be closed?"

"She tacked up some of them signs a couple of days after the election at the heads of the trails. An e-mail went out to everyone in the club within the week."

"So she was swift in her justice."

"That's one way to put it. Women can really mess you up, you know?"

"So I've been told." I decided I'd heard about all the things worth telling that Hanley might have in stock. It was time to take off before he invited me into the office a second time. "So you'll find time soon to come up to Greener Pastures?"

"I'll be there. Unless I decide to take advantage of Alanza's unfortunate demise and take my ATV for a spin up to the camp instead of working." Hanley patted his gut and flashed me a smile. I put him in the mental column of another one who was glad to see Alanza tucked neatly into a crisper drawer at the state morgue. I wondered if he and Jill were lying when they gave each other an alibi. And if Alanza had decided to close the snowmobile trails to keep Hanley from carrying on at his camp with Jill. I climbed into my car and drove off lost in thought. It made me wonder who else might have felt the same way and whether or not they would be as inclined to admit it.

Village Hardware's display of fencing choices involved snippets of wire mesh, and an assortment of dusty pickets overlaid with old minutes of town meetings and flyers for long past bake sales and tractor shows. I wanted to pick up a couple of samples to take home to show Grampa, but I wasn't convinced either would keep out a ravenous mountain lion. After seeing what happened at Connie's, it seemed like we would be well served to get hold of a zoo designer. The mountain lion wasn't likely to get any less hungry as the winter drew on.

Up at the counter, Piper's latest squeeze, Dean Hayes, leaned his gangly frame near the register looking like he didn't have a thing to do except wait for Piper to get off work. He looked up from a sudoku book he was filling in with a carpenter pencil when I approached, and he gave me a smile. I didn't think he was right for Piper but he wasn't a bad guy. Or maybe I was just a little envious of the way my friend picked up new men the way I pick up a cold.

"Hi there, Dani, that sure was some time over at Piper's on Saturday, wasn't it?"

"It was. Even without the kangaroo, it was turning into a night worth talking about. Your band sounded great. You guys must practice every available minute." I felt a little embarrassed at how much I sounded like a small-town groupie.

"No, we usually practice on Friday nights, but we didn't even get a chance to this week."

"You could have fooled me. I would have been certain you'd been practicing all week. I know Piper was impressed." If I was going to pull the groupie card, it might as well be the right groupie.

"Well, normally that would have been the case, but the percussion player, Byron, is off at his wife's folks' house, and then Roland called to let me know he couldn't make it either so we decided to cancel. Not much sense holding the practice with only two of us there to do any practicing." Dean tucked the pencil behind his ear along with a stray lock of dark curly hair. Piper always was a sucker for curls. The color never much mattered; it was just the wiggle of them that got to her.

"I thought Roland was totally committed to his music when he wasn't working on the inn. I hope he wasn't sick or something."

"Well, the stress with Alanza was taking a toll on him, but he didn't say he was sick, just that something had come up and he couldn't make it." But that wasn't what he told Felicia. What could have been so important it made him miss his practice? Could he have been at the grange hall sticking something toxic into my syrup? "But you didn't come in here to talk about Roland, so what can I do you for?" he asked, which is exactly why he isn't good enough for Piper.

"I was hoping you could cut me off a couple of samples of fencing and give me an estimate of what it will cost to run it round the pasture and up near the barn."

"That's gonna cost you a whole lot of money. How come you're feeling like such a big spender if your business is tanking?"

"Aren't you in the business of selling stuff? Why do you care why I want it as long as the checks clear?"

"Okay, you don't need to get huffy about it. I really just meant the job must be awful important to make such a big effort." Dean rummaged around under the counter and brought up a few small squares of fencing.

"I expect she thinks it is a matter of life and death." Mitch stepped out from behind a display of rakes, a new steel one clutched in his hand.

"That's right, I do. So the price is irrelevant."

"Life and death for whom?" Dean shut the sudoku over his finger and gave me his full attention.

"Livestock, of course," I said.

"What is it you think they are in danger from?" Dean asked.

"Chupacabras? Was it? Jersey Devils? UFOs?" Mitch asked. I wanted to bash him over the head with the rake.

"Ask Connie about the fencing she wished she'd bought." I wanted to deflect attention from my own mountain lion in the vain hope the rumor of it might at least stay away from Celadon.

"Hanley's wife Connie?" Dean asked.

"Yes. And her goats. She lost a goat to something on Friday night."

"Lost one?"

"Airlifted right out of the enclosure and another one clawed all up along its haunches. So yes, I am interested in fixing up the fencing so I don't have to experience the same thing at Greener Pastures."

"What kind of thing could grab up a goat and take it away?" Dean leaned forward across the counter like he was afraid he'd miss something.

"I've heard a mountain lion could do something like that," Mitch said.

"But everyone knows there aren't any mountain lions in New Hampshire," Dean said, rolling his eyes.

"That's because they all got eaten by chupacabras," I said, scowling at Mitch.

"No way. Chupacabras eat goats. I saw a program about it on TV."

"Mountain lions are real. Chupacabras are imaginary," I said.

"You only think that since no one has ever caught one. I'd love to go on one of those cryptozoology hunts one day," Dean said.

"You ought to ask Graham for some tips on wrangling wildlife. Ask him about the best way to catch three-toed sloths." I grabbed the fencing samples and scooted out the door.

Thirteen

 "Brantley Sims here, calling from the State." Hearing the gnome's chirpy voice filled my ear with a cheerful sound and my guts with a sloshy carnival ride feeling. Here it was, the moment of truth.

"Yes sir, this is Dani." I gripped the arm of my desk chair for support and hoped for the best. I was glad he had called me when I had reached the privacy of my office and not back in the hardware store in front of an audience.

"I've got some good news and some bad."

"Give me the bad first." I'm a "get on with what needs doing" kind of a person and I've found knowing what you're up against early on helps with that. I hoped the website update in front of me was not going to need heavy revisions.

"Can't give you organic certification until this poisoning thing is all cleared up." At least he didn't apologize or mince words. Still, a small part of me had hoped he was going to say he was just going to have to wait until after the holiday to mail my certificate because they were out of printer ink.

"So you aren't shutting me down permanently? Is that the good news?"

"That's not my job. I can't say yea or nay on that subject."

"So what is the good news?"

"If the police get to the bottom of the poisoning and you aren't to blame, things should go through without a hitch. Your operation looks good, and I'd be delighted to pass you just as soon as the other thing is resolved." I heard him mumbling something to someone in the background. I wondered again if it could be another one of the dwarves or Snow White.

"Well, that's something at least."

"It's a whole lot of something. You wouldn't believe the kinds of stuff I see during my inspections. The poisons people keep sitting around in their barns and sheds for livestock and kids to get into scare the life right out of me sometimes. Many's the time I've given landowners what for, for their sloppy and dangerous practices." I heard him harrumph like an animated dwarf.

"You'd think people would know better, especially if they are producing things for consumption."

"Not a lick a sense, most of 'em. I'm not one bit surprised that woman at the pancake breakfast was killed by a pesticide. It would be all too easy to do if you ask me, accidentally or otherwise."

"Well, there wasn't anything accidental about that toxin ending up in the syrup."

"No, I'm sure there wasn't if it came from your property. At least not if you didn't clean something up between the time the syrup got poisoned and the time we had the inspection. Like I said, it looks like you have a very clean operation."

"I'd appreciate your spreading that kind of rumor around if you feel like you can and the opportunity crops up. I'm afraid my business is going to suffer a serious blow on account of this mess."

"I'm not one to hold my tongue when I think something is worth shouting about. I'll tell you what, if the police clear this up and it turns out you aren't in the middle somewhere, I'll put in a good word for you wherever I can."

"Thanks so much. I could use all the help I can get. Alanza Speedwell's death may be the death blow for Greener Pastures."

"Alanza Speedwell. I knew I'd heard that name from somewhere besides the evening news. She called my office about a sugaring operation."

"When was this?" Excitement buzzed in my brain, like a fly trapped against a sunny pane of glass.

"Let me think. I am pretty sure it was last week."

"Can you be more specific?"

"She called just as I got back from my trip to the dentist for a filling. I get a little too into my work sometimes and test a bit more maple candy than is strictly necessary. I remember that I had a spot of trouble getting her to understand me at first because of the Novocain, but as the conversation went on, things improved. That would make it Thursday afternoon." Thursday. What could have happened as a result of her conversation with the organic inspector that could have led to someone deciding to kill her?

"Do you remember what she asked you about?" It was worth a shot.

"Generally speaking, I wouldn't feel comfortable telling you something like that. But seeing as how the dead woman has landed you in such a heap of trouble, I'll tell you."

"Thanks for stretching your limits."

"Is that a short joke?"

"No sir. I am in no kind of position to be looking down on anyone else."

"I'm just fooling. Where were we?"

"Alanza's call. Her questions."

"Right. Now let's see. It was her second call to the office, now that I come to think of it. Such an unusual name, I should have thought of it right off, but my memory isn't quite what it used to be."

"When did she call the first time?"

"Maybe a month back. She wanted to know all about the rules regulating sugaring operations and how difficult it would be to start one up." About a month earlier would have made it just around the same time she lost the snowmobile election.

"Difficult how?"

"Oh, permits, equipment, fertilizers, and tree maintenance issues."

"So nothing out of the ordinary?"

"Nope, not really. I gave her a brief rundown of what

was required in terms of equipment to get started. I told her not to get all worked up about spending on the most advanced stuff before she had tried her hand at it at all."

"Was she listening to your advice, do you think?"

"Well, she called back again, didn't she?"

"What would she have needed a second time?"

"Fertilizers."

"Fertilizers?" There wasn't too much call for fertilizers during the late fall in New Hampshire. And maple sugaring doesn't rely heavily on fertilizers the same way many other commercial crops do.

"She wanted to know the average schedule for fertilizing a sugar bush."

"What did you tell her?"

"I told her what you would expect, that a sugar bush doesn't need too much in the way of fertilizers and that she would want to look for certain plants growing in the bush alongside the maples which indicate soil fertility. I recommended she hire a forester to give her property a once-over and make recommendations."

"Did she ask anything else?"

"She wanted to know if pesticides, herbicides, and fertilizers had to be registered with the state in order to be available or professionally applied."

"They do, don't they?" Our motto may be "Live Free or Die," but we do have some limits.

"Of course. I told her there was a listing right on the website of all the registered fertilizers in the state, but when she asked me if I had heard of one in particular, I went ahead and checked it for her. It was easy enough for me to do instead of asking her to navigate the website herself."

"Can you remember the name of the fertilizer?"

"It was kind of cutesy, with a funny spelling that stuck in my memory. Best Bett All in One. I wrote it down because there was nothing with that name listed and we are eager to track down people selling nonlicensed fertilizers or pesticides. Those things are regulated for a reason, missy." The gnome harrumphed again, with an even more exaggerated throat clearing than before.

"Did she tell you where she heard of it?"

"Nope. As a matter of fact, she hurried off the phone right quick like. I wondered at the time if she was trying to avoid answering my questions."

"And you can't ask her now." Was that the whole reason she died? She knew too much about an illegal fertilizer operation? Could it be enough to kill someone over?

"No, I can't, and I feel just terrible about it."

"If I turn up anything, I'll be sure to let you know." And I had a couple of decent bets where to start.

I was grabbing my car keys almost before I had hung up the phone. Lowell needed to hear there might be something to lead the investigation away from Greener Pastures, the sooner the better. I promised Grandma I would be back within an hour or so to help with more pie baking and set off for town.

The police station is just one block off Sugar Grove's main street. It sits tucked back behind a shady clump of rhododendrons that are unique in the fact they are being used in a commercial setting and don't look like they are suffering because of it. I sometimes think petty thieves and IRS auditors get reincarnated as rhododendrons. I can't think of anything more miserable than being one of those plants that get a reputation as an easy-care, hardy evergreen.

I rolled up to the corner of the station and parked the MG near the back so as not to take up any spaces needed for actual emergencies. I was sure Lowell would want to hear what I had to say, but I was not sure it justified plopping down in front of the building like I was a mayor on crutches or something. The door swung silently on its hinges and I walked in past the reception desk without spotting Myra. She ought to be at her desk fielding calls about police emergencies as well as the kind involving turkeys that were still frozen the day before they were scheduled to be the main event. The door to Lowell's office was halfway open, and I could hear him talking to someone. I didn't want to interrupt or disturb him so I stepped up quietly.

He was speaking softly, and at first I had a hard time making out his actual words. I was about a foot from the door when the forced hot air heating system shut off and the building suddenly became much quieter.

"How about if I call Mitch in a little early and we go over to my place for a little bit? He's always looking to pick up a few more hours and I never take my vacation time." Lowell's voice had a softness to it combined with a rumbling sultry quality I had never heard him use before. I heard a woman giggle just a bit. Lowell has never had a girlfriend I have ever met as long as he has been my godfather. Sure, I've heard my father and grandparents asking him about dates he had been on, but there was never anybody he brought out to the house for a family dinner or even anyone whose name he brought up in conversation. I was intrigued and felt like he was headed into new territory that would do him a world of good. I crept just slightly closer to the doorway, hoping to catch a glimpse of the woman who caused him to behave so recklessly.

Her back was to me and her face was obscured by Lowell's but I would know her anywhere. After all, it's hard not to recognize your own mother.

I backed away from the door so quickly I bumped into a chair and fell to the floor. Myra came out of the small room at the end of the hall, where they kept the microwave and the extra paper goods. She was holding one of those frozen diet entrées in her red beefy hands, a startled look on her face.

"Dani, are you all right?" She moved toward me like she was going to help me up. I jumped to my feet and continued on without a word. I heard her calling after me in tones a lumberjack would use to alert the others a tree was on its way to the ground. I had gotten to the car, shut the door, and had even turned the engine over before Lowell and my mother appeared in the doorway of the police station. The look on my mother's face in the rearview mirror was one I had not seen since my father's funeral. She looked stricken and small. The last thing I saw before I rounded the corner was her turning in toward Lowell's chest and him wrapping his long arms around her shoulders.

Fourteen

The only place to go was Piper's. Even if she wasn't home, her place was never locked. Her parents used to scold her about it until she pointed out that if anyone wanted to steal her stuff, they could easily take it all by hitching her RV to a truck and towing the whole thing away. Once she promised to lock it at night when she was inside, they stopped nagging. They did buy a surveillance service for the campground, but they argued it was a business expense and for the campground so it wasn't really about her anyway.

Piper's parents own and operate a kitschy campground right off the highway. It was built about the same time as the Stack Shack. and it has a no longer politically correct cowboys and Indians theme. There's a wagon train and a teepee village coexisting much more peacefully than happens in children's games. The wagons, which are actually small cottages, are circled around a main bonfire area and a horseshoe-pitching pit. The teepees make up a second circle around another bonfire area and a shuffleboard court.

The campground is open from Memorial Day weekend until, in an ironic twist, Columbus Day weekend. Piper's parents spend a few more weeks doing repairs and winterizing and then head down to Florida to spend the winter. Now that Piper is an adult and runs the Stack, she also keeps an eye on the place in the off-season. Usually, she has some guy or other helping to keep her company while she's at it. The relationships always seem to melt away with the snow come spring and the return of her parents. I'm not sure exactly what that says about her relationship with them, but at this point it was certainly better than mine no matter what. With one parent dead, and the other lip locking with the deceased's best friend, it was hard not to be on rocky ground.

Piper's RV was set back out of the main camping areas so as not to detract from the effect the Wild West Wagons and Wigwams was trying to achieve. I parked in the parking lot and noticed her car wasn't there. I wandered to her RV and stopped on the stoop Piper had built in front of the Airstream and used the raised vantage point to look out over the teepees and wagons. Alongside one of the teepees, a bit of wash flapped on a clothesline. A pair of trousers, some boxers, and a long-sleeved T-shirt waved at me as I turned to enter Piper's private space.

It doesn't matter how long we've known each other or how many times I have been in Piper's RV, each time I enter it, I get a startled feeling. Everything is neat, everything is tidy, and almost everything is covered in vintage leopard print. From the flooring to the drapes to the knobs on the golden maple cabinets, leopard spots cover so much, it can be difficult to see where one surface ends and another begins. If life were fairer, Piper would have been the one to encounter a big cat instead of me. She would have been thrilled. I yanked off my jacket, flipped on the electric teakettle, and threw myself down on the built-in leopard print couch. I tugged the leopard throw off the back of the couch and curled underneath it.

What was my mother thinking? I knew there was a possibility she would start dating again someday, but I hadn't thought any of us were ready to consider it. Dad had been gone only five years. And to become involved with his best friend? I felt like everything I knew about either of them was now called into question. I had to wonder if they had been carrying on while my father was still alive. Could he have found out about the two of them? I was so hurt and angry my blood was pounding behind my eyes like the bass beat at a rock concert. I started crying, and the sound of my sobs bounced around the confined space like a ball bearing in a clothes dryer. I wore myself out entirely and fell asleep like a toddler who'd thrown a temper tantrum that had run its course.

I awoke to the scrunch and crunch of tires on the ground outside. It was dark in the tiny home except for a leopard-spotted night-light. I wondered if Piper had brought any of the daily special home for dinner. The door opened and the figure silhouetted in the doorway didn't look like Piper. I thought again about her parents' door-locking policy and wished I'd followed through. It occurred to me I had no idea who the person was staying in the campground. For all I knew, it could be a dangerous squatter with a desire for clean clothes.

"I thought I'd find you here." Celadon's voice cut through the tiny home even more efficiently than my sobs had. I squished back down and pulled the throw over my head. "Oh no you don't. You are going to sit up and head home if I have to throw you over my arm and carry you there." Celadon has been saying things like this since we were kids. It used to work but now that her back has started giving her trouble, the threat is as hollow as a jack-o'-lantern without a candle.

"Go away." It's best to be direct with my oldest sister. She is sort of like a small child or a dog that way. My mother listens better the longer you speak, like an old-fashioned radio that needs to warm up to tune in. Celadon would rather receive her messages as telegrams. It's like she thinks there are only so many words you are allowed to hear in a lifetime and she doesn't want to outlive her supply.

"Not without you. Mom's a complete basket case and your little discovery today at the police station is threatening to ruin Thanksgiving for everyone."

"My little discovery. What about you? Did you already know about the two of them?" I sat upright on the couch. If anything, the situation was getting even worse. Was it possible members of my family knew about this all along and deliberately decided to keep it from me? Celadon dragged her hands along the walls until she encountered a light switch. Leave it to her to make an already difficult situation even more unpleasant. My eyes were bleary from all the crying and the light only made them sting even more. At least she had the grace to look a bit sheepish before pulling on her indignant mask and going on the offensive.

"As a matter of fact, I did. I encouraged it even. After all, both of them have been missing the same man. Who better to understand that aching spot than each other?"

"I don't want to hear another word about Mom consoling her aching spots with Dad's best friend. And I don't want to hear anything else from you either. I can't believe you knew about this and didn't tell me." I felt another sob trying to burble to the top of my throat, but I didn't let it. It was a nice catch, I can tell you, considering how little distance there is to travel along my very short neck.

"They're both grown people entitled to a little happiness. It would do you some good to grow up, too. Do you think any of us have liked keeping this from you?"

"Any of us? Does everyone else know?" I felt even sicker. I would never have thought my grandparents would be in on something like this. After all, Dad was their son. "Did all the rest of you know about this?"

"Everyone except the children."

"So I'm still one of the children?" It was something I had struggled with all my life. Every family has a way of behaving; everyone has a role to play no matter how much time has gone by. The mother's helper, the Goody Two-shoes, the athlete, the black sheep, all continue throughout life when spending time with family. In mine, I'm the baby and everyone else tells me stuff last, trusts me least to act like an adult, ladens me with unsolicited advice. This was the most egregious example, but I had been almost surprised that anyone had even told me about my father's death and hadn't tried to keep it from me thinking it was grown-up business.

"Maybe if you didn't act like one most of the time, you wouldn't get treated that way. What you need is to grow up, find a husband, and take your place in the town like the rest of us."

"So that's what you think?"

"It is. Which is why I invited that passably attractive man from the Fish and Game Department to come to the house for Thanksgiving dinner."

"You what?" My stomach began pulsing with a low dull ache.

"And of course, Knowlton will be there so you should have a bidding war on your hands if everything goes well." Celadon dug around in her purse and pulled out her keys.

"I'm not for sale."

"Yes you are, and since women don't fetch higher prices when they become antiques, we need to get you pawned off on someone before your value slips even more." I found myself in the unique position of being perceived as an aging baby.

"Is that what Mom is doing? Selling out before her value slips?"

"Our mother doesn't need to prove herself. She has a family and a position in society. The problem here is you."

"The problem is an outdated worldview. In case you hadn't noticed, in this century women are valued for more than their ability to snag a man and crank out some offspring. I'm perfectly happy just as I am." Celadon cocked an eyebrow at me and clucked her tongue.

"Your bloodshot eyes tell a very different story. Get yourself together and get on home before I tell Grandma you were not willing to try to resolve this with Mom." Celadon knew how to pull out the big guns. No one wanted to get tattled on to Grandma. And no one wanted to be the one to do the tattling either. The consequences were almost as steep to be the one carrying tales. It had better be a good one if you were planning to share it with her, or she would shame you for being evil to your sibling. I was counting on this to work in my favor when I answered. There was no way I was heading home right now.

"I'll get home when I am good and ready. You tell anyone you want, anything you want. I'm not leaving."

"Suit yourself then. You be the one to deal with the consequences of worrying your mother sick and throwing the rest of the household into a tizzy at the busiest time of the year."

"It's only the busiest time of the year because all of you make it be that way. All your Christmas crap is purely optional."

Celadon pursed her lips so tightly it was like they were a star beginning to implode. "Maybe it is better if you don't come home for a while. Perhaps you will begin to appreciate what you have that way." Celadon slammed the door behind her so hard the leopard print lampshade on the ceiling fixture swayed like there was a sudden storm. I huddled beneath the blanket again and thought about my options.

I didn't want to go home and I didn't want to face the family until we all had an opportunity to calm down. I could stay at Piper's most likely for at least a couple of days, but no matter how angry and hurt I was, it would just get worse if I had to explain why I hadn't done my fair share of the work to prepare Thanksgiving dinner. And not being at the actual event was unthinkable. As hurt as I was, there was no way I could do that to myself, or the rest of the family.

I fixed myself some cheese and crackers from Piper's cupboard and had settled in with a book I found in her bathroom on weird New Hampshire history, witches, and strange phenomenon when Piper was at the door, tugging Dean into the RV behind her. They were giggling and pawing at each other in a way I was sure they wouldn't be if they were aware they had an audience. For the second time that day I was an unwelcomed presence in an otherwise romantic interlude. Piper asked me what was wrong and encouraged me to stay but I told her it was just holiday craziness at the house and that I was refreshed and ready to leave. I'm not sure I convinced her, but Dean seemed pleased to see me leave so at least I had made someone happy.

I was deep in thought about my love life or lack thereof and all the rest of the things Celadon had said. Maybe I wasn't as mature as the average person my age. After all, I was almost twenty-seven and still had no marriage prospects, no thought of children besides a vague idea that someday I might like to have a couple of my own. I wondered if I looked as unsuccessful as I felt. Was public pressure finally going to wear me down and cause me to marry Knowlton and mother a troupe of taxidermy-loving children? I rounded the corner to where I had left my car and spotted Graham plucking his laundry off the makeshift line. He caught sight of me and waved.

I waved back with as little enthusiasm as possible to still not count as ignoring someone and trotted to my car as fast as I could manage. Unfortunately, Graham moved even faster. It must have been his long, lean legs and decently muscled back end that gave him the advantage. Not that I noticed much about his back end, but I was human after all. He tapped on the window, all professional, like a cop. Did I mention I am no longer interested in cops? I didn't roll down the window.

"Yes?" I asked through the glass.

"I just wanted to thank you for the invitation to Thanksgiving."

"I didn't invite you so there is no need to thank me."

"But you will need to put up with me at the dinner, and I think maybe I left things a bit rough round the edges the last time we spoke."

"If my family invited you, it is no business of mine. They do whatever they are going to without consulting me." I hadn't intended to share that much but it just slipped out. I must have been more stressed out than I had realized.

"Are you sure you're safe to drive? You look a little crazed. Distracted and not quite yourself." I rolled down the window so I could be sure he could hear how indignant I sounded when I came up with a snappy retort.

"Every time I run into you, you think I'm crazy. Is it just me or is it women in general?"

"It's just you. I can't remember any other woman ever making the sort of impression on me that you seem to." That knocked me off balance. I wasn't sure if he was flirting with me or insulting me again.

"If you think I'm crazy, you're going to enjoy meeting my mother on Thursday."

"Does she see imaginary animals, too?"

"She sees auras, ghosts, and spirit guides." Last week, she had tried to get me to join her for a sacred cleanse session in preparation for the toxins we would be experiencing over the holidays. It involved drinking algae shakes and standing knee-deep, naked as jay birds, in a stream at the edge of the property under the glow of the full moon. I had declined, citing the ill effects of frostbite on my already too tiny bustline. "And for the record, I may have more proof about the mountain lion that was anything but imaginary."

"Uh-huh."

"No, really. The same night I called you, another woman in town had something break into her goat enclosure."

"What makes you think that means it was a mountain lion? Lots of things could have done that."

"Could lots of things have slashed the haunch on one

goat and carried a second one off over the top of the twelve-foot fencing?"

"Are you sure about that?"

"I was over there myself talking to Connie. She was all torn up about it."

"People leave their gates open a lot more frequently than they realize they do. That is a lot more likely than something dragging a goat over a fence that high."

"Connie treats her goats like her own kids."

"They are her own kids."

"Very funny. You know what I mean. She wouldn't forget to do anything that had to do with their safety. She crochets blankets for each of them to coordinate with their fur. She even designed a goat bonnet for the ones she thinks have cold ears."

"So most of the women in Sugar Grove are crazy by the standards of most other places."

"I don't know about that, but Connie is devoted to her goats."

"Did she actually see anything?"

"She discovered it after the fact."

"Unless she saw something, I've got animals people are actually seeing that need to be rounded up."

"I remember calling about a mountain lion I had actually seen, but my eyewitness report didn't seem to convince you I wasn't crazy."

"I'm still not convinced. And considering how long it's taking to round up the rest of those animals, I am not sure I'll get out to check on the report anytime soon. I'd suggest taking some photos."

"Which you'll just say are doctored."

"Most likely. I've seen a lot of those. I'd be thrilled to discover mountain lions in New Hampshire, but there is just no evidence and I don't think there is going to be any."

"I think it is safe to bet you won't be the one to make a discovery. I don't think you can see things that are right in front of your face."

"Oh, I'm not so sure about that." He stared down at me with his deep blue eyes, little laugh crinkles around the edges standing out against his fading tan. I felt flustered and unsure what to say. After so many years of fending off Knowlton and his absolutely clear stance on his interest in me, I didn't quite know what to think about this. I was out of practice with flirting and out of practice with most men in general. It's not like I am a pariah, but I don't leave town too often now that Internet shopping is a thing and eligible men are about as rare as mountain lions in Sugar Grove and about as startling.

"So if I hear about any more mountain lion sightings in the area, you'd want to know about them?"

"Absolutely. If I'm not up to my armpits in missing tortoises and monkeys."

"At the rate you're going, you'll be chasing creatures around this village until you're ready for retirement."

"Even after the exotic animals are all rounded up, I may still be chasing around a local creature, a small one with a feisty attitude and a surly disposition." He smiled at me again. I gulped. I wondered what Celadon told him when she invited him to Thanksgiving dinner. He seemed like he was more interested in me with each sentence slipping through his lips. Had she said I was desperate? Had she told him I was interested in him? Had he decided I was lying about what Knowlton had said and that I was, in fact, very passionate and flexible? The day had been too long and too emotionally exhausting to tangle with him. I needed to get out of there, and even going back home seemed like a good idea in comparison with sticking around any longer.

"I've got to go." I cranked on the window and he stuck his finger in the remaining crack, preventing me from closing it all the way.

"What's the hurry? Was it something that I said?"

"It's fine. I'm in a hurry." There was no way I was going to get into the details of my family life at the end of such a terrible day. Especially not with someone who'd left me feeling as off-kilter as Graham had.

He held up his hands and backed away like I was holding a gun on him. "Until tomorrow."

Fifteen

Standing in the dining room on Thanksgiving at about two o'clock, I could almost hear the old oak table groaning and gasping for air under the weight of Grandma's week's worth of work. I noticed with pleasure the maple cranberry sauce, the yeasted pumpkin rolls snuggled down all cozy into a towel-lined basket, the steaming bowl heaped with mashed sweet potatoes dressed up with butter and maple syrup.

What I was not at all pleased to see was a place card sitting dead center in the plate nearest me. I leaned in for a closer check. My grandmother doesn't usually worry about place cards, saying people will pretty much sort themselves out in just the way she would have done anyway. This had to be Celadon's doing. It was definitely her handwriting. I wouldn't have put it past my mother to be involved, but this had Celadon written all over it. And I think I could guess why.

I had circled the table looking for my name. Sure enough, tucked into a corner, down at the end next to a place card with my name, was one with Graham's. I picked his up and was looking for a new place to put it when he walked in carrying a plate of stuffed mushrooms. Evil. The whole family knew I couldn't resist a stuffed mushroom. They must have been betting on the messenger receiving credit for the message. I wasn't going to fall for that, but I was going to get a mushroom.

With a table this long, it can be difficult to get every dish passed in your direction unless you jump up on your seat and holler. I learned early on not to make that mistake a second time. No matter how cute she tells you she thinks you are, no one is allowed to stand on one of Grandma's dining room chairs hollering for more turkey like a drunken lord in a mead hall. Or so I've heard.

"Your grandmother asked me to make sure you got one of these before the rest of the guests eat them all. She mentioned not wanting a repeat of your fifth Thanksgiving." He lowered the platter toward me, and I looked at them like I was pretending to decide. As I went to load up one hand with the other, I noticed I was still holding Graham's place card. He noticed it, too. That's another thing I didn't like so much about policemen—they were always noticing something but usually not the thing you hoped they would, like a new haircut or the way a pair of earrings set off your eyes. They were much more likely, in my experience, to notice the bit of steak between your teeth left over from lunch or how you misused a new vocabulary word from your word-a-day calendar. "Why are you holding my place card?"

"I was just checking that Celadon spelled your name correctly. I can't stand it when people don't pay attention to details." I snatched a piping hot mushroom and stuffed it in my mouth before I could stick my foot in there instead.

"Did they spell it just like the cracker?" He waited for me to swallow. I made a big show of checking the front of the card and ended up getting some mushroom juice from my fingers on it while I was at it.

"Looks just fine. Now where did I find this? The table is so big, I may not be able to get it back in the right place."

"It goes over in the corner right next to yours." Drat. He really did notice all the wrong details. I was going to get my sister back for her tinkering around in my social life. "I came in a little while ago and swapped it with Knowlton's." He offered me the platter once more. I couldn't think of anything to say to that so I took another one and popped it into my mouth. "I figured if he was going around pretending to be your fiancée, a big family occasion like this would only help him delude himself further." So maybe he didn't only notice the wrong things. That was exceedingly chivalrous of him. I suppose he could have swapped Knowlton's name with someone besides his own but I'd let that slide. Maybe he had no idea if there was someone else I was trying to avoid even more than Knowlton. I chewed slowly, trying to craft a response.

Fortunately, the rest of the room began to fill with

revelers, and Graham squeezed the platter into an open spot, plucked the card from my fingers, and steered me to the end of the table we were supposed to occupy. I was pleased to note Knowlton sat at a point at the table so far away he couldn't speak to me even if he did conduct himself like a mead hall reveler.

Grampa said grace, Grandma gave the tour of the menu items, and we were off and running. Graham on the one side of me and Tansey on the other, I felt like maybe I was in a dinnertime version of the pancake breakfast. I like a man who can eat, but as I watched Graham out of the corner of my eye, it was like seeing someone who was starved. And not just on a physical level. He ate steadily but he seemed to be in a bit of a food trance, like he'd never done something quite like this before. I made a note to ask him about his own Thanksgiving traditions when he had slowed down enough that it wouldn't feel like I was interrupting a man at prayer. Which did beg the point of why he was able to be available to enjoy dinner with us. He obviously didn't have to be on duty if he was able to eat with someone. Was his family all too far away? I looked around the table at the assembled faces and thought about how conflicted I'd felt about my own family over the last couple of days.

And that's when I noticed what I would have realized straight off if I hadn't been so distracted by Graham and where Knowlton ended up. Lowell was nowhere to be seen. With the exception of the year he was in the hospital, for my entire life, Lowell has sat at our Thanksgiving table. And Christmas and Easter, too. He was as much a part of the family as the rest of us. I wasn't sure who to be mad at, myself or Lowell and my mother for messing everything up. It was upsetting enough to make me lose my appetite right in the middle of the best food day of the year. I was so upset, it took me a minute to notice Tansey herself had switched from eating mode to socializing.

She had finally slowed down enough to speak to Grandma even though she was across the table and Tansey needed a bullhorn to be heard over the din. She managed it, though, even without standing on her chair.

"We missed you the other night at the quilting circle." Tansey was one of those rare people who could turn her hand to about anything in the physical world and make it come out right. She farmed her fields, tapped her trees, built her own barn, and was a quilt artist. Her work was a source of envy in the quilting circle, and she had been featured in more than one magazine with her original designs. I had been on her about selling her quilting patterns, so many of which featured maple trees, at the sugarhouse shop, but so far she had refused, saying anybody could make up their own and you'd have to be an idiot wasting good money on a thing like that.

"I was sorry to miss it but you know I always help set up for the pancake breakfast," Grandma said.

"The turnout was pretty good for a holiday week. You and Felicia were the only ones absent." Tansey slathered a pumpkin roll with enough butter to caulk a tub and bit into it with gusto.

"I'll be there next time. I've got that Christmas table runner I am trying to finish up," Grandma said. That's when it hit me. Felicia told me she was at the quilting circle

Friday night when the syrup was poisoned. Why would she lie about a thing like that?

I'd lost my appetite and I needed to think. As soon as I could slip away unnoticed in the after-dinner cleanup frenzy, I snuck out the door. I was about a mile up an old logging road when I heard rustling in the long grass at the side. I wished I were walking a dog. A dog would be a good way to know if I was imagining things. Dogs are amazing heifer dust detectors. And they seem to love their favorite people anyway. We never had a dog because Celadon was allergic. It was just one of the many things we didn't see eye to eye on. Ever since the exotics had been let loose in town, I'd wanted a dog worse than any time since I was eleven and pretty sure no one in the world would ever understand me. A dog seemed the only solution at the time. Most days it still seemed the best.

The rustling continued and so did the gentle waggle at the tops of the timothy hay where an unknown was trampling it. I gathered my courage with as much enthusiasm as a child picking up sand toys after too little time spent on the beach. Stepping forward, I sent a silent shout out to the universe detailing how appreciative I would be if the creature involved would not turn out to be a snake. I must have gotten onto a good list with the upstairs management because snakes don't have four legs and a shell. The leopard tortoise. That didn't seem so bad. The background of its large shell was colored like maple sugar and the detailing of darker splotches on each knobby segment made it beautiful.

As I bent even closer, it slowly rotated its leathery neck and trained its dark eye on me. It let out a hissing, leaking sound like the air was squeezing out of its body, then it pulled its legs and head inside the handsome shell. Graham had mentioned it the morning of the pancake breakfast. I hadn't seen any native amphibians or reptiles in weeks so I felt certain this big guy couldn't be too comfortable. In fact, it was probably surprising he had survived this long.

I squatted behind the creature and tried to wrap my hands around its shell. I confidently gave a heave and felt nothing but the sting of defeat. I looked down in surprise. How much could the thing weigh? I stood and gave it a closer look. The shell looked to be somewhere in the neighborhood of two feet in length. I routinely lifted five-gallon buckets of maple sap as a part of the sugaring process and they weigh around forty pounds each. I hadn't been able to budge the tortoise more than an inch off the ground so it had to be far heavier. I looked down at the shelled creature and thought about my options.

I could run all the way back, get help, and return, hoping to find this big guy again. I could keep watch over him until someone came looking for me even if it took all night. Or I could figure out some way to carry him back to the house. Since asking for help is even less appealing than sticking myself in the eye with a nut pick and the temperature with the sun still slanting above the horizon was dropping close to freezing, I decided finding a way to transport it was clearly the best option. All those childhood hours wiled away reading adventure and survival books came in handy. I slipped my arms out of my jacket and then put the orange vest back on just in case someone didn't respect the fact our land was clearly posted. I positioned the bottom edge of the jacket near the tortoise and moved it inch by inch onto the jacket. I puffed and panted my way along until the whole creature sat entirely on the back of the garment. I took a moment to catch my breath then grabbed the end of each sleeve and started dragging the animal slowly out onto the logging road.

The going was slow and the light was fading fast. I felt a shiver of worry when I thought about the other creatures that could be prowling around as the night came on. Primarily mountain lions. Like most cats, they hunt at night, and I was acutely aware that not only did I not have a shell to retreat into, I didn't even have the meager protection of a jacket.

I had gone about halfway back down the logging road and had repositioned the tortoise on the jacket three times when I started hearing noises. Quiet, crackling twig type noises. Birds being startled up out of the grass and shrubs noises. I stopped and strained my ears, wondering what I would be able to do to protect myself if a mountain lion crouched between the house and me. I had been so eager to leave and now I wondered if bits of my partially digested ponytail would finally provide the coughed-up hairball proof Graham and the rest of Fish and Game would need to prove there really were mountain lions in New Hampshire.

A rustling, crunching ahead of me on the path made me crouch behind the tortoise frozen in place, wondering if I was about to become lion chow. I racked my brain for bits of trivia concerning fending off large cats. All that ran through my mind was a television commercial for super-absorbent kitty litter. My knees went weak when Graham came into view and not in the way a girl hopes when landing her peepers on an available man with a decent job. I hovered in a semisquat above the tortoise, not sure my legs had what it would take to rocket me back up into a standing position. I was saved from decision making by Graham dropping to his haunches next to me, giving the tortoise the once-over.

"It's like you're an exotics whisperer." He ran a square, still tanned hand over the bumpy ridges of the creature's shell, tracing the rectangular pattern of dark and light browns with a gentle finger. My knees started to feel a little wobbly again and this time it might have been for reasons other than a shot of adrenaline. Even out in the open air, he smelled like wood smoke and pumpkin pie.

"It's not like I'm doing it on purpose."

"It wasn't a criticism. I appreciate all the help you keep giving me."

"I'm doing it for the animals and the town."

"Duly noted. I've come to realize it is unwise to make assumptions about you."

"What kind of assumptions?"

"You're not entirely what you seem on the surface."

"You mean crazy? Or a liar?"

"I mean normal."

"What's that supposed to mean?"

"It's Thanksgiving. Everyone else in the country is lifting forkfuls of pie to their already overstuffed lips with friends and family. You're out here attempting to lift a turtle which probably outweighs you and I don't even think you plan to eat him."

"It's a tortoise."

"You know what I meant."

"No. I don't. I'm not sure how much time the average Fish and Game official spends with criminals, but I'd like to think there is nothing odd about helping out other creatures, especially those in need. Especially today."

"Not everyone would help. You look exhausted. Where did you find this guy?" Graham turned his head and glanced at the waving pasture edged by trees.

"A ways up the logging road. I wasn't expecting it to take so long to get him back, but then a lot of things don't turn out the way you would expect them to." I turned my gaze back to the tortoise. My nose was burning a bit in just one nostril, the way it does whenever tears are threatening.

"He looks heavy, especially for someone your size."

"I'll have you know the average woman can easily lift half her body weight." I flexed my arm in a bodybuilder pose. Graham reached over and gave it a firm squeeze, and my knees did that wobbling thing again.

"So that must mean hoisting a forty-pound sack of potting soil is about your limit."

"Hey, buddy, I'll have you know I weigh over a hundred pounds so you'd better make that a fifty-pound sack."

"I didn't think we knew each other well enough for you to tell me your weight."

"I tell everyone how much I weigh." And I do, just to reassure myself I'm not shrinking. My maternal grandmother is four-foot-eight and dwindling. The last I'd heard from Aunt Colleen, Grandmother O'Malley was eating an entire frozen cheesecake and a takeout pizza every day to maintain a weight of eighty-three pounds. With a metabolism to shame a hummingbird, you just can't be too careful.

"So I guess that means I'm not special." I thought under the fading glow of Graham's tanned cheek that there was a bit of a rosy blush darkening it. How bizarre. And possibly flattering. If I was interested in that sort of thing.

"I'm sure you're special to someone. Like your family." I glanced at him as slyly as I could and realized I'd made a mistake.

"I haven't got any." That explained why he was available for Thanksgiving with people little more than strangers.

"I'm so sorry, I shouldn't have said that."

"You didn't know. No harm done." But there had been. I was flip about something that could have been sweet and I'd ruined it. And I'd hurt someone on a holiday that revolved around family.

"I still had no right saying that when your personal life is none of my business."

"Well, if we are speaking our minds and overstepping our bounds, I'll even the score and say I think it's too bad you're avoiding your family today of all days."

"I'm not avoiding them."

"Then what are you doing up here instead of sharing the day with the type of family some of us have wanted all our lives?" You know how sometimes it is easier to tell a stranger about deeply personal things? This wasn't one of those times. With those strangers, you know it is a onetime exchange, and after the catharsis of confession, the odds of encountering them again are so slim the risks feel irrelevant. With the way his roundup of the exotic animals was going, I had no confidence Graham was going to be out of my life soon enough to share anything but half a peanut butter sandwich. But having stepped in it the way I did, I couldn't be churlish about it.

"I'm trying to figure out how to deal with some changes I don't like, and I am not doing a very good job of it." I gave the tortoise a pat just to do something with my hands.

"Anything I can help with?"

"I doubt it."

"Give it a try. You wouldn't believe how many times I get called out for domestic disputes because I am the nearest officer on duty." I looked at his face and decided to risk it. There was no one in the family I could talk to, and Piper had opted to spend the holiday in her RV with Dean, celebrating in a less orthodox manner.

"The problem is my father."

"But he wasn't there."

"Nope. He missed his favorite holiday for the fifth year in a row." That pesky nostril was stinging so bad it felt like a hornet had crawled up in there and was tap dancing its way back out.

"I can't imagine him giving all of you up willingly."

"Only his heart gave up and I doubt it was willingly. He had a massive heart attack right in the middle of his sugar bush. Loden found him when Dad didn't come to supper."

"I'm sorry to hear it."

"So was I when they called me at college to let me know."

"That must have been a hard call to make and an even harder one to receive."

"I didn't take it at all well. Celadon says that's one of the reasons the family babies me so much. Why they don't always tell me things."

"So is that what this is about? Someone's not telling you things?"

"The family didn't bother to let me know my mother was replacing my father with his best friend, Lowell." I sat with a thump down onto the ground. My knees may not have reached thirty, but they were starting to hurt. A stone in the path dug into my backside and pretty much summed up my day, a pain in the butt. "I decided to head out here before I said something I'd regret. You can't really ever take things back."

"From the reaction to your exit, I'd say it looked like the silent treatment instead of a mature choice to mind your words."

"Are you sure you weren't imagining things? Everyone was so busy they probably didn't even notice I left." Graham sat down beside me and stretched out his legs. He had dressed neatly and respectably for Thanksgiving dinner but his trousers probably could have stood up to an emergency animal-wrangling session and come out none the worse for it in the end.

"I'm pretty sure of what I saw. You're the one with a

vivid imagination. Anyone who sees mountain lions in New Hampshire is possessed of that."

"Is that your attempt at lightening up the tone of this conversation?" I stretched forward to tug the tortoise back within arm's reach.

"It is."

"It's a good thing your specialty is animals. Your people skills could use some work."

"Maybe I just need the right person to give me some pointers. Know anybody who might be willing to give me some private lessons?"

"My friend Piper loves fixer-upper men. Why don't you try her?"

"Perhaps I'll do just that." Graham stood and reached a hand down to me and gently pulled me to my feet. "We'd better get this guy under cover before it gets any colder and darker. And I don't know about you, but I want another piece of pie before I head out." He bent over the tortoise and lifted it easily. I was both impressed and annoyed. We silently covered more ground in ten minutes than I had in half an hour and arrived back at the house just as the sensor light winked on over the kitchen door. I helped Graham settle the tortoise into a wooden crate in the back of his truck. Then wondered what I was going to do with myself.

"Come in with me while I angle for another slice of pie?" Graham asked, nodding toward the house. Through the windows I could see my family moving about, talking and laughing. I wanted to be done being angry, but I just didn't know how.

"I'm not hungry."

"Now that can't be right. You picked at your dinner and dragged oversized wildlife a mile down a cart track. You must have worked up quite an appetite." I watched the tortoise slowly find its feet and poke the front of its nose out every so slightly. Could it be so easy to adapt and start over?

"I don't know what to say to them. I don't know how to act like nothing happened."

"I think you won't have to say anything if your mouth is full of pie." A chiming sound erupted from Graham's phone and his attention went elsewhere. He finished up quickly and returned his attention to me. "Someone's reported lemurs swarming all over the Dumpster behind the general store."

"Sounds like you had better get going. Do you need any help? I believe you called me an exotics whisperer just a little while ago."

"You're just looking for an excuse to avoid your family."

"Does that make my help any less valuable?"

"Mitch is the one who called it in. He's waiting for me there."

"I think I hear my grandmother calling me. I'll say your good-byes for you." I waved at him as he backed down the driveway, then I headed out to the sugarhouse. I may have said I'd tell her good-bye, but I never said when.

Sixteen

The next day was the first opportunity I had to ask about the Best Bett All in One fertilizer. I didn't want to be caught anywhere near the police station so I went looking for Myra at the Stack. She's usually there for lunch and ends up eating half her other meals there as well. She was the first stop on my journey to get to the bottom of the Best Bett All in One question. If anyone was going to know the score with all things Bett, it was Myra.

Even from the doorway it was easy to spot Myra's purple polka-dotted, stretch knit clad backside oozing over both sides of a counter stool. Piper waved at me from her usual spot behind the counter. It was all the encouragement I needed. Her own family might be the only topic Myra didn't gossip about, but if there was one thing I knew about her, it was that she wouldn't be able to resist correcting false information. It might be her nature or it might be something developed through her time with the police department but she was incapable of letting it pass. I figured I could use Piper as my sounding board. Myra also couldn't resist listening in on a bit of gossip she hadn't heard and then trying to top it with something better of her own.

"Hi, ladies. What's good today?"

"Everything, as always. I'm surprised to see you in here, though, with all the leftovers I'm sure are still floating around your place. Nothing's happened to your grandmother, has it?" Myra looked alarmed and then eager for a bit of news.

"She's as fit as a health spa spokesperson. I just wanted a break from turkey."

"I recommend the special," Piper said, pointing to the chalkboard painted in the shape of a giant maple leaf on the wall near the door. Sweet potato and kale stew with a cranberry corn muffin.

"I'll take it. So, Piper, what have you heard about the new Bett family fertilizer business?" I studiously avoided glancing at Myra. It was just like fishing; this was the tricky part with wiggling the bait. Piper shrugged hard enough to slosh the coffee in the pot she was holding.

"Nothing. I've never heard of such a thing. Are you sure you've got that right?"

"I heard about it from the state ag inspector. He heard about it from Alanza."

"Small world. How'd the inspector know Alanza?"

"She must have called him about her sugaring

business," Myra said. I knew she wouldn't be able to resist joining the conversation and especially sounding like she knew more than the next person. "Which Bett did he say was involved?"

"He didn't but I am hoping to find out so I can buy some from them. And maybe even sell it at the shop. You know how I like to use local products whenever I can." Community spirit is strong in Sugar Grove and it seemed a likely story.

"I know all the Betts and I can't think of any in the fertilizer business. There's Felicia, and Connie and myself. Even Knowlton is a relative, which makes Tansey one by marriage." Myra stirred her coffee so agitatedly she sloshed some over the side. Piper wiped it up before it had a chance to spread.

"I didn't know Knowlton was related to you," Piper said, looking up from her work.

"His father's mother was a Bett before her marriage. Lewis Bett was Knowlton's grandmother's cousin." Myra drummed her pudgy fingers on the Formica.

"I don't know how you keep them all straight," I said. "I guess with so many of them running around, no one would be able to know what they were all up to." I hoped Myra recognized a gauntlet when it was lying on the ground right in front of her.

"If remaining close to family is important enough to you, it's easy." Myra gave me a look that I'm sure was meant to make me feel chastised about what had happened at the police station the other day.

"Communication helps keep everyone tightly knit,

don't you think? Look at this situation with the Bett fertilizer business. Who would have ever thought you wouldn't be in the loop for a thing like that?"

"I'll look into it and let you know what I find out." Myra plucked three grease-stained paper sacks from Piper's outstretched hands and trotted out the door. As I watched her go, I asked myself if the person who murdered Alanza had just offered to help me get to the bottom of the crime. She had an alibi for the night of the poisoning, but she also had the best access to the grange hall. After all, who would think anything of the head of the Sap Bucket Brigade touching the syrup jugs? Who would be suspicious if she got to the grange earlier than everyone else and was there alone in the morning? It would be more suspicious if she hadn't been there first than if she had. And Myra's reasons for getting rid of Alanza were strong. Myra's pride in being a Bett knew no bounds. Saving Bett's Knob from being defiled by an interloper was something she would consider a privilege as well as a duty. I might be able to get the information I wanted from her, but it felt like I might be making a deal with the devil.

Graham's state-issued truck was pulled into the lay-by the chamber of commerce had built to view Bett's Knob. As I approached, I saw Graham holding a net and moving closer to the viewing machine. I pulled over for a closer look. Knowlton was there, too, and the opportunity to get some things straight and to ask about Hanley was too good to miss. As I got out of the car, I got a better look at what Graham was trying to capture.

A small black monkey sat atop the viewing machine, chattering and holding an empty soda bottle in its paws. Graham was within swooping range with his net when the monkey turned its attention to him and flitted effortlessly away. Graham ran after him, reaching with his net and leaping like a lord in the Christmas carol. Knowlton ran around the other way, trying to drive the monkey toward Graham. Knowlton caught sight of me and dropped his hand to his head and smoothed his hair. He plastered a goofy grin on his face and made a beeline for me, leaving Graham to carry on with his leaping and his net. The little monkey didn't seem ready to let Knowlton out of the game, though. It changed course and ran straight after Knowlton. It swarmed up his pant leg, sprinted up his torso, and paused long enough on his head for Graham to swoop his net at it. His net crashed down over Knowlton's face just a second after the monkey leapt from his head and into my arms.

The monkey tilted its wrinkly little face up at me and I felt an odd tug like maybe my family wasn't so wrong in trying to convince me to marry and start a family of my own. The monkey snuggled in close, and I felt my heart melt a little more as its small paws gripped my jacket. Out of the corner of my eye, I saw Graham yank the net off Knowlton's head then stealthily creep toward me. A call went up and the little monkey sprang from my side and disappeared into the trees. Monkey chattering faded away like so many birdcalls in the wind. I felt a little sense of loss and then asked myself if the monkey could have given me fleas.

"I've been chasing those monkeys since the crack of dawn." Graham stood his net on end and heaved a deep sigh as if all his hopes for the future had been pinned on capturing the little creature.

"And I've been here, too, helping out," Knowlton said.

"That's right. He's been here the entire time." Graham had his back turned to Knowlton so there was no way he was offending him when he rolled his eyes so far up into his head I worried they'd get stuck up there.

"It's nice the two of you have gotten the chance to renew your acquaintance."

"What do you mean?" Knowlton asked.

"Graham told me the two of you had met before he arrived here for this visit."

"He did?" I saw Knowlton's Adam's apple give a little bob like a float on a fish line.

"He mentioned you're engaged to be married and that everyone at some sort of carcass exchange is impressed with your bride-to-be."

"He told you all that?"

"All that and more. Apparently, she's so flexible she's practically a circus freak."

"Are you jealous?"

"Why would I be jealous of being insulted like that?"

"I can't see why any woman would be insulted by my compliments."

"Are you sure? I know I'd die of embarrassment if my

fiancé blabbed to anyone who would listen that I liked to get naked and twist myself into a knot capable of lashing a cruise ship to a dock." Knowlton's apple bobbed like he had hooked a blue whale.

"When you put it that way, it does sound a little embarrassing."

"Does this girl know you talk about her like that? You might want to be careful or she might back out of the marriage."

"I see what you mean."

"When's the wedding? I haven't heard Tansey saying anything, and knowing your mother, she should be all a-dither planning and shouting the news from rooftops all over town." Out of the corner of my eye I saw the net Graham was holding beginning to flutter like it was jiggling from some giggling. Silent and manly giggling, but giggling nonetheless.

"I haven't told her about it yet." Knowlton was having trouble lifting his gaze above my kneecaps. Which was a new experience. Usually I can't get him to lift his eyes above my nonexistent bustline.

"To hear Tansey tell it, the two of you are still as close as the days you were taking up space on her insides. How could you deny her the pleasure of this news? Especially with such a special girl." Graham must have decided to take pity on him.

"His descriptions of his fiancée wouldn't necessarily make a good impression on a mother-in-law. A father-in-law maybe, but certainly not a mother."

"That's it exactly. I wanted them to be able to be close."

"How is it that after all these years I had to hear about the love of your life from Graham? When Graham first told me you were engaged to such an extraordinary woman, I thought for sure he was lying to me. But since you aren't denying any of it, I'll have to go home and tell Celadon that you're off the market and we'll need to set our sights elsewhere." Knowlton held out hope that if I wouldn't marry him Celadon would even though she'd been married to her husband for years.

Knowlton shuffled his feet along the dirt for a moment before speaking again. "Uh, Dani, could we talk in private for a moment?"

"It doesn't seem appropriate for me to be chatting tête-à-tête with a man whose heart belongs to another," I said. He looked so miserable I was rapidly losing my anger at him. We all want to show off for our peers sometimes, to be the source of envy. The only thing I was still sore at him for was using my real name and besmirching it all over the state.

"I think I see one of those monkeys up in that tree way over there." Graham gestured with his net and stepped quickly out of earshot. It was a small kindness to be sure, but a telling one, and it raised him in my estimation more than anything else I had seen him do so far. A look of relief flitted across Knowlton's face as if a cop with the blue lights on had just barreled past him and had stopped a car a few ahead of his own.

"I lied, Dani. You know you and Celadon are the only girls for me. There isn't anyone else. Please don't tell your sister I have a fiancée. She'll never give me another glance." The only glancing around for Knowlton that

Celadon had ever done was to be sure he wasn't hanging around before she ventured to leave the house, but it wasn't going to do anyone a bit of good to share that with him.

"Is that right? I hope you knew enough not to use some real girl's name when you went around making stuff up. If what Graham told me was even half as colorful as what you'd been saying, I'd hate to be the girl anyone thought was involved in those stories." I kept my eyes fixed right on his face as it turned the color of a male cardinal. He opened and shut his mouth several times but nothing came out. I think Graham had positioned himself downwind and was still able to hear a lot more than it seemed like he could, given the distance, because he picked that precise moment to show up and rescue Knowlton from having to come up with a response.

"So did you just stop in to help us lose a monkey or did you want to talk to me about more imaginary animal sightings?" That dropped his points back down to zero and gave Knowlton a terrific topic change.

"I heard about that from Mother. She said Myra was spreading it all over town. What was it you hallucinated again? A Sasquatch?" This is why it was impossible to like Knowlton. As soon as you started to feel the least bit softened toward him, he said or did something that crusted you all over once more.

"It was a mountain lion and I did not hallucinate it. I saw it being walked on a short lead by your fiancée." That snapped his jaws shut like a leghold trap on a fox. "And yes, I did have business to discuss with Knowlton that didn't involve his athletic sex life."

"Okay, what was it?"

"Are you sure you didn't see either Jill or Hanley on Friday night?"

"I'm sure. Neither of them was up at the camp. It's black as the inside of a bull moose out there when there's no moon and it's overcast. Even with the distance between camps, you can see lights winking away and the noise travels, too. There weren't none of either one on Friday." But if he didn't see anyone, then no one could say they saw him either.

Seventeen

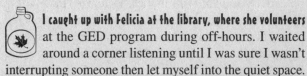 **I caught up with Felicia at the library, where she volunteers** at the GED program during off-hours. I waited around a corner listening until I was sure I wasn't interrupting someone then let myself into the quiet space.

"The library's closed," Felicia called over her shoulder automatically, her attention focused on packing a tote bag with books and papers.

"I came to see you," I said, feeling strange at how loud my voice sounded.

"Dani, I would have thought you'd be out at the Black Friday sales getting some Christmas shopping done." She smoothed a stack of papers with a small hand and gave her attention to me. I caught myself wondering if that same hand had twisted the top of one of my syrup bottles and slipped in poison. It made me sick to my stomach to wonder such a thing about a woman so long a friend of the family. But wonder it I did. When you watch the news or read the newspaper and become aware of a crime, you don't really give much thought to the ways it impacts a community. Sure, you think of the victim and their immediate family. If they left young children behind, it is easy to consider how lives are changed. If the murderer is revealed to be someone close to the family, everyone understands the sense of betrayal.

But what you don't know, until it happens in your own town, is how small things shift and feel tainted. How the offhand comments of long-term acquaintances take on shades of meaning you would never before have assigned them. How quirks and habits suddenly look like something potentially fraught with malice. Before Alanza took a plunge into her pancakes, I never would have wondered if a mild-mannered innkeeper who helped increase her fellow community members' chances of job success would bop someone off.

Standing there with Felicia, I felt angry that someone would do something in my town so terrible I would change the way I looked at my friends and neighbors. So far, I had been looking for ways to slide my questions into conversations as nonconfrontationally as possible. The anger I was feeling prompted me to plunge ahead with my queries without apology.

"With everything going on with Greener Pastures, I didn't feel much like shopping, no matter how good the deals."

"I'd be upset, too. What brings you by the library?"

"I wanted to ask you about last Friday night."

"What about it?"

"You said you were at the quilting group but you weren't. Tansey said so at Thanksgiving dinner." It was hard to do but I kept my eyes locked on hers instead of staring at my shoes, which would be my usual inclination when embarrassing someone. Felicia remained quiet for a moment, her hand frozen in mid smooth across the stack of papers. Then her eyes dropped and her shoulders sagged. She sank into the seat beside her.

"You caught me. I didn't want anyone to know." My hearted bounced around in my chest. I tried to remember where all the exits were in case she decided to bolt, or worse, if I needed a quick escape route of my own.

"So where were you really?"

"Out at the Loon Lodge with Jim Parnell." A tear rolled down her pink cheek. Her sagging shoulders started shaking. I looked over at the librarian's cluttered desk and spotted a box of tissues. I grabbed them and handed the box to her. I could understand why she would be upset. Maybe she wasn't going to confess to murder after all.

"So Roland doesn't know about it?" Loon Lodge was a grubby motel and coffee shop on the far side of town. To be there with someone other than your husband spoke volumes about the state of your marriage.

"Of course he doesn't. He was off practicing his music with Dean and the other guys like he does every Friday night." I tried to imagine Roland's blood pressure readings if he had been privy to his wife's goings-on. Felicia started sobbing even harder. I wondered how best to comfort her but, given my limited experience, didn't feel competent to advise her on things marital or extramarital. And really, I was here to find out if she had killed Alanza, not to hear a confession about anything else. Her choice of bedmates had no bearing on my syrup-making business. Time to get back on track.

"So was this brought on by the stress of Alanza raising a ruckus next door to your place?" Felicia honked her nose delicately.

"What else would it be about?"

"I'm not sure. I've never been in your situation." I thought briefly about my mother and Lowell. What they were doing felt like they were betraying my father and he wasn't even part of the picture anymore. How could anyone do something like that to someone who was still around to be hurt by it?

"It was all Alanza's fault. For weeks all Roland could talk about was how everything we had worked for was being destroyed."

"He did seem bitter about it all."

"You don't know the half of it. It was the first thing he said every morning, the last thing he said each night, and the only topic of conversation in the hours in between."

"I can understand how you would be tempted to do something rash."

"Yes, it was very unpleasant but mostly I was worried about Roland and his heart condition. I spent all my time monitoring him for signs of a stroke. It felt like living with a time bomb." Now I was confused. It sounded like she could easily have had reason to do away with Alanza, but how did a secret rendezvous with another man help keep her husband from popping something in his brain? It sounded like she was trying to do away with him, too.

"Having an affair with Jim seems like a weird way to keep Roland from keeling over." If I was butting my nose in, I might as well go all the way.

"An affair? With Jim?" Felicia's tears turned off like the city was repairing the water main, and her shoulders began shaking even harder, but this time she was laughing.

"You did say you met with him at Loon Lodge and Roland didn't know." I felt my cheeks flushing. It wasn't as if I wanted to discuss Felicia's sex life. Or anyone else's for that matter.

"I met him in the coffee shop to talk about putting our place on the market." That explained it. Jim owned the most respected real estate brokerage in town and specialized in antique and choice properties.

"Without talking to Roland?"

"I wanted to run it past Jim first. If there wasn't enough value left in our property, then I wasn't going to mention the idea to him. If there was enough to sell up and put a hefty deposit down on another place, I was going to risk telling him."

"It doesn't seem like you told him since when I was here getting the pickles, he still seemed to think you had been at the quilting group."

"Jim said with the real estate market the way it is and the destruction Alanza was planning on Bett's Knob, we would be lucky to recoup our initial investment. There wouldn't have been enough money to start over. We would be lucky to pay off the remaining mortgage once Jim took his commission."

"So I guess it was lucky for you that Alanza died when she did."

"It certainly was. I couldn't believe our good fortune." She made it sound so unconnected with her own actions. But was it really? And did Roland really not know where she had been, or was he just playing a part that provided both of them with alibis? And even if she were telling the truth, there would still have been time for her to slip into the grange hall and poison the syrup. She'd have even more reason than ever to do so.

"Roland looks better, too."

"Oh, he is. Now he's talking about new ways to plant the garden to distract people from the view of the storage facility and even adding some things like package deals for sugar-making weekends, etc. . . . . He wanted to talk with you about it if you can ever reopen with all that's been going on." Felicia gave me a warm smile. It seemed that unburdening herself agreed with her. With so much new information heaped on my shoulders, why did I feel like I knew even less for sure than when I first started questioning her? Maybe talking with her husband about his own lies would be more enlightening.

Roland stood in the drizzle poking at a smoldering pile of brush with a long green stick. The smoky wood smell rose up and hovered in the air, an autumnal country smell if ever there was one. My stomach clenched at the idea of confronting Roland about his lie, but there was no way I was losing my business because I had been taught to respect my elders at all costs. I was sure Grandma would understand.

He looked up at me as my feet came to a stop a little distance from him. His dark canvas jacket was smeared with soot and darkened in patches by the damp. I caught sight of someone's outline in the kitchen window and waved. Even if Roland were a crazed poisoner, would he really do away with me right in front of his witness? I hoped she was squeamish or religious or something and he wouldn't dream of upsetting her. I drew a deep breath and broached the topic. In a roundabout way. I had no desire to actually accuse him of lying. Especially if he was hiding the fact he committed a murder.

"Well, what brings you by this morning?" Roland waved his big hand in front of his florid face, and I hoped the color was due to the heat of the fire and not another bout of high blood pressure. I didn't want to say anything to push him over the edge.

"I've been thinking about my business."

"That's the plight of the small business owner. You don't realize it is going to consume you entirely. There ought to be a health warning when you file papers with the state to go into business for yourself." Roland turned a bit of sizzling brush over with his stick and sparked a blaze.

"I'm sure you can imagine the news about Alanza hasn't been too helpful for a company like mine."

"Even when she's dead, that woman is still messing things up for people around here." Roland shook his head like a person who had seen too much in his time.

"I'm hoping things will get back on track for Greener Pastures just as soon as this whole mess gets cleared up about who was really responsible for putting the poison in the syrup."

"Good attitude. I hope you find a way to turn things around. A good reputation is the best thing a company can have."

"I hoped you'd say that. I have been thinking of some ways to bring people into the sugarhouse so they can see our operation firsthand and get to find out how clean and wholesome the place is, not at all the sort of place to worry about buying edibles. And that's where I thought maybe you could help."

"What is it that you need?"

"I thought since you guys are so popular at the Griddle and Fiddle, I might be able to convince your band to play at Greener Pastures at sugaring time. You guys really draw a crowd." So maybe that was stretching things just a little, but they did sound good and he would have a hard time not feeling kindly toward me after I had slathered all that butter on him.

"I don't know about drawing a huge crowd, but I like to think we are competent enough and our hearts are in the right place."

"Don't be so modest. You guys are the favorites every month at the Griddle and Fiddle. Dean tells me you even have a regular rehearsal schedule. That takes a commitment to your craft that goes above and beyond the casual players that account for most of the performers at the Stack."

"I never thought of it that way. I guess we do make it a priority more than some."

"And your efforts seem to really stick even when you don't have the chance to get together. Like last Friday night." Not the smoothest of segues but eventually I needed to get to the point or just get on home instead.

"We did practice last Friday night. We practice every Friday night."

"But not this Friday. Dean told me you canceled and so they didn't have practice." Roland stabbed the stick he was holding into the center of the smoldering pile with enough savagery that it seemed he was imagining Alanza in there somewhere toasting to a crisp.

"No. Not this Friday. And I would appreciate it if you wouldn't say anything about it to Felicia." Well, that was just getting better and better.

"I can't promise something like that until I know what you were doing instead. You had a serious bone to pick with Alanza and that was exactly when the syrup was being poisoned." Roland gave me a long look.

"You really do have the makings of a ruthless businessperson inside that diminutive package."

"Thanks, I think. So where were you?"

"At a bar."

"At a bar?" I felt sick to my stomach. Was every marriage I admired on the brink of disaster? "With another woman?"

"No. Nothing like that."

"So why can't Felicia know?"

"I've been in AA for years. We always had the plan to open an inn, but Felicia finally told me one day that she was not going to go down that road to her dream life with a guy too drunk to help. If I wanted it, I was going to have to clean up and stay that way. When I hit five years' sobriety, we celebrated by purchasing this place."

"So what were you doing at the bar?" I held my breath. I didn't think I wanted him to answer. Five years' sobriety before the inn purchase plus the six since they bought the place was a long time to toe the line. I'd hate to know he blew it.

"I was sitting in my car trying to talk myself out of going in to drown my sorrows and to forget all about Alanza."

"Did you go in?" It wasn't going to be good for his drinking or his promises to his wife, but if he had been spotted in the bar, it would at least give him an alibi for the time the syrup was being poisoned.

"I'm not proud I got so far as the parking lot, but I am proud to say I got no farther. I stayed in my truck deciding what to do until closing time."

"So you were in the parking lot until around one a.m.?"

"I was. Then I dragged my sorry self home and snuck into bed next to Felicia and tossed and turned all night long." At least that's what he said he did. There were a few hours between then and the time the breakfast started to slip into the grange hall and poison the syrup. And like almost everyone else in town, Roland had a key to the place.

"Well, that explains why you looked so beat the next morning at the pancake breakfast." At least, it could explain it.

"It explains my performance, too. I'm gonna beat your grandfather some year if it is the last thing I do." Roland nodded his head like he needed convincing. Which everyone would. Grampa was a force of nature when it came to pancakes.

Eighteen

Since it was just next door to Roland and Felicia's inn, I decided to poke around at Alanza's property. It was silent when I pulled in and stepped out of the car. Even the birds and squirrels seemed to be giving the place a miss. I wasn't sure if it was a sort of commentary on Alanza herself and the energy she had put forth while living there, or even the natural world's commentary on storage facilities. The squat little office building for the storage facility was set back enough to obscure it from sight of passersby out on the road.

If someone was going to kill Alanza, I wondered why he or she decided to do it in such a public fashion. Why not just sneak out here and clunk her over the head in the middle of the night? Why would someone need to implicate my business in their beef with her? Was Alanza even the intended victim or was Greener Pastures? Maybe she was just someone easy to dispose of because of her unpopularity in the community. No one would miss her and she was doing her best to cause problems.

But what reason would anyone have to bother Greener Pastures? I didn't think I had any enemies particularly, but maybe I was being shortsighted. Knowlton had been chasing me for so long, it was a town-wide joke. Maybe he was tired of being mocked and tired of being rejected. And Tansey wasn't any too happy with me either. As far as she was concerned, I had missed the boat by passing up what her darling son had to offer. She also might have blamed me for another sugaring operation starting up in Sugar Grove.

I thought about Lowell and whether or not he had considered the possibility that killing Alanza with Greener Pastures syrup was much more deliberate than I had first thought. I would have asked him about it, but since I was avoiding him like I avoided people with the stomach flu, I couldn't very well do that.

I rounded the corner of the building and spotted Jill Hayes pulling a box out of her jeep. In the bright clear light of day it was still possible to make out her bruising under a heavy cover of makeup. I called out to her and she dropped the box on the ground, spilling most of the contents.

"You scared me half to death." Jill and I both squatted down at the same time to retrieve the scattered tree-tapping supplies, and we smacked heads. Now I was going to have a bruise.

"Sorry. I'm glad to see you out and about. Are you feeling better?"

"I was until you banged heads with me. What are you doing here?" I had to think fast. Then I thought of the perfect excuse.

"I lent Alanza a book about sugar making and I thought she might have left it here. I wanted to get it back before whoever inherits starts clearing out the place."

"Good idea. Once that happens, you probably won't see it again," Jill said.

"So what brings you by?" Jill had no better reason to be there than I did.

"I was just checking on some of the equipment I had here for tapping the trees. You know how busy it gets during sugaring season."

"It looks like you were bringing supplies in, not checking on what was already here." I handed her a spile. She blushed and took it.

"I guess I don't know if I'm coming or going lately."

"That would explain the problem with your story about being at Hanley's camp Friday night."

"What do you mean?" Jill stood, the box forgotten on the ground.

"Knowlton says you weren't with Hanley on Friday night like you said you were. He said no one was up there at all."

"Knowlton is a fruitcake who talks to a stuffed woodchuck when he's looking for some company."

"He may be an eccentric but he doesn't tend to lie." Except for all that stuff he said about me and the contortionism to anyone in the world of taxidermy who would listen.

"What did Hanley say?" Jill gave me the same cornered but still fighting look my niece and nephew do when they're trying to wriggle out of trouble and it isn't looking good for them. Even though I hadn't asked him about it yet after speaking with Knowlton, it was time to see what she thought of their relationship.

"What do you think he said?" I watched her shoulders sag and the brave leaked all out of her.

"I think he said I was with him at first and then he told you the truth the minute you applied any pressure."

"Well, if he is willing to hit you, I don't think the relationship is all that good, do you?"

"He didn't hit me. I lied when you came to see me that day."

"You aren't going to tell me you walked into a door, are you?"

"It was someone else." Jill started to speak then stopped herself.

"Did another man hit you? It wasn't your brother, was it?" Suddenly I feared for Piper's safety. She might do a lot of things that felt unsafe to me, but she had never put up with an abusive man and I didn't want to even consider the possibility that she could start.

"It was Alanza." Jill sagged against the wall as if the weight of her secret had thrust her off her feet.

"Alanza hit you? Why?" The idea of a physical altercation between grown women in a civilized town was so tacky it nauseated me. It had been hard enough to think about Hanley using his fists on Jill, but to credit the damage to another woman was hard to wrap my mind around.

"It was about the trees."

"The trees?"

"Lewis Bett had allowed me to tap the trees here for years since my own property isn't big enough to produce the amount of sap I need to run a thriving business."

"How does that lead to Alanza giving you a black eye?"

"As soon as Alanza decided to go into the sugaring business herself, she didn't want anyone else to tap her trees. I reminded her I had a long-standing arrangement with Lewis and that he had promised me when he died it would still stand. He wanted the property to go on being an asset to the community."

"What did Alanza say to that?"

"She said a whole lot of things were going to change on the property and that the townspeople ought to get used to it. I wasn't the only one who would be affected and I should grow up about it." I could relate to that conversation. It sounded like Celadon had been taking interpersonal relationship lessons from Alanza.

"That sounds threatening." And like a reason someone might decide to get rid of her before she did any more damage to his or her interest in the property. "But you still haven't explained the black eye."

"I shoved her. She was right in my face, shaking her finger at me and calling me names. I snapped and I put both hands on her chest and shoved her into one of the very trees she didn't want me to tap anymore." Jill started panting a little, like she was reliving the experience.

"And then?"

"And then she hauled off and decked me. She knocked me right off my feet. My eye started to swell shut and my ears were ringing. I'd never experienced anything like it."

"Why didn't you go to the police?" Lowell was forever being called out to domestic incidents. As a matter of fact, in the annual town report the police log listed four times as many domestic disturbance calls as any other single category.

"I started it. She could have pressed charges against me, too. It was ugly and embarrassing. And I hoped it would all blow over. It wasn't likely she would change her mind about me tapping the trees if I set the police on her."

"Is that the real reason why you weren't at the pancake breakfast?"

"I didn't want to show up with my face all swollen and I certainly didn't want to run into Alanza." But was Jill telling the truth now? It sounded too far-fetched and embarrassing to be made up, but she had lied in the first place about Hanley hitting her.

"So this happened on Friday night when you told me you were with Hanley at his camp?"

"That's right. I had been planning on going up with Hanley that night, but he said since Alanza had closed her property to use by off-road vehicles, it wasn't worth it to go up." So neither of them had an alibi for the night the syrup was poisoned. Where was he if he wasn't with Jill or Connie and he wasn't up at his camp? And was Jill so angry with Alanza, she went to the grange and poisoned the syrup to get back at her for the fight and to regain the use of the trees? She wasn't actually around to see the death, which made her look all the more suspicious to me. As much as I hated the idea, I was going to have to talk to Hanley again and try to worm out of him what he was up to.

Hanley was standing over a fallen tree, cutting it into stove-length pieces, when I arrived home. Sawdust covered his lucky plaid shirt like snowfall. I wasn't looking forward to asking Hanley where he really was on Friday night. Asking him while he was wielding a chain saw was even less appealing. But it had to be done. And besides, Grampa was in the nearby barn kitting out the reindeer in his herd with their seasonal bells. He'd be sure to come running if I started squawking.

Hanley noticed me standing nearby but made me wait fifteen minutes while he finished up. I would have given him grief about it, but I figured calling him a liar was going to be enough punishment. Once the sawdust finally stopped raining down, I stepped up to the task at hand without preamble.

"Jill says you weren't with her on Friday night, and Connie mentioned you weren't home either." There, I'd said it and I lived to tell the story. I did keep one eye on Hanley and the other on the barn.

"You sure are a snoopy little thing, aren't you?" Hanley used the chain saw like a pointer and gestured in my direction. I was so glad the thing was no longer running, I felt more emboldened than frightened.

"That's why I'm asking you again where you were and I'm hoping you tell me the truth this time."

"You're not my wife. As long as I show up and do the work I say I'll do, what's it to you?"

"If my business goes under because it looks like I poisoned people with my syrup, I won't have any more work for you to do. So I guess it's more about what it means to you."

"Syrup making or not, this is still a tree farm, and unless I missed some sort of memo, your grandfather is still in charge of who works on it." Hanley spat a big gob of something awful within an inch of my favorite work boots.

"Right you are. And my grandfather only hires people he wants to have around. He isn't a fan of liars or men that cheat on their wives. I'd hate to have to disillusion him about you." I batted my eyelashes at Hanley and shrugged. From the way he scowled at me and tossed a perfectly good chain saw on the ground like a toddler having a tantrum, I'd say we had come to an understanding.

"I was up at Alanza's tinkering with my equipment."

"What does that mean?"

"I was sabotaging my heavy machinery."

"You were doing what?" How could that be? Sure, he had just mistreated his saw but generally Hanley was meticulous concerning his tools.

"Have you seen the clearing I've already done near the storage facility?"

"Yes. I saw it when I was up at Roland's the other day. It looks ghastly."

"So you know why I had to do a little damage that would stop the clearing up at Bett's Knob but would still be easy to fix once I'd managed to get Alanza to change her mind."

"Why did you sign on to do the work in the first place if you didn't agree with it?"

"Alanza was one of my biggest clients, just like Lewis Bett before her. If I refused, she would have fired me and given the contract to someone else. With the economy being as bad as it is, I needed the business." I could see that. At Greener Pastures we were still hiring Hanley whenever we needed him, but someone in different financial circumstances might look on forestry services as a luxury expense.

"If you were up there, did you see Jill and Alanza having a fight?" Maybe he and Jill could still give each other an alibi.

"I heard a bit of a ruckus, but it wasn't like I was going to investigate. I didn't want Alanza to know I was there."

"What made you think you were going to be able to change Alanza's mind about clearing Bett's Knob?"

"She had a sweet spot for me." Hanley widened his stance and patted his oil drum gut. Which was exactly what Tansey had told me.

"Sweet enough that she'd give up her business plans? I doubt it."

"Maybe not, but I figured if I put her off long enough, the snow would fly and the project would get stalled. I was kind of hoping she would lose interest over the winter and the whole thing would just fizzle." Or maybe he knew she wasn't going to be around long enough to order him to complete the work on Bett's Knob.

"I guess you got your wish then. Alanza's plans are about as fizzled as they could get."

Nineteen

I decided rather than enduring the awkwardness of dinner with my family, I would go to the Stack for my evening meal. I hadn't gotten more than a couple miles down the road when I heard a thumping coming from underneath the car. Praying I'd run over a branch and was dragging it, I pulled over and got out to investigate. Using the little flashlight attached to my key chain to get a better look, I knelt at the back of the car searching for the source of the noise. No branches were caught up in the underpinnings of the vehicle, but there was a piece of metal hanging down that seemed closer to the front of the car. I stood and made my way around to get a better look.

I reached with the flashlight as far as I could, trying to see what was the matter. My arm felt like it slid out of the socket and still I couldn't get a good view. I turned my head, trying to flatten myself enough to slither farther between the lumpy ground and the underside of the car. My legs were still sticking out the end when I caught sight of someone else's legs. And feet. But most important, claws. Running toward me. Wrinkled, gray-tan bird legs with a long, long claw on the end of each toe.

I dropped the flashlight and wriggled backward as fast as I could. Jumping to my feet, I saw what looked like an ostrich wearing a dinosaur costume. Black glossy feathers draped like an old lady's shawl over its bulbous body. Its royal blue and red head had a bony ridge on the top. It towered above me. The thing must have been six feet and probably outweighed me by quite a bit, too. Although to be fair, so do a lot of family dogs. The bird hissed like a Gila monster and began to run in my direction. My mind went blank, my legs lost function, and I simply watched as it bore down on me. I still don't know what snapped me into action, but I was grateful my reptilian brain made the decision for flight, not fight, without consulting the rest of me.

I whipped round the side of the car, keeping the tiny vehicle between us. I made a grab for the passenger door but found it locked. The bird rounded the front of the vehicle and I made it to the back, then the driver's side. I jerked the door open, slammed it shut behind me, and sat trembling.

I reached into my pocket for my keys but found nothing. I tried the other jacket pocket, then each pocket in my jeans, all the while keeping an eye on the bird tapping at the glass with its beak. That was when I remembered dropping the flashlight with the keys attached under the car, outside, where the bird was. I lunged for my purse

Jessie Crockett

and dug out my cell phone. Desperate times called for desperate measures.

"Officer Paterson speaking."

"It's Dani Greene. I'm out on County Road and I think I've spotted one of the animals you are looking for."

"Thanks for calling, exotics whisperer. Which one have you seen?" He sounded friendly and eager for information this time instead of superior and condescending. It was miraculous how much more attractive that made him seem. I felt a shivery little tickle on my neck on the same side I was cradling the phone.

"It's a really big bird. Like a black-and-blue ostrich."

"You haven't stopped, have you?" I heard a note of anxiety in Graham's voice. My stomach dropped low enough to operate the clutch.

"I'm pulled over on the side of the road. I don't make calls while driving. As a police officer, you ought to know how dangerous that is." Typical. I can't tell you how many times I've seen Mitch yakking on his phone as he blew past me on the highway.

"Has it spotted you yet?" Again, I heard the worry. It came through like a physical caress, only not so pleasant. And what about this guy made me think of caresses in the first place?

"It has."

"Dani, you've got no business messing with cassowaries."

"I thought the point of you asking for community involvement was that we spot them and call you."

"The point is you shouldn't stop for cassowaries. Even

the Australian government websites say so. They're very aggressive when provoked and they take gawking as provocation." I looked over at the bird, which was circling the car. It looked bigger all the time.

"Where are you?" The anxiety in my voice was more than a match for Graham's.

"Two minutes away, three at most, according to my GPS. Whatever you do, don't get out of the vehicle." Graham hung up and I sat huddled in the seat humming "Amazing Grace" when the bird stopped at the driver's side window, its long-lashed eye cocked inside searching around like a beat cop at lover's lane. If only the thing had a flashlight and a patrol hat, the picture would have been complete. I took a deep breath and told myself there was no way it was getting inside. And that, of course, was when things took a turn for the worse. Like a scene from a low-budget martial arts movie, the creature lifted one foot off the ground. Balancing on the other, it flashed a claw at me the likes of which I have never seen. Its foot held three toes and the middle one had a built-in dagger. It waggled it at me like we were in a production of *West Side Story*. My heart hammered around and I suddenly needed to pee worse than I had since that time in the third grade when the neighbor's Doberman chased me up a tree and no one noticed I was missing until suppertime.

It raked down the window with the claw. The sound wasn't exactly like the noise of fingernails on a chalkboard but it was close and much more frightening. The bird didn't stop with the window, though. When it got to the metal of the door, I actually heard it rip.

I leaned away from the door as far as I could, wondering why I never drove the minivan until I remembered I didn't have any kids and now probably never would. The bird didn't give any sign that the door had injured it in any way. It lifted its foot again and began another pass down the side of the car. I was beginning to take the attack personally when the thought occurred to me that I had no idea what the thing wanted in for. Was it a carnivore? It hissed and slashed some more and I felt like I was in a science fiction novel that was not going to end well for me, one where the island inhabitants wall themselves up in a city to avoid the perils of the giant beasts beyond. I was worried for my safety but I was also angry about my car. It was a classic before the bird decided to open it like a can of kippered snacks.

The bird reached the bottom of the door and I watched with relief as it moved away. Now if it would just wander back into the woods, I would risk retrieving the keys and keep driving no matter how much the exhaust system dragged on the ground. That was when things started to get really bad. The bird leaned down and began to investigate the tires. There was some tapping and thumping and then a bang and a hiss. I felt the car settle lower on one side as the air leaked out of a tire.

Instead of scaring the thing off, the popping noise startled it into even more aggressive action. It jumped onto the hood of the car, offering an even better view of its clawed feet. With a striding, leaping motion, it disappeared from view and the entire car shook as it landed with a thud on the convertible's soft top. I heard the ripping before I saw the claw coming through the fabric.

I was bent low in the seat when I heard a horn blaring over the sound of the tearing fabric. I looked through the gap in the steering wheel and spotted Graham's state-issued truck racing into view. He parked a hundred or so feet away and slid out on the passenger side. He busied himself with something in the back of the vehicle then headed toward me carrying a rake. As he drew closer, I could see it was missing a bunch of tines, like it had been under a running lawn mower. He held the rake aloft like a king's standard bearer and advanced toward me at a steady pace.

I wasn't sure where to look, up at the claw coming down toward my head or out at Graham. Soon enough, I didn't need to choose. The ripping noise ceased and the claw pulled back out of the fabric. I could see through to the sky. As suddenly as it had jumped on, the bird took a flying leap off the roof of the car and began running toward Graham. He stopped moving forward but he didn't back off. He just stood there bobbing the rake up and down like a picketer at a demonstration. I'm not sure what Graham had hoped it would do for him, but whatever it was didn't seem to be working. The bird was bearing down on him steadily, determinedly hissing and opening and closing its beak.

I didn't want to attract it back in my direction, but I didn't see what choice there was. I laid on my own horn and kept at it in staccato bursts. The bird appeared disoriented. It dashed back toward me and then raced once more toward Graham. It shot past him and began pacing near his truck. Suddenly, out of the woods emerged a second bird, even bigger than the first. It joined the first bird and they appeared engrossed in each other.

Graham took advantage of the birds' short attention span and ran toward me, not even keeping his eye on them. He just pelted along like he was training for the Olympics. If the U.S. teams added these birds to their training regimens, we would probably bring home an even larger array of glittering medals.

He paused next to the MG long enough to notice the flat tire, pop open the door, and grab me by the hand.

"Is there anywhere nearby we can take shelter?" he asked as he dragged me along behind him.

"Tansey's place is just over the rise a little ways. She has an outbuilding Knowlton uses for his taxidermy at the edge of the property. Tansey doesn't like the dead animals so close to the house."

"How long to get there?"

"Three minutes, if we hurry."

"Oh, we're going to hurry." Graham picked up his pace and I was almost dragged off my feet. His legs had to have been twice as long as mine the way he was moving. I wished I had taken time for a snack in the afternoon because my energy levels had been flagging even before the cassowaries showed up. Now I was running on pure adrenaline.

"What will happen if they catch up with us?" I didn't think I wanted to know the answer, but the question blurted out before I could stop myself.

"Have you seen *Jurassic Park*?"

"Enough said." I broke into a jog and then turned on the turbo. What I lack in stride, I make up for in a willingness to try harder. We ran the whole way to the little shed. Fortunately, few people in Sugar Grove worry about locking their outbuildings. Many don't even lock their houses. Graham pushed open the door and shoved me through it. I stood there looking around at all manner of dead creatures in various poses before I could catch my breath. The place smelled of skunk. It made me wish I were still out in the open air even if it meant I was running from those feathered dinosaurs.

Graham was tipping his cell phone this way and that trying to pick up a signal. Despite the smell filling my nostrils, I was so hungry I peeked around for something to eat. Knowlton's workshop seemed like he had stolen the space. His taxidermy tools were clean and laid out on a workbench in an orderly fashion. The rest of the shed looked like a purgatory of delayed decisions. Ice skates with broken blades, belts with missing buckles, rusty handsaws with missing teeth heaped up in piles and leaned against the walls.

Here and there among the mess a perfectly preserved creature struck a pose. From the top of a stack of plastic milk crates a stuffed raven prepared to swoop down on me. A bobcat crouched between a wicker chair with a busted seat and a child's wagon. A coiled snake wrapped convincingly around a chunk of granite on the floor in the corner. It was so realistic I could have sworn I saw it twitch just a little.

My eyes roamed the room for a box of crackers, a sleeve of fig bars, a slightly withered apple, anything that would slake my hunger. I lifted plastic bags left from a defunct discount store, balls of grubby used string, and cans of greasy bolts and washers. Graham startled me with his voice just as I was yanking open a metal cabinet door.

"Do you remember the name of the poison that killed Alanza?" I looked at him, trying to determine why he would ask such a thing. He was stooped over a metal toolbox, the large red kind on wheels. One of the drawers was opened and he gestured at something in it. I stepped over to look.

"It was called Compound 1080, I think. It has another name, too. Like flouro something. A pesticide and rat poison was what Lowell said."

"Could it be called fluoroacetate 1080?"

"I'm pretty sure that was it." I started to pick up the box he pointed at, but he shot out his arm and circled my wrist with strong fingers.

"Don't touch it."

"Why not?"

"Because Lowell said a few salt-sized particles of this stuff were enough to kill a fully grown woman and that means it would be twice the amount needed to kill you." I shrank back. If Graham hadn't been there to remind me, I would surely have picked it up. Even if just handling it hadn't killed me, it might have if I had found something to eat and wasn't able to wash first. Which given the amenities in the shed, I wouldn't have been. With the way my stomach was growling, I wouldn't have stood on the formalities.

"Thanks. I was foolish."

"Just enthusiastic. Besides, you wouldn't want your fingerprints found on what might have been used to kill Alanza."

"You think this is the actual poison used to kill her?"

"It is the same sort. Since it isn't a commonly used murder weapon, I'd say that ups the chances considerably."

"You don't think Knowlton killed her, do you?"

"Someone killed her, this is the sort of poison that was used, and this building was not locked when we arrived. How many people in town would have known this wouldn't be locked?"

"A lot probably knew and anyone would have guessed. People just don't bother with locks on outbuildings, especially not those filled with stuff they'd just as soon see get stolen."

"Which makes this serious."

"But there is no saying the poison even belonged to Tansey or Knowlton in the first place. Anyone who knew it was open could have snuck it in here and left it where it would look like it belonged to the Pringles." I was feeling hot and then cold and all over shaky. If someone like Tansey could kill a person, then probably anyone could. I felt like someone had snatched my rose-colored glasses off my face and stomped on them with steel-toed boots right in front of my stinging eyes.

"We need to call Lowell."

"I'm not speaking to Lowell."

"Well, I am, and as soon as I can get a signal, I'm calling him. Stay away from that box, and for God's sake don't eat anything you find in here. We've got no idea if any of that stuff has gotten spread around." Graham resumed his lift-and-check dance with his cell phone and I stood in the corner looking out the nearest window. In the distance, with the light fading as fast as it was, it was hard to say for sure but I thought I saw two large birds slipping off through the trees. Graham began to speak in that peculiar telephone call tone people use when talking to those they do not know well. "He says they'll send someone out right away."

"Did you ask them to bring snacks?" My body felt like it was experiencing an earthquake the way I was shaking from all the stomach growling.

"It wasn't the thing most on my mind. Besides, how could you even consider eating with the smell around here?"

"Police officers are always shown on television standing around dropping doughnut crumbs on battered corpses. Should you really be so dainty about a bit of a skunk?"

"Do you believe everything you see on television?"

"Not what I see on the news, but I do have a soft spot for those alien abduction shows."

"That explains the mountain lion sighting. I bet you like crop circles, too."

"If my sugaring business goes bust, I may start a new business laying out fake circles in the far pasture. There can be a swift trade in such things."

"Should I worry your mountain lion sighting was merely crass commercialism at work?"

"Of course not."

"Good. Because that would count as wasting police time and then I would have to arrest you." Graham took a step closer, his eyes locked on mine, a slight smile curving his already curvy lips.

"You'd have to catch me first."

"Are you saying I can't?"

"Not to burst your bubble, but so far the only things you've caught in Sugar Grove are the ones I've helped with." I crossed my arms over my sadly flat chest and wondered what he'd make of that. I felt a little bad reminding him how little he'd gotten done on his own steam, but he was the one who'd mentioned arresting me.

"As a keen observer of animal behavior, I'd say you're helping me to catch you. Right now, your pupils are slightly dilated and you're using your arms across your chest pushing things up and showing them off to best advantage." Graham wiggled his eyebrows at me like an old-time movie bad guy. If I didn't get out of here soon, I expected to be tied to a train track for not paying my mortgage. All he needed was a mustache to twirl and the image would be complete.

Luckily, the police arrived before I had to think of a response. I never expected to be happy to see Mitch, but for once, I welcomed him with enough enthusiasm to surprise the both of us.

Twenty

I was in the office at the sugarhouse the next morning trying to pretend I still had a business to attend to when the call from Myra about the fertilizer came in. After having spent a couple of hours kidding myself it was going to matter what I planned to order to stock the shop, it was a relief to have any sort of distraction.

"Zip. That's what I got from all my digging around." Myra exhaled forcefully then coughed. She must have been calling me during a smoke break. I imagined her leaning her stretch pants covered backside against the peeling clapboards of the old wooden police station, flicking ash close enough to worry the fire department.

"No one knows anything. How can that be?" I was astonished. Myra never failed to turn up the dirt on anything she set her mind to finding. She was like a human truffle pig when it came to delicious nuggets of knowledge. The only way I could imagine her not finding what she was looking for was because it didn't exist. Or maybe the only people who knew about it had a very compelling reason to keep quiet. But why would anyone want to keep quiet about his or her business? I yakked about mine to everyone in my path. I paid for advertising and conducted free talks anywhere that would have me just to get the word out about Greener Pastures.

"What I'm wondering is if your guy at the state was wrong. Maybe he remembered the name incorrectly. Or maybe he is just messing with you."

"He wrote the name down when the call came in and read it back to me so I don't think he got it wrong. And what possible reason would he have to make something like that up? He volunteered the information."

"Maybe Alanza lied to him when she called. You never knew what that woman was up to or why, but you knew it was to stir up trouble for someone."

"What could she gain from lying about an unregistered fertilizer business?" It didn't seem worth her bother.

"I'm going to mention this to Lowell."

"But I thought you hadn't discovered anything."

"Dani, if someone doesn't want anyone to know they are making or selling fertilizer, what might that mean?" Myra's voice had taken on a worried note I never associate with her. She is bossy, pushy, brash, and nosy but never worried. My stomach got squishy and my legs felt like the bones had turned into licorice whips as I understood what she was implying.

"Explosives."

"Exactly."

Jessie Crockett

* * *

I drove to Tansey's hoping to hear how things had gone with the
police questioning her and Knowlton about the rat poison
in her shed. She was sitting on her porch, her feet in her
usual gardening boots, a cat in her lap. Her greeting felt
more forced than usual and I can't say I blamed her.

"How's Knowlton?" I asked. With Tansey there is no
need to bother with the usual niceties. She's content to get
to the point and respects others who do the same. Tansey
and small talk mix about as freely as church deacons and
biker gangs.

"Tired and upset, no thanks to you and the guy trying
to replace him in your affections." For such a practical
woman, she had a blind spot the size of the Atlantic when
it came to her son and me.

"Did you want us getting killed by a giant angry bird?"

"How you manage to fit so much bull pucky into such
a small package, I will never know." Tansey stroked the
cat harder and harder until the poor thing's eyes bugged
out of its head and it squirmed to the ground in a well-
timed act of self-preservation.

"You run into a couple of them as night approaches
and then let me know how scary they are. Besides, I didn't
find the rat poison and I didn't call the police about it
either."

"So you didn't turn your back coldly on your one true
love?"

"I didn't say anything approaching that. I said I didn't
rat you guys out to the police for having some old

chemicals in your shed. For all I knew, they weren't even yours."

"They were ours, all right. When the studies came out about how dangerous that stuff was, I stopped using it around the farm. But you know how it is; you plan to get to the hazardous waste day at the dump but something always comes up and you don't get there. So it has sat, along with all sorts of other junk in the shed, until I finally get around to it. It's been kicking around so long I didn't really remember it was there until Lowell came to ask us about it."

"But Knowlton must have seen it since he spends so much time in that building."

"Knowlton only has eyes for his mother, animals he might want to stuff, and you Greene girls. Nothing else matters to him. He still doesn't even notice when his teeth need brushing." She said that like it was something that would have escaped my attention. Knowlton's lack of personal grooming was among the chief reasons he was more popular with dead animals than live people.

"Are the police just questioning him or did they arrest him?"

"They asked him questions for about an hour last night and then turned him loose. The poor thing was so upset he didn't even go out looking for roadkill." He must have been rattled. Gale force winds, nor'easters, and hailstones the size of biscuits never kept Knowlton from roaming around at night. Which was another reason he hadn't snagged a girlfriend. Women in New Hampshire like their men to stick around at night if for no other reason than to take the chill off the sheets. Nights are too cold here to spend them all alone. I know from too much experience.

"Did they question you, too?"

"Of course they did. There were enough questions here to have fueled a television game show. They even got around to asking some fool thing about fertilizers."

"Best Bett All in One?" I asked, thinking Myra had made good on her decision to tell Lowell what she knew.

"That's the one. Lowell wanted to know if I had ever heard of anyone producing or even buying a product with that name. I told him the same thing I said to Lewis Bett when he asked me about the trust; I was only connected to the Betts by marriage and their business was not really mine." Tansey crossed one grubby jean-clad leg over the other and stared off into space like she was remembering something.

"Lewis Bett asked you about a trust?" You know that buzzy feeling you get when you are starting to pick up a thread on an idea? I was buzzing like a bunch of wasps had started construction on a paper nest inside my head.

"He did indeed. Several years ago, when he was getting on and feeling his mortality, he asked me if I would serve as a trustee for his estate. He said he liked the way I took care of my own land and he felt I would do a good job helping to protect his."

"But you refused?"

"I did. The whole thing sounded a lot more complicated than I really wanted to be involved in. Something about a living will and assets and making sure things all stayed like they were even if the people he left the place to wanted to make changes. I told him he ought to talk to someone related by blood, not by marriage, but really it just seemed like about as much fun as pulling burrs off a poodle."

"So who did he ask?"

"First I suggested Myra but he said she had a big mouth so I suggested Felicia. I didn't really want to talk about it again in case he had trouble finding someone so I never asked if she said yes. You'd have to ask her."

Which was exactly what I decided to do.

I caught up with Felicia just outside the post office. Her arms were full of parcels and I caught one on its way to the pavement. As I helped her load them into the car, I noticed they all were marked with the return address *Grow Right Garden Supply Company*. What was she doing with something like that at this time of year? The ground had frozen up enough that there was no way she was planting perennials or bulbs outside, and it was a bit early for most people to have placed their seed orders. Besides, there would have been enough seeds in the boxes to plant a good-sized Midwestern commercial farm. Roland and Felicia were enthusiastic gardeners, but they only had just so much room around their place and it was mostly planted with low-maintenance trees, shrubs, and flowering groundcovers. Rather than question her about that, though, I decided my priorities lay elsewhere so I took advantage of her gratitude and started in asking about Lewis Bett's trust fund.

"He did ask me. It's been a while, though."

"Did you say yes?"

"I thought about it long and hard. Lewis was a distant relative and a nice old man. But in the end, I turned him down."

"Why?"

"We had just bought the bed-and-breakfast, and as Roland put it, if we weren't close enough family to leave the place to, then why were we close enough to be responsible for it? In the end, I agreed with Roland that it was more responsibility than I wanted to take on."

"Do you know who did?"

"I suggested Connie. She is related in some sort of shirttail way to the Bett family and she used to do a great job with our books so I knew she had more experience with that sort of thing than I did. I suggested she might be an ideal candidate for the job." Felicia slammed her lid down on her trunk.

"Do you know if she accepted?"

"She did. When Alanza first got to town, Connie introduced me as another member of the family, and when I asked how they had met, Alanza told me Connie was a trustee of the trust fund."

"Do you think Lewis Bett is rolling over in his grave after what Alanza did to his property?"

"I wondered about that. When all the trouble with Alanza started, I went to Connie and asked her about what the trust covered and if she could stop Alanza."

"And?"

"She said if I had wanted to be the one to deal with the trust, I should have said yes when Lewis asked me.

She told me her hands were tied and she wasn't about to discuss the terms of something so private with me."

"I noticed some coolness between the two of you at the pancake breakfast."

"I told her after Alanza announced her plans to put in the storage facility that I regretted suggesting her to Lewis, and if that was the way she was going to handle things, I would get someone else to do our books." That couldn't have been good news for Connie. Roland's position as the president of the Chamber of Commerce might cause others to reconsider keeping Connie on as their bookkeeper if he fired her. Roland and Felicia were well liked and well respected. I felt like every time I got one question answered, it brought another three or four to mind. Finding out more about trusts seemed like the next step. Fortunately, I knew just who to ask.

Whenever Loden wasn't taking long rambles through the sugar bush or visiting the local library, he could be found in his train room. With a house as large as ours, with as many different people in charge of remodeling over the years, there were always unfortunate outcroppings of bad taste. Loden's train room took up what the rest of the family considered to be a home unimprovement. Verdant Greene, arguably the looniest of us all, had stuck a leaking little wart of a thing onto the back of the house in 1923. He built the pyramid-shaped structure as a tribute to the discovery of King Tut's tomb and had covered the entire thing with galvanized tin. It overheated in summer and encouraged frostbite in winter, as he hadn't wanted anything as utilitarian as windows or a heat source to mar the effect of his creation.

Loden claimed the space as his own almost as soon as he could walk, and rare was the day he was not found in it for at least an hour or two. Personally, I think that might go a long way in explaining why he's still not married either. I knocked, and upon hearing permission to enter, I tugged open the door and began wriggling through the opening. What met me on the other side of the birth canal of a hallway was not the golden splendor of Tut's hoard but a wonderment of another sort.

Loden is a model train enthusiast whose dedication to his hobby borders on obsession. What most of the family does with Christmas, he does with trains. He's handcrafted most of the buildings and the land formations, too. No one can make tiny trees look as realistic as Loden can, and his miniature stone walls are so convincing, I always expect a rock adder to slide out from one of the cracks and hiss at me. In a rare moment of self-revelation, Loden once confided that the hardest part of law school for him was being too busy to work on his models. But for my purposes that day, his law school experience was exactly what I needed. Unfortunately Loden also has a fine set of principles so getting the information from him was going to take a bit of blackmail.

"I thought you weren't talking to me."

"You didn't think you should tell me about Mom and Lowell?"

"No, I didn't. You reacted exactly like everyone expected. Which is why no one wanted to tell you."

"Tell me what any of you have gained by keeping this from me."

"I guess that's a good question. Looking at it that way, I don't suppose there was anything improved by that."

"Well, that's something, at least. It's more than anyone else will admit. I'm the bad guy because I loved my father and don't enjoy my family keeping secrets from me."

"How can I make it up to you?"

"You can't."

"That's not fair."

"You're a lawyer; you understand how little fair matters anytime there is a disagreement."

"So what can I do to get back on your good side?"

"As a lawyer, what would you suggest?"

"Compensation for pain and suffering."

"So I should ask for something I want in order to forgive you?"

"That's right. Ask for something much more valuable than you expect to receive and bargain down from there." He flicked an imaginary speck of something off a miniature picnic table.

"Ask Piper to marry you."

"What?" His finger bore down on the table and snapped it in two.

"Since the family is running around airing out hidden depths of emotion, I thought it was time to mention you have been in love with Piper since the first time I brought her home after school and she liked what you did with this place." I waved my hand around the pyramid.

"You can't be serious."

"You said aim high and work down from there. How about a tempestuous weekend fling?"

"Dani."

"Then I want you to ask her out on one date."

"Why now?"

"I don't like her latest boyfriend. I'm worried she's going to start thinking about settling down. If she is going to settle, I would rather it was for you."

"Thanks."

"Not that she would be. Settling, I mean. You are a great catch. I just hate seeing you shrivel up like a slug hit with table salt whenever you spot her zipping around town in another guy's car."

"Are you saying you want your friend to settle for a disintegrated slug?"

"You know I'm not. I think she keeps picking losers because in her heart of hearts she doesn't want things to work out with them since she is secretly waiting for you to pursue her. You've got to be the only man in town under seventy not trying to get her to give them a private tour of what's beneath her waitress uniform." Loden blushed so deeply it was like a beautiful sunset was taking place right across his face.

"I can't."

"Okay, then you'll have to tell me what you know about trusts instead," I said, watching him put the finishing touches on a covered bridge.

"You mean like a legal thing?" He gently put down the paintbrush he was holding and gave me his full attention.

"Yes. What are they exactly and why would someone have one?"

"The reasons for creating a trust are about as varied as the people who create them. There are a number of different types. One of the most important details is whether the trust is revocable or irrevocable."

"I assume one is permanent and the other is subject to change?"

"That's right. Once a trust is irrevocable, it is no longer possible to get the entrusted property out of it. Why are you asking?"

"Lewis Bett left his property in trust."

"I know. He consulted me on it." Loden didn't have an active legal practice, but he was a member of the New Hampshire Bar and he happily took pro bono cases that interested him from time to time.

"What did he say?"

"You know I can't tell you that. I shouldn't even have told you he consulted me about a trust."

"Then I'm not forgiving you. Your choice."

"You drive a hard bargain."

"You know how I like to get my Christmas shopping done early, and I want to know whether or not to keep you on my list. Besides, Lewis is dead and so is Alanza. You don't have a client in this situation at all, and my business is flapping all over the riverbank gasping for a bit of air."

"Since you put it that way, I guess a bit of information

won't do any harm. Lewis Bett came to me several years ago to ask about setting up a trust for his property. He wanted to leave it to a family member, but he didn't want them to be able to run through all the money in a hurry. He wanted them to be able to leave the bulk of the wealth to the next generation."

"He was a well-known cheapskate."

"He preferred to be called thrifty. He said he had seen too many people go through their money buying any bit of glitz that caught their eyes."

"Didn't he have a very expensive wife at one point? A much younger wife?"

"He did. Alanza's mother was her sister."

"So Alanza wasn't really even a Bett?"

"Not by blood. But he wasn't particularly keen on any of the blood relatives he knew around here. He said they weren't willing to help out with the property so he didn't feel obliged to leave any of it to them."

"So Alanza was the one he thought of."

"Yes. But he wanted the trust set up in case the spend-thrift nature of her aunt was a genetic thing. So that's what we set up, a spendthrift trust."

"So it wasn't a land trust?"

"Not at all. I tried to convince him a land trust would be the best thing for everyone since he valued community use of his property, but he wouldn't hear of it. For him, tying up the money was his main priority."

"So how did it work?"

"He appointed a trustee and all access to funds associated with the trust went through her."

"So Alanza couldn't get her hands directly on any of Lewis's money?"

"No. We set up a small stipend for Alanza per month in addition to the use of the house. Everything else had to be approved and authorized by Connie."

"Why Connie?"

"She was a relative of sorts and had been doing the books for Lewis for years. She was the one who informed him of how far Alanza's aunt was driving him into the ground. And Hanley worked his property as the arborist so the two families were quite close."

"So what was in it for Connie?"

"You mean financially?"

"Yes."

"She earned a trustee fee for her services, but it was modest enough to have passed muster with Lewis so you can imagine it wasn't very large."

"So she was mostly doing it out of the goodness of her heart?"

"I believe so. But I wouldn't have been surprised if Lewis would have fired both her and Hanley if she had refused so it was probably more valuable to her than it might have been to someone else."

"He had a reputation as a person who didn't like to be refused."

"He did indeed. Lewis Bett was an odd duck to be sure. I wouldn't have wanted to tell him no and then have to deal with him about anything going forward."

"So Connie was in a hard spot."

"I'd say so. He wasn't too easy to work for either. As

much as he was very generous to the town as far as access to his property was concerned, he was not anywhere near as pleasant behind closed doors."

"So Connie and Hanley were pretty well stuck with what Lewis wanted?"

"He held a lot of sway in town, and if he decided to fire her, he would not have been above encouraging other people to do so as well."

"You sound pretty sure of that."

"I can't mention specifics, but I have had more than one person over the years come to me to ask if there was anything they could do about Lewis Bett targeting them."

"That sounds unpleasant."

"It was and there was never a way to really prove any of it. And look at the way he passed over so many other more closely related family members in town in favor of Alanza."

"That was odd."

"It was because he liked things his way and he knew enough about a bunch of his relatives nearby that he found reasons to exclude them. With Alanza, she wasn't close enough to ever have offended him."

"It's a wonder Alanza got killed instead of Lewis."

"Maybe people kept hoping he would change his will in their favor and that kept him safe."

"Did he change it a lot?"

"More often than you change the oil in Dad's MG." Wow. I change the oil faithfully every two thousand miles, just to be on the safe side.

"So even if he was cheap with everything else, he was willing to splash it around on legal fees?"

"Did I say that? He filled out those do-it-yourself forms he bought in bulk at the office supply store then he would bring them around here for me to check."

"For a fee?"

"No."

"Why didn't you refuse?"

"Because it wasn't worth the trouble and he was a sad and pathetic old man who was losing his grip on life. It took me almost no time at all to look them over."

"So did he switch to paying you when he decided to go with a trust instead of a will?"

"I did charge him a bit for that. As a matter of fact, that section of track over there is compliments of that particular job." I looked at where he was pointing and was pleased to see an elongated section of track that must have amounted to a nice chunk of change. "It took me longer to decide how to spend it than it had to earn it so the job wasn't exactly onerous."

"So now that Alanza is dead, do you know who benefits?"

"I wasn't Alanza's attorney so I have no idea about the disposition of her own will, but I do know the trust named the town as the beneficiary if Alanza died."

"Looks like you're back on my Christmas list."

Twenty-one

I knocked as loudly as I could on Connie's back door, considering my hands were full of pickle jars. I hollered her name and got nothing but Profiterole scratching at the door from the other side like he was desperate to get out. I tried the knob, and like the doors to most houses in Sugar Grove, it turned easily in my hand. Profiterole shot past me and was gone into the side field toward the barn before I could stop him.

I let myself in and sat the jars on the table. I looked around the kitchen for a piece of paper and a pen to compose a quick note thanking her for the pickles and letting her know how much of a hit they were, especially with the kids at the dinner. I looked around the heaped-up kitchen for a piece of scrap paper and a pen. The kitchen was in no better condition, clutterwise, than the rest of the house. It seemed, at first, like everything in the world was in that room besides something to leave a note with in a hurry. Then I noticed a notebook, a roll of stamps, and some envelopes shoved between a cookie jar shaped like a goat and a pot containing a dead houseplant on the hutch. I reached for the notebook but managed to knock into the cookie jar. Letting go of the notebook, I made a grab for the cookie jar before it hit the floor. I didn't think Connie would appreciate me returning pickle jars in order to break her collectables.

I carefully placed the frolicking goat back on the hutch, pushed it a little farther back from the edge than I had found it, and bent to retrieve the notebook. Loose papers of all sorts had fallen out and it took a bit of doing to gather them back up. I had no idea what order they had been in or even if there was an order. I decided to turn them all faceup and heading in the same direction and then slip them behind the front cover.

I picked up the notebook and got a look at the cover. Marked across its front in heavy marker were the words *Lewis Bett Trust Fund.* I gave the papers a bit more attention than was strictly necessary for getting everything tidied away. Among the property tax, fuel oil, and electric bills, there were several invoices from Hanley's forestry business. I ran my finger along the column of numbers and the accompanying text detailing the services and supplies Lewis's trust was being billed for.

According to the invoices, Hanley had spent considerable time on Bett's property. He had removed damaged limbs, cleared away underbrush, and even taken out entire trees deemed detrimental to the health of the overall forest. The property was large, almost as large as Greener Pastures, but to my knowledge, our tree farm had never been presented with a bill by Hanley, or any other forester, for even a third as much. I looked even more closely and noticed he also had fertilized on six separate occasions using a product called Best Bett All in One. I stuffed the papers into the notebook and shoved the whole mess back onto the hutch. I wasn't sure what any of this meant, but I felt certain I didn't want to get caught in the house with Hanley.

Profiterole was nowhere to be seen. As a farm dog he was used to being outside but I didn't feel right about leaving him to run loose. If anything happened to him, I would feel guilty and Connie didn't need any more animal trouble after what had happened to her goat Susannah. I called and called but he didn't come. I closed the kitchen door behind me and began wandering the yard looking for him.

The barn door was partly opened and I slipped inside, waiting for my eyes to adjust to the low light. Once again I noticed the goats huddled together in the corner of the barn, quaking all over. I had never thought of goats as stupid but I hadn't given them credit for such long memories either. It was hard to believe they were still so spooked by what had happened more than a week earlier. Although, I had to admit, if only to myself, that I was uneasy being out in the dark and I had only seen the mountain lion through a window. I couldn't imagine how afraid I would still be if I had seen my sister dragged off to her demise, even if it had been Celadon.

I advanced toward the goats, making a clucking noise like Grampa always did when coaxing a horse or a cow. I hoped it would comfort them but they remained steadfastly terrified. Clementine's eyes were darting wildly. I stretched out my hand for her to sniff, hoping to get to the point of patting her. She seemed to have liked that when Connie did it the last time I visited.

Just as I was reaching for her, I heard Profiterole barking behind me. The frightened goats pressed farther toward the splintery barn wall behind them. If anything, they seemed even more terrorized than before. They somehow managed to get most of the flock squeezed behind the wooden-runged ladder that connected to the hayloft above. One of them poked its snout through the rungs and let out a desperate-sounding bleat. Between the barking and the bleating, my soothing clucking sounds were never going to be heard. But at least I had found Profiterole. Or rather, he had found me. I turned toward him to grab his collar in order to get him back into the house safely before I headed out. There didn't seem to be much I could do for the goats, and while it might sound cold, watching them feel miserable was not how I wanted to spend my day.

Profiterole was stiff and his barking was interspersed with deep-throated growls. I felt intimidated by the idea of grabbing him by the collar but made a lunge for him anyway.

"What's gotten into all of you?" I asked him, locking fingers around his thick leather collar. He twisted his head up toward me then snapped it forward again like he was trying to point something out to me. I followed his lead and wished I hadn't.

Rearing up from the scattered straw bedding in the corner of the barn was a snake. A very large and very exotic-looking snake. It swayed and bobbed in my direction and its tongue wiggled out at me like a sentient kite tail. I dropped my grip on Profiterole's collar and reached for the ladder instead. I shot up the rungs like a child born into a circus family. Camels, cassowaries, and kangaroos were one thing. Snakes were another. My ability to display courage did not extend to snakes. I perched at the top of the ladder, keeping my feet as high up as possible, and looked down on the snake. It was still moving, and while it didn't seem to be interested in me any longer, it was paying a lot of attention to the trembling goats. Profiterole was doing his best to be distracting but he looked small and insignificant next to the snake.

I dug into my pocket and grabbed my cell phone. I hit the contacts number for the police station and was surprised to hear Lowell's voice on the other end.

"Dani, I'm so glad you called." As angry as I still was with him, I couldn't think of anyone I'd rather speak to in a crisis. Not even my dad. Lowell just had a way of keeping a steady hand on the tiller that helped everyone around him. Being angry with both him and my mother was taking so much energy as well as robbing me of the pleasure of his company. And right now, I needed him.

"No time to go into things right now, Uncle Lowell. I'm in trouble." I reached out with my free hand and felt for something, anything to hurl down at the snake to distract it from gobbling the goats. My hand made contact with an old coffee can full of screws. I lobbed it with all my strength but the snake zigged as the can zagged. Screws bounced all over the floor like a game of jacks. The snake seemed momentarily jarred then returned its attention to Clementine and the rest of the flock.

"It's not Mitch again, is it? I told that boy if he bothered you any more, I was not only going to fire him, I was going to personally make sure he couldn't get a job as a security guard at a strip mall."

"It's not Mitch. I need you to call Graham." I scootched a little farther from the top of the ladder and closer to the pile of junk stowed in the loft. I could only imagine what would have become of the house if the overflow storage had not been available.

"Graham? What did he do to you? I'll grab my gun and be right over."

"It's nothing like that." Lowell must have taken my silent treatment hard. He never was much of a talker, and now I couldn't seem to get a word in edgewise.

"Well, I'm sure glad to hear that. I thought the two of you might really have a shot at getting along. I don't want you to end up like me, Dani, waiting around forever for the person of your dreams. I never want you to know how hard it is to be alone." Despite my attention being taken up with the swaying of the snake, I still registered the pain and the caring in his voice. I felt crummy to have contributed to it in any way.

"We can talk about this later if you'll just call Graham. I'm trapped up in the loft of Connie's barn with a snake longer than your driveway coiled up below me threatening to come up and give me a cuddle."

"I'll call him and I'll get out there, too." Lowell disconnected and I stuffed the phone back into my pocket. I used both hands to grab and hurl things down from the loft. The goats made a pitiful sound and Profiterole began darting at the snake. I tossed a hammer, a rusty barbell so light it could have doubled as a baby rattle, a greasy bicycle chain, and several cans of spray paint. The cover popped off a can of turquoise gloss as it connected with Profiterole's back. I would have apologized but my voice was frozen in place by the sight of the snake raising itself up even higher. It lifted itself enough to look down on the goats and they sounded even more desperate.

Even over Profiterole's constant barking and the pathetic noises of the goats, I heard a vehicle door slam. I felt torn between wanting to hide from Hanley and a desperate desire for help with the snake. After what I had found in the kitchen, I was not at all sure everything about him was on the up-and-up. I was certain something was wrong with his fertilizing program, and I wondered a great deal about why the fertilizer he was supposedly using wasn't registered with the state. But I also didn't want him to walk in on the snake and not give him some sort of fair warning. Still undecided, I lay down in the loft and peered down at the scene below. I heard footsteps, then Connie's voice.

"Calm down, dog, you've scared the goats so stiff I'm going to need a hairdresser to put the curl back in their beards." Connie advanced on the shivering goats completely oblivious to the snake within feet of her.

"Connie, stop!" I yelled, finally finding my voice. Her neck twisted and she glanced up at me, an even more terrified look than the one the goats were exhibiting on her face.

"What are you doing up there?" She looked angry in addition to frightened. No one likes trespassers and she was clearly no exception.

"Snake!" I yelled, pointing at the reptile bobbing and weaving like a boxer in the middle of the seventh round of a heavyweight fight. She shook her head at me like I was crazy and ignored my warning.

"Dani, come down from there this instant. It's really not safe."

"It isn't safe down there either. Turn around." I pointed again. This time, she paid attention. It was like watching a movie where as a viewer you are seeing the face of a character that suddenly realizes everyone else is seeing something dangerous that they never noticed. She looked at the goats, then at the dog, and finally, like she didn't want to do so, turned to where my finger was pointing. I thought she would jump back, but she lunged forward, between the snake and her flock of goats. It darted at her and I did what came naturally. I started throwing more things at the snake. Connie looked up, even more shocked than before.

"Dani, stop it." She looked frantic and her voice pitched well above all the other sounds. How could she not want help?

"This is the only way I've been able to distract it from eating anyone. I'll try not to hit you." I lobbed a brick someone had covered in a crocheted granny square, probably to turn it into a doorstop. It nearly hit Clementine and I had to ask myself if Connie had a point.

"Don't throw another thing from up there." She sounded even bossier than Celadon and I felt myself getting huffy. The snake arched itself even higher and I disregarded her concerns. I stuck my hand back into the pile and wrapped my fingers around something made of glass with a bit of heft to it. I raised it to shoulder height and prepared to lob it like an Olympic shot-putter.

"Stop. You'll kill us all!" Connie screamed as if the situation could actually have gotten any worse. I looked at my hand. In it was a syrup bottle shaped like the state of New Hampshire. A paper tag cut in the shape of a maple leaf with Alanza's name on it was tied around the neck. I recognized Celadon's prim but elaborate script. The bottle appeared to contain grade B amber syrup. I'd been eating it all my life, but had never seen anyone react like it was life threatening. Fattening perhaps, if used to excess, but never life threatening. Unless this was connected to Alanza.

I lowered my arm and looked at the pile. I knelt in front of it and noticed another couple of items I recognized in among the detritus. Two more bottles of maple syrup from Greener Pastures and a few more maple leaf cutouts were there along with a jar of small pellets that looked like the ones I had seen in Piper's attic and a zipped-top plastic bag with a pair of heavy-duty rubberized gloves tucked inside.

"What is all this?" I asked, holding up the bottle of syrup in one hand and the zip bag in the other.

"It's the poison that killed Alanza. You can't even breathe the stuff without getting sick, maybe dying. Whatever you do, don't throw it." More footsteps clattered into the barn and I had never been so glad in my life to see anyone as I was to see Lowell at that moment. Unlike either Connie or myself, he knew to look for a large snake and spotted it straight off.

"You all right, Connie?" See what I mean about remaining calm? He was overwhelmed enough to release his grip on the galvanized trash can he held. Connie burst into tears and I wondered if she was hoping the snake was going to swallow her down whole or squeeze the life right out of her. Graham was hot on Lowell's heels with his loop-on-a-stick contraption. With as much ease as the snake wrangler guys you see on television, he slipped it over the snake's head and cinched it down, then pulled the giant reptile's head toward the floor of the old barn. Lowell stepped up to help with the thrashing, and with less fuss than I would have imagined, the snake was coiled up in the bottom of the trash can, the lid, complete with a few airholes punched in the top, firmly in place.

Connie sank to the floor, her flock of goats clustered around her. Profiterole stood next to the trash can growling and poking his nose against it. I expect the snake was lucky to be deaf since I can't imagine how terrible the noise would have been if it hadn't been.

I gently placed the bottle of syrup on the floor of the

loft and sat at the top of the ladder, glad not to need to support my weight on my trembling knees any longer. Now that the adrenaline was seeping away, the stiffness had gone right out of all my bones.

"It's okay now, Dani. It's safe to come down," Lowell called up to me. Graham nodded in agreement.

"I don't think I have what it takes to do the ladder yet. Besides, there is something up here you need to see." Lowell climbed the ladder and sat next to me. He draped a protective arm across my shoulders, and I felt the backs of my eyes start stinging and my nose began to drip. I leaned against the fabric of his uniform and just let loose. I felt all the scared and hurt and angry flow out of me and run in a messy stream down over him. He just sat quietly, a warm sturdy rock, one that deserved a chance to be happy with someone he loved, until I'd emptied myself out of all the toxic feelings I'd been dragging around for a while.

"Now what is it you need me to see?" he asked, handing me a handkerchief for my nose even though the damage had already been done to his shirt.

"See that pile of stuff?" I asked.

"Yes."

"That's what's left of the tinkering project that pushed Alanza to the other side of the veil."

"How do you know?"

"Connie told me. If I were you, I wouldn't let her leave until she answered some questions." Lowell nodded.

"Connie," Lowell called down, "is there anything you want to tell me about all this?" She looked up at the loft for the first time since the snake was captured.

"Alanza was blackmailing me. She found out I was billing Lewis for products and services Hanley never provided and that I kept right on doing it when Alanza took over the place."

"How'd she find out?" Lowell asked.

"She got all the information she needed from me. She asked to see the trust accounts, and as the trustee, I had to let her have them. I figured it would make her more suspicious if I refused. Besides, I thought I had covered my tracks pretty well."

"So what gave it away?" Lowell asked.

"It was the Best Bett All in One, wasn't it?" I asked. Connie turned her attention to me, a look of surprise on her face.

"It was. She remembered how you praised maple trees as a low-maintenance crop at the talk you gave to the Chamber of Commerce. When she looked at the bills paid from the trust to Hanley's tree service, she knew I was skimming."

"What did she want in return for keeping quiet?" Lowell asked.

"Money from the trust. She got use of the house and the land and a very small stipend. Blackmailing me was probably the easiest way to get more money from the trust."

"But why kill her?" Graham asked. "She wasn't taking your money."

"She started wanting other things, too, right?" I asked.

"Yes. She got me to persuade the other board members on the planning committee to approve her storage facility and then she got me to give up my seat and to convince them to appoint her in my place."

"Still, that wouldn't be enough to take that sort of risk."

"She decided to clear Bett's Knob and she was making Hanley do it. Do you know what that would have done to his business?"

"I know my family would have had a hard time not holding that against him," I said.

"Still, the trees would have grown back and people might have understood," Lowell said. Connie stared at the ground and clutched at Clementine.

"I think it was more personal. When did you find out about Alanza and Hanley?" I asked.

"Friday morning. Alanza told me she wanted me to come by the house because she had something she needed to discuss with me. When I got there, she told me she and Hanley had been seeing each other behind my back and she wanted me to give him a divorce. She said if I didn't, she would expose me, and since the penalty for embezzlement is seven and a half to fifteen years in prison, she would have him all to herself for a long time anyway." Connie began weeping in earnest. She was so loud and fractious about it, Clementine tried to pull away.

"Where did you get the poison?" Lowell asked.

"The attic at the Stack Shack. I remembered Piper had warned me to stay away from it when I was putting the tax returns I help her with up there. I told Alanza I needed to think over what she said and I went to the Stack. I told

Piper I needed something from the box and I helped myself to the rat poison."

"What made you decide to doctor her syrup?" I asked.

"As the treasurer for the Sap Bucket Brigade, I was there on Friday night when your family brought in the syrup. As soon as I saw the tag with Alanza's name on it, I knew just how to do it. When no one was looking, I grabbed a couple extra bottles from the box next to the contestants' table. I brought them home and added the poison to three of them, just to be sure I had at least one if something happened."

"Where did you get the caps to reseal the bottle?" Lowell asked.

"I had them. I never get rid of anything, and a few years ago I started selling bath products made from goat's milk. I had a bunch of caps in different sizes."

"I thought that was how the poison got into the bottle." Despite everything else I was relieved the rest of the syrup supply was safe.

"Graham, I assume you've got a pair of cuffs with you and a working knowledge of the Mirandizing procedure?" Lowell gestured toward Connie with a quick thrust of his chin. She looked up at me as Graham headed her way.

"You'd better get an expert in here to handle that stuff. I'd hate to be responsible for anyone else getting hurt. And Dani, I am sorry about what this did to your business." Graham snapped the cuffs in place as Connie bent her head down for what I guess she expected to be a last nuzzle with Clementine. Profiterole followed Graham out of the barn dancing along at his heels like a child behind the Pied Piper. I suppose Graham is a banquet for the senses if you are a dog.

"Looks like I've got a job to get on with, and not a pleasant one either. Are you going to be all right?"

"I think I can manage the ladder now."

"That's not what I meant." He gave my shoulder another squeeze.

"I'll be fine."

"Maybe what I should have asked was, will we be all right?" For such a calm man, he looked mighty worried.

"We will be." And I meant it. It was time to move on, to change, to grow up. My mother had found a way to get over my father's death, and I should follow her example and do the same. "As long as you promise to be good to my mother."

Twenty-two

After giving my official statement at the police station, all I wanted to do was to sit in the sugarhouse office and play mahjong on my computer. The driveway was empty of cars when I'd pulled up, and I managed to sneak down to the sugarhouse without being spotted. I was in no mood for any more emotions coming off any more people. What I needed was to just be alone.

I paused on the porch thinking about where everything had started and wondering what had become of the mountain lion and what would become of Graham once the last monkey had been rounded up. A metallic glint caught my eye. A fluttering shred of tinsel was snagged on a rough spot on a floorboard. In all the excitement I had completely forgotten the Christmas typhoon that had laid waste to the sugarhouse. Where had it all gone?

I pushed open the door and sniffed the air. No

cinnamon, no pine. A stiff fresh breeze blew in from the back and I went to close whatever window had been opened. My mother knelt in a corner, a red and green peasant skirt swirled out around her, carefully lifting sparkly ornaments from an artificial tree. All around the room, surfaces that had been smothered by her efforts to cheer the place up were once again cleared. When she turned to face me, I noticed glitter sprinkling her face like metallic freckles.

"Lowell called," she said.

"I expect he had a lot to say."

"He said that Connie confessed and Greener Pastures is in the clear."

"I know. I was there when it happened."

"He also said the two of you settled your differences." She leaned a little toward me, like a well-behaved dog eyeing the turkey platter. Restrained, but hopeful. I sank to the floor next to her, close enough to feel the peculiarly unnatural itching fake trees cause.

"Uncle Lowell and I are all patched up."

"But you and I are not." She clutched at the ornament box like it was a life preserver.

"Why didn't you just tell me?"

"I wanted to, Dani, but I just didn't know how."

"You could have just come out and said it. I can't see what was so hard about that."

"I didn't want you to be hurt. You've been through enough with what happened with your father."

"And whose fault is that, do you think?"

"Do you blame yourself for what happened to him?"

She dropped the box in her lap and gave me her full attention.

"I'm the one who had to go to college so far away."

"What was so wrong with that?"

"There are plenty of great schools within a two-hour drive. I broke his heart and the rest of you paid for it."

"I loved your father and I never had a word to say against him. But he was wrong to discourage you from making your own choices. If I hadn't decided to visit new places, he never would have met me. Not all your genetics come from your father's side, you know." Which was hard to remember sometimes with the way there were Greenes all around me all the time.

"That doesn't change the fact he had a heart attack."

"Your father ate a pound of butter and half a cow every other day. And don't get me started on his ice cream habit. It's pretty hard to keep your heart working properly when your arteries are flowing with fudge ripple."

"I still didn't have to upset him."

"Dani, his heart attack came after you'd been gone more than three years. Trust me, he'd gotten used to it. And he was proud of you for going."

"Celadon blames me. She said I was guilty of killing him."

"Celadon told me about your argument. Did she say you killed him or that you felt guilty for killing him?" Mom reached out and took my hand in her own. Despite everything else that had happened, the ugly conversation with Celadon was still fresh in my memory.

"She said I only started the business because I felt

guilty about Dad's heart attack. And then she broke a wooden spoon and stomped out of the room."

"See, she doesn't blame you. She said you felt guilty, not that you were guilty. She's been worried about you. We all have. I was chatting with your father about it just the other day."

"He's dead, Mom."

"What does that have to do with anything? We talk all the time." Usually I just smile and nod when my mother gets started in on her spirit world mumbo jumbo, but this time it got a rise out of me.

"Really? What does he have to say?"

"He said you should stop in at Mountain View Food Mart for some snacks. And while you're there, you'll find something worth discovering in the pet supplies aisle."

"That's the message my father wants me to receive from beyond the grave? An 'I love you' would have been nice. An 'I'm proud of you.' Even a little confirmation that the afterlife lives up to the brochures. But not a reminder to run errands." I couldn't help but feel ripped off. My mother just shook her head at me.

"He also says just because you don't look at things the same way as someone else doesn't mean you shouldn't listen to what they have to say."

"Is this exactly what you heard or is it an interpretation of one of your visions?"

"Information from the other side always has to be interpreted. It isn't like communication with words. It mostly comes in pictures. And you know how your father was a man of few words."

"So what exactly did you see?" I might not believe she was really in touch with the great beyond, but her impressions when she visited the sugarhouse earlier were hard to ignore.

"I saw you standing on a big hill holding a box of animal crackers and waving excitedly at Aunt Hazel's fat old cat Petunia."

"So, of course that means I should stop for snacks at the grocer? And maybe a flea collar?" I asked as my mother rose to her feet.

"What else could it be?"

Even though it was still late afternoon, it was November so the light was starting to fade as I grabbed my keys and headed for the minivan. So help me, I pointed it in the direction of the Mountain View Food Mart. While I wasn't quite ready to believe my mother had received a message from my father saying he wanted me to go to the grocer, I wasn't willing to discount it entirely. I parked out front, picked up a box of animal crackers, and grabbed a bag of cheese curls for good measure. I stood in the pet food aisle pretending to scrutinize the ingredients on the cans of cat food for as long as I could stand. As much as I love to read, lists of glutinous barley meal and poultry by-products have only so much power to fascinate. While I knew it had been a long shot, I have to admit I was disappointed there was nothing more exciting at the store than a fifty percent discount on name-brand toilet paper.

I started for home the long way, slowing as I passed

Jessie Crockett

the footpath leading to Bett's Knob. I put the van into park and stuck the snacks in the pockets of my down vest. If my errand wasn't going to lead me to anything important, at least I could enjoy something for my efforts. I picked my way through the leaf litter and fallen branches, listening to the wind and noticing how the autumn light slanted through the bare branches of the trees. At the top of Bett's Knob, a rocky outcropping offered a natural seat from which to view Sugar Grove spread out below. I settled myself in a dimple in the largest boulder and soaked up the warmth radiating from the sun-soaked stone.

From my perch I could see the rooftops of the Congregational church, the grange, and the library. A curl of smoke wound its way out of the butter pat shaped chimney at the Stack. Acres of maples and beeches and cow-dotted fields met my eye. Even in the bleakness of late November, the beauty of my hometown was as easy to see as the sunlight sparkling on the lake at the foot of the hill.

Behind me, I heard a rustling and cracking twigs. Graham emerged from around the side of the outcropping. His official uniform jacket bulged as if he had indulged in few dozen too many Thanksgiving pies.

"What have you got there?" I asked.

"The last monkey for the barrel." Graham opened his coat and the little monkey he'd been chasing the other day stuck its head out. "What brings you up here?"

"I was out on a fool's errand and thought I would stop and take in the sights." I patted the rock next to me.

292

"There's a seat here free if you and your friend would like to watch the sunset."

"Don't mind if we do." Graham stretched his legs out in front of him and settled the monkey on his lap.

"How about a snack?" I pulled the packages from my pockets. "I've got two choices." I held up both, and the little guy slipped a hand out above the jacket zipper and reached toward the cheese curls. "I'd say that's a yes." I handed the monkey a cheese curl and the bag to Graham.

"I'm pretty sure that wouldn't be the sort of thing his mother would approve of," Graham said before crunching into a curl of his own.

"Just make sure to wipe off all the orange sawdust before you reunite them. That's what I do with Celadon's kids. She never catches on." I carefully opened the animal cracker box, and pulled out a zebra.

"If he holds still, I'll give it my best."

"So, I guess you'll be headed back to wherever it is Fish and Game officers go now that you've caught your last fugitive." I kept my eyes fixed firmly in the middle distance, not wanting to look either eager or disappointed.

"Where we go is mostly up to us as long as we patrol our territory. Sugar Grove happens to fall within mine so I can be through here as often as I wish or as often as someone here needs me." I felt him scooch just the tiniest bit closer. I felt my stomach go all cold then hot. Before I could think of a thing to say, I spotted something long and lean and ending in a swishy tail picking its way through the trees on the hill opposite us. I jumped to my feet and, without taking my eyes from the mountain lion, grabbed at Graham's arm.

"Do you see it? Now do you see it?" I waved my free arm, jabbing it in the direction of the big cat.

"See what?" Graham asked.

"The mountain lion. It was right there." And then, it was gone. I strained my eyes but the light was fading fast and the buff-colored leaves provided perfect camouflage. I turned toward Graham, his arm still held tight in my grasp.

"I'm sorry, Dani, the only thing I'm looking at is you." I started to laugh. There I was standing on a big hill, waving wildly at a cat while holding on to a man named after a cracker. Now what else was it my father wanted me to know? Then I remembered: Don't discount what someone says just because they aren't looking at things the same way as I do. I turned back to the valley and breathed in deeply, inhaling the scent of wood smoke drifting up from below. Graham and I might not look at things the same way, but somehow it felt like my father approved.

Celadon was right, at least in part. I had started the business because of my father. But it hadn't just been guilt. I wanted something I had shared with my father to continue and even to grow. After the way I felt when it looked like Greener Pastures was doomed to close, I realized the business meant more to me than it had when I had first proposed it. I was proud of what I had accomplished, and as I looked out over the place I knew I belonged, I felt sure the pasture was greener right here in Sugar Grove.

Recipes

Maple Magic Martini

Makes 2 cocktails

>   2 slices pound cake, but extra is always even better
>   2 slices bacon, cooked until crisp
>   2 fluid oz. vodka
>   2 fluid oz. maple liquor
>   2 fluid oz. pure maple syrup
>   ice

Preheat oven to 250 degrees F. Cut slices of pound cake into cubes and place spaced slightly apart on a parchment-lined baking sheet. Bake, for 12–15 minutes, or until dry to the touch, stirring a few times to ensure even toasting. Allow to cool completely. Can be prepared several days ahead if stored in an airtight container.

In a martini shaker filled with ice, combine the vodka, maple liquor, and pure maple syrup. Strain into two martini glasses. Thread pound cake croutons onto 2 cocktail picks. Place one pick in each glass. Lay a bacon strip across each glass for use as a swizzle stick. Serve and enjoy!

Who'd a Thunk It

Makes 1 sandwich

    cooking spray
    1 small apple, peeled, cored, and thinly sliced
    **2 waffles, homemade are preferable but frozen will
        do in a pinch, each the size of a slice of bread**
    a small amount of softened butter
    2 strips bacon cooked until crisp and broken in half
    **¼ cup shredded sharp cheddar or maple flavored
        cheese**
    pure maple syrup

Spray a small sauté pan with the cooking spray and place over medium heat. Add apple slices to the pan and cover with a close-fitting lid. Stir occasionally, cooking until slices are softened but still hold their shape. Remove from heat. Heat a second pan or griddle over medium heat. Butter one side of a waffle and place it buttered side down in the pan. Add the apple slices, spreading them out to the edges. Top with the bacon slices. Add the cheese. Butter the second waffle and place on top of the cheese, buttered side up.

Continue to cook for approximately three minutes, or until bottom waffle begins to brown on the underside. Press gently on the top waffle with a spatula to secure the layers before flipping the sandwich over and toasting the second side for approximately three minutes. Remove from heat and serve with a knife, fork, and generous quantity of maple syrup.

The first slice is magic . . .
The second slice is murder . . .

FROM

Ellery Adams

Pies and Prejudice

A Charmed Pie Shoppe Mystery

When the going gets tough, Ella Mae LeFaye bakes pie. So when she catches her husband cheating in New York, she heads back home to Havenwood, Georgia, where she can drown her sorrows in fresh fruit filling and flaky crust. But her pies aren't just delicious. They're having magical effects on the people who eat them—and the public is hungry for more.

Ella Mae decides to grant her own wish by opening The Charmed Pie Shoppe. But with her old nemesis Loralyn Gaynor making trouble, and her old crush Hugh Dylan making nice, she has more than pie on her plate. And when Loralyn's fiancé is found dead—killed with Ella Mae's rolling pin—it'll take all her sweet magic to clear her name.

Includes pie recipes!

facebook.com/ellery.adams
facebook.com/TheCrimeSceneBooks
penguin.com

M1198T1012